BETRAYAL

A CAPT. MARK SMITH NOVEL

Cover Design and Interior Format

© **KILLION**
THE GROUP, INC.

BETRAYAL

A CAPT. MARK SMITH NOVEL

DAN STRATMAN

THRILLER NOVELS BY DAN STRATMAN

MAYDAY

HURRICANE

DEDICATION

To Cyndi. My dear sweet wife, my best friend, my lifeblood.

CHAPTER 1

NOELLE PARKER VISIBLY TREMBLED. THE pounding of her beating heart echoed in her eardrums like thunder as she stood in the middle of the small New York City apartment. She dreaded having to deliver the horrible news to her sweet, innocent millennial-generation niece. Just the thought of telling her brought tears to Noelle's crystal-blue eyes.

She considered going with the *rip the bandage off quickly* approach and just blurting it out. *"April, you just inherited one BILLION dollars!"*

She held back verbalizing the shocking news, knowing it was the least important of the explosive, life-altering secrets she was about to reveal to her niece.

There was more.

Much more.

The traumatic events of the past week had exposed dark secrets she thought were buried long ago.

Looking for moral support, Noelle reached out for the hand of her ex-husband, retired airline captain Mark Smith. Even while recovering from a bullet wound to his leg, and relying on crutches to get around, Mark still gave off an aura of strength. His handsome masculine features and fit physique dominated the room.

Although he stood at her side during this difficult moment, recent events had dealt a serious blow to Mark's earlier thoughts of reconciliation with his ex-wife.

Noelle had been ready to give up her maiden name

and become Mrs. Noelle Smith for the second time. Now those plans were stuck in an indefinite holding pattern. Still, Mark took her hand and gently squeezed it twice—a silent sign of encouragement.

Noelle's only sibling, Tommy Parker, and her sister-in-law, Stephanie, stood nervously arm in arm on the opposite side.

April Parker looked up from the couch, a dusting of freckles dotting her ivory cheeks. Filled with apprehension, her eyes darted back and forth between her parents and Noelle. After everything that had happened, she expected her aunt to deliver bad news.

April shared the same red hair, tall, slender body, and crystal-blue eyes as Noelle. Eyes that still projected an innocence untarnished by the harsh realities of life. Eyes too trusting to believe that sometimes people weren't always who you thought they were.

The time had come.

Noelle desperately needed to unburden her soul of the secrets that had haunted her for almost three decades. She took in a deep breath, glanced at the family members assembled next to her, and swallowed hard.

Noelle turned her gaze toward April. "I need to tell you…" Before she could finish her sentence, Noelle broke down in tears.

CHAPTER 2

TOMMY AND STEPHANIE EACH TOOK an arm and supported Noelle as she sobbed. They nodded knowingly to each other. The pair gently led her across the worn wooden floor to a nearby bedroom and closed the door.

Mark and Noelle's twenty-four-year-old daughter, Mary Smith, had been an innocent victim of the events that had unfolded in France a week prior. But she too was completely unaware of the bombshells about to be revealed by her mother. Confused, she sat next to April on the faded orange couch and clung tightly to her cousin.

She looked up at Mark and demanded, "Dad, what the hell is going on?"

Like father, like daughter. Mary had inherited Mark's blunt, direct personality and communication style.

Mark shook his head. "I'm sorry, girls. I can't be the one to tell you."

"Tell us what?" April asked, the blush on her neck rising along with her voice .

Mark just shook his head again and hobbled off on his crutches toward the bedroom to console his ex-wife.

Feeling confused and shaken, the two attractive twentysomethings sat speechless on the tattered couch. They didn't know it yet, but the world they had known their whole lives was about to be turned upside down. Even their current surroundings seemed foreign.

Mark had recently moved back in with Noelle and

Mary. Wedding plans had been made. The Smiths were on their way to becoming one big happy family again.

Then everything changed a week ago.

The memory of the violent altercation in Mark and Noelle's old apartment, and the murder of the brave building superintendent there, were more than anyone could be expected to easily move past. Their landlord had quickly volunteered to relocate them to a different apartment in the building without raising the rent, hoping his action would head off any thoughts of a lawsuit. The new apartment was slightly bigger, but it had seen many families come and go since the Prohibition era, when it was constructed. Worn was a generous word to describe its condition.

Family and friends had hastily set up the new place before Mark, Noelle, and Mary returned from France. Tommy and Stephanie salvaged the few family pictures and mementos that weren't damaged, or stained with blood, and relocated them to the new apartment.

Andy Wilson, JetBlue copilot and hopeful suitor of Mary, was put in charge of finding replacements for the damaged furniture. A typical bachelor, he'd procured an eclectic mix of thrift store and garage sale leftovers to do the job—all for under fifty dollars. After he'd finished moving the pieces in, Andy thought the place looked warm and comfortable. A side career in interior decorating was not in the cards for Andy.

———◆———

Mark went to Noelle's side and sat on the bed. A troubled look filled his sea-foam-green eyes. As most men seemed genetically programmed to do, he desperately wanted to "fix" the situation they found themselves in. Struggling to come up with words that would magically do the trick, he wrapped his strong arms around Noelle's trembling shoulders, hoping that would suffice.

Tommy tilted his head toward Mark then asked his sister, "He knows?"

Noelle nodded then looked back at the floor, tears streaming down her soft cheeks.

"I know *now*," Mark clarified. "She told me while we were in France."

"And?" Tommy asked, trying to gauge Mark's reaction to the shocking news.

"I'm pissed off." Mark removed his arm from Noelle's shoulder. "Why the hell didn't you guys tell me?" he asked no one in particular.

Noelle, Tommy, and Stephanie looked back and forth between themselves. Each hoped someone else would come up with a plausible explanation for twenty-eight years of lies.

Finally, Noelle spoke up. "It's my fault. I should have told you before we got married."

Using the crutches to lift himself, Mark stood up. "Damn right, you should have. Even your best friend knew before I did." He wedged the foam padding on top of the crutches under each armpit and tried to turn around and face Noelle. The tiny bedroom, stuffed with four people, made maneuvering impossible.

Stephanie offered him a helping hand.

Frustrated that he'd gone from jogging five miles a day to now having to rely on others to get around, Mark angrily waved her away. "I'm a big boy. What's done is done. Noelle and I will deal with it." After taking a breath, his angry expression softened a little. "Look, I was no saint when we were married. God knows she's forgiven me more times than I can count for all the things I've done." He pointed toward the door. "What matters now is what are we going to tell *them*?"

Noelle kept her head cradled in her hands and didn't respond.

Tommy went over to Noelle and gently laid his hand

on her shoulder. "It's time, Sis."

She looked up; her cheeks stained with mascara. Noelle nodded. "I know."

She forced herself up off the temporary safety of the bed, straightened her blouse, and grabbed a tissue from the box on the dresser. As she looked in the mirror to wipe away the mascara, Noelle hesitated. Her body was physically present in the room, but her mind was thirty years in the past. She couldn't help but think about how different life would have turned out if she'd listened to her father and not taken that modeling job in Paris when she was twenty years old. As stubborn as she was beautiful, Noelle did as most young people tended to do and ignored his wise advice. Three decades later, regret—the emotion that leaves the most bitter aftertaste—overwhelmed her heart. She took a deep breath, forced a weak smile, and pulled open the door to the bedroom.

The four walked back into the room, avoiding eye contact with April and Mary. The young women stood up, still clutching each other.

"You guys are freaking us out. What were you talking about in there?" Mary asked.

April looked achingly at Tommy and Stephanie for an explanation. "Mom? Dad?"

Tommy reached out for April. "Sweetie, it's really important for you to understand that we love you very much."

She lurched back. Her eyes widened. "Oh my gosh. Love me very much? That's the kind of thing people say right before they tell someone really bad news. Tell me! What is it?"

Noelle, Tommy, and Stephanie looked back and forth at each other. The awkward silence was deafening.

Mark blurted it out. "April, Noelle is not your aunt. She's your mother."

CHAPTER 3

"MARK!" NOELLE WAS SO ENRAGED at his blunt handling of the delicate situation she considered slapping him across the face. "How could you?"

Mark lifted his hands, palms turned up, defending himself. "Somebody had to say it. The poor girl was going to explode if you three didn't stop tiptoeing around the news."

April stood frozen in place. She stopped breathing. The floor under her feet felt like it had just shifted. Her peripheral vision disappeared as the walls of the small apartment seemed to close in on her. April Parker couldn't determine if the traumatic revelation she'd just heard, or an impending broken heart, was causing the tightness in her chest. It didn't matter. What mattered was that the adults she'd admired and trusted her entire life had kept a life-altering secret from her. Secret was too nice of a word. They'd lied to her.

She planted her hands on her hips and glared at Noelle. She grasped for the right words. "Wait, I don't... understand. Are you saying...are you saying my whole life you've been lying to me about who you are?" Tears welled up in her blue eyes. "About who I am?"

Then she turned her ire on her parents—well, the two people she'd thought were her parents until thirty seconds ago. April tried desperately to formulate coherent sentences to express the overwhelming sense of betrayal she felt. Conflicting emotions whirled around in her mind. She grabbed the sides of her head with both her hands. When the spinning sensation finally ended, her anger was replaced with a torrent of questions.

"I'm...*adopted*? Who else knows? Were you guys ever going to tell me? Or were you planning on keeping this from me my whole life? And why tell me now?" April slumped back down on the couch and hugged her knees tightly against her chest. She slowly rocked back and forth.

Mary hurried over, sat down, and wrapped her arm around April's shoulder. "Take deep breaths. It'll be okay. I'm here for you." Mary stopped and tilted her head. "Wait a minute. If Mom is..." The reality of the situation finally registered in Mary's brain. "We're *sisters*?"

CHAPTER 4

APRIL LIFTED HER HEAD FROM her knees and turned toward Mary. Her tear-filled eyes narrowed. Mary leaned back and focused on April.

Both girls examined each other's faces.

Then they looked up from the couch at Noelle. Slowly, they stood up, forming a triangle. The world around them no longer existed.

All three women were tall with athletic, slender builds. April wore her red hair in a cute, stylish, rounded bob. At age fifty, the color of Noelle's flowing shoulder-length red hair had faded over the years but was brought back to its original tint every six weeks with the help of her stylist. Mary's long blonde hair was tied back in a ponytail that swung freely side to side whenever she moved.

The tip-off that they shared bits of the same base nucleotides in their DNA was in their eyes. Although slightly different, the eyes of all three women shared a similar shade of an enchanting blue color. It was a unique hue that subconsciously drew in every person that looked their way. Especially men.

April turned to look at her supposed parents. Tommy Parker was tall, thin as a sitcom plot, and had curly red hair. When she looked at the person standing next to him, April cocked her head. Stephanie Parker was different. Short and pudgy, with wiry black hair, she bore no resemblance to anyone in the room. April and Stephanie looked nothing like each other. Not one physical attribute was similar. Seeing her standing there in the New York City apartment, it was as if April's eyes had truly been opened for the first time in her twenty-eight years.

She slammed her eyes shut and pressed the palms of both hands against them, hoping to completely block out the light. And the truth. "Oh my gosh. Oh my *gosh*! This can't be happening. There must be some kind of mistake." Drawing in a deep breath to keep from hyperventilating, April opened her eyes again and looked around the room.

Words can be manipulated and twisted. Body language can be controlled. But the eyes don't lie. Looking into the eyes of the adults she wholeheartedly trusted five minutes ago, April saw not only a window into their souls, but the truth.

"It's true!" April burst out in tears. "I can't believe this. I hate all of you!" She flung open the door and sprinted out of the apartment, trying to outrun the pain in her heart.

Noelle and Stephanie collided into each other as they each started for the door, their protective maternal instincts going into overdrive.

Hands gently grabbed their arms.

"Wait. Let her go," Mark said as he held back Noelle.

"She'll be okay. We just need to give her some space right now," Tommy said as he held back Stephanie.

"He's right. April needs some time to process all of this," Mark added. "How would you feel if you just had a bombshell like this dropped in your lap? Suddenly finding out you are adopted at twenty-eight years old."

Their hearts told both women to run after their daughter and hug her tight. To comfort her in this time of confusion and pain the way only a mother can do. As difficult as it was, the two resisted their urge to dash to the rescue. Instead, they embraced each other and wept.

Mary gave the four parents a searing glare then ran out after April.

"What have we done?" Stephanie asked between sobs. "I'm so sorry. It's all my fault."

"April will never trust us again after this," Stephanie predicted, shaking her head.

"If I could just look my daughter in the eyes, hug her tightly, and explain to her why we did this. What the circumstances were at the time. I'm sure she would eventually come to understand," Noelle lamented.

Stephanie Parker recoiled from the embrace with Noelle with an aggrieved expression on her face. Her tears stopped and her eyes narrowed. "Your daughter? Hold on a damned minute. You might have given birth to her, but April is *our* daughter, not yours."

CHAPTER 5

MARY SEARCHED THE HALLWAY OUTSIDE the apartment for her...cousin? Sister? It had all happened so fast. Minutes ago, she was an only child. Now she had a big sister. Someone who had treated her like a little sister all these years: protecting her from bullies at school, telling her in no uncertain terms when she disapproved of her choices in boyfriends, borrowing her favorite outfits without asking.

Ever since she could remember, Mary had secretly wished for a sibling when she said her prayers at night. As a kid at Christmas, she would wrap up presents she bought herself and pretend they had been given to her by her imaginary brothers and sisters. Mark and Noelle went along, knowing the doctors had told them they weren't able to have any more children.

Mary started down the hallway for the stairs. As she approached the first step, she suddenly froze and thought, *Why aren't I running after her? April needs me.* Her wishes from childhood had come true. She had a sister.

Mary felt conflicted. Being an only child could be lonely at times, but it also meant you always got all your parents' love and attention. The jealousy and conflict that came from sibling rivalry were a non-issue. But learning to share wasn't an easy thing for an only child. Now, she'd have no choice but to share her parents.

Mary shook off the questions swirling around in her head and galloped down the steps in search of April.

The old lady in 4C walked in the building as Mary reached the foyer. She pulled a beaten-up wire basket on wheels behind her, loaded with grocery bags from the Kroger down the street.

Mary screeched to a halt to avoid knocking the frail woman over. "Hi, Mrs. Crenshaw. How are you today? How is Petey doing?"

She adjusted her thick glasses to get a better look. "Oh hello, dear. That lazy dog is eating me out of house and home," she grumbled. "I told Carl it was either him or Petey. One of you has got to go. I can't afford to feed you both on my meager Social Security check. Just the other day—"

"Okay, Mrs. Crenshaw. It was great talking to you. Bye." Mary slipped around the woman and escaped out the door before she could delay her search any longer.

Mrs. Crenshaw's memory wasn't what it used to be. Her husband, Carl, had been dead for over ten years.

Mary bounded down the steps two at a time in front of the rundown brownstone. She looked up and down the sidewalk for April. Residents of the Borough of Queens crowded the narrow and crumbling sidewalk in both directions, going about their difficult lives. Mary weaved in and out of the sea of bodies, searching. April was nowhere in sight.

Assuming she'd gone home, Mary jogged to the end of her block then one block north to April's building. Her pace quickened as she recalled how devastated April was when she heard the shocking news. Mary's imagination conjured up frightening actions her big sister might take in her fragile state of mind. By the time she reached the apartment building, Mary was in a full-out sprint.

She slipped in the front door as a young couple walked out arm in arm, oblivious to their surroundings.

Mary rapped on the apartment door, not sure what she was going to say when April opened it.

No one answered.

She knocked harder, then listened for any sounds of movement in the apartment.

Dead silence.

Mary pulled her phone from her back pocket and dialed April's number. She pressed her ear up against the door, listening for a ring tone. No sounds came from inside the apartment.

Leaving the building, Mary asked everyone she passed if they'd seen April. Residents either hadn't seen her or didn't even know who April was. Mary wandered the streets of Queens searching for her new sister.

On a hunch, Mary walked to a nearby coffee shop. It was furnished with leather chairs and distressed wooden tables arranged in small groupings—the corporation's attempt at creating a cozy ambiance. The chain hadn't invented coffee, but it had certainly made billions catering to its ardent fans.

When she entered, Mary scanned the shop. Unfamiliar faces were scattered about the room, sipping their exotic blends of overpriced caffeine.

She paused her search for a moment to slowly inhale. The olfactory receptors in her nose rejoiced as each molecule of the pleasant aroma passed by. She wandered through the coffee shop then spotted April sitting alone at a small round table in the back, isolated from the other patrons.

Mary walked up. "Why are you crying? Did the barista mess up your venti, soy, half-caf, no-sugar caramel drizzle latte, hold the whipped cream?"

April snorted out a laugh between her tears at the inside joke. Plain black coffee was their preferred beverage whenever the two spent hours talking at their favorite hangout. They'd snickered in the past at picky customers who'd placed ridiculously intricate orders.

"The more complicated, the more obnoxious," was April's

standard wisecrack when some diva made the barista's eyes roll with an overly demanding order.

Mary pulled up a chair and sat down.

"That seat's taken," April said half-heartedly.

"Oh okay, be that way. In that case, I'll leave," Mary said, faking offense. She stood up and turned back toward April. "If you see a sweet but sometimes overly protective girl with red hair come in, would you please have her call me? She's had a crazy day, and I think she might need a shoulder to cry on." Mary tilted her head to the side and peered down at April to see if her attempt at humor had worked.

April turned away and forced back the beginnings of a grin. "Nobody like that around here." She waved dismissively at the empty chair. "If you promise not to talk to me, you can wait here for her."

"Thanks." Mary plopped back down in the chair and waited.

April was in no mood to talk.

After a few minutes, Mary broke the silence by humming a tune and drumming her fingernails on the wooden table. The annoying behavior failed to have the desired effect, so with each passing minute Mary hummed a little louder.

April shook her head, rolled her eyes, and let out an annoyed groan. Then she turned toward Mary and grabbed her in a tearful hug. The young women cried in each other's arms for what seemed like hours. Customers sipped their drinks and pretended not to notice.

"How could they not tell me?" April questioned through her tears. "How?" She pulled back from Mary. "Did you know?"

"Trust me, I'm just as shocked as you are. My parents told me *some* things in France, but not that."

April pulled away and wiped her nose with the back of her sleeve. "I'm sorry, I'm being selfish. Here I am crying over finding out I'm adopted while you and your folks just went through hell. You should be the one crying. What in the world happened over there?"

Fresh tears welled up in Mary's eyes as the painful memories she thought were locked away raced forward again. She began to shake. "I was so scared. I was sure they were going to kill me. This nutjob French guy sent his bodyguard to kidnap me. He wanted to get his revenge on Mom for dumping him years ago when she was a model. Mr. Simpson, our building super, tried to stop him, but…" Mary's words caught in her throat. She closed her eyes and took a deep breath. "He killed Mr. Simpson."

April put her hand to her mouth. "What kind of person would be so bitter after all those years? I'm so sorry you had to go through such an awful thing. You don't have to tell me anything more if you don't want to."

"I need to tell somebody. If I don't, I feel like I'm going to lose it."

April nodded and patiently listened.

"The last thing I remember is being tackled by the jerk. The bodyguard must have tranquilized me. I woke up bound and gagged, lying in the dark in some old mansion outside of Paris." The expression on Mary's face shifted from pain to pride. "But Mom and Dad flew all the way to France in a jet they borrowed from their charter company and rescued me. They landed the plane right on the rich guy's lawn. He was so pissed when he saw they'd messed up his perfect grass."

April rolled her eyes. "Rich people are so lame. I'm glad I'm not like that."

"After they landed, I heard yelling in the room next door, a scuffle, then gunshots. I figured the bodyguard had just murdered my parents and that I was next. I started screaming and crying. But then my folks burst in and untied me. They told me no one was going to hurt me anymore and that we were going home.

"The police arrived a few minutes later. The head of the French police was furious at Dad for some reason. He questioned Dad for a long time, but they let us leave after we were treated in the hospital." Mary lightly touched the dark purple bruises on her cheek, painful reminders of the violent event she's endured, reminders that would fade away long before the traumatic memories. "But you have to believe me, April. I had no idea."

A sympathetic smile formed on April's face. "I believe you." She looked down at the floor and shook her head. Her jaw tightened. "But not them. Our whole lives they've been lying to us. I'll never trust any of them again." After silently fuming over the betrayal she felt in her heart, April looked over at Mary, and let out a soft chortle. "My little sister. Can you believe it? If I'd known, I wouldn't have teased you so much when we were little."

Mary laughed. "Yeah, you would have. I deserved it. If I'd known, I wouldn't have been such a spoiled brat."

"You want to hear something weird?" April asked.

Mary nodded.

"My whole life I've had this nagging feeling in the back of my mind that there was something not right. Something different about me. But I couldn't put my finger on what it was. Now"—she exhaled a long, emotionally drained sigh—"I know why."

April's cell phone rang a familiar tone.

She pulled it from her pocket and checked the caller ID. "Great," she said sarcastically, "it's my mother." Thinking about the last word she just uttered, April's head sank. She massaged her temples with her fingertips. "This is going to be so confusing."

CHAPTER 6

WITH CELL PHONES PRACTICALLY SURGI-
CALLY attached to members of the millennial
generation, Stephanie Parker was surprised that April
didn't answer. She rightfully assumed April was in no
mode to talk after the shocking revelation about her
adoption.

Stephanie tapped her iPhone screen, disconnecting the
unanswered call. She looked at Tommy. "*Our* daughter
didn't answer. Can you blame her?"

Noelle bristled at the snide comment, her face flush
with anger.

Mark hobbled over on his crutches and stepped
between the two women to prevent the situation from
getting out of hand. At six feet two inches tall and broad
shouldered, he made an imposing barrier.

He turned to Tommy. "Look, I think it would be best
if you guys went home. If April is there, she's bound to
have lots of questions. Let's talk later, after everyone cools
down."

Tommy nodded, wrapped his arm around his wife's
shoulder, and steered her toward the door.

Stephanie angrily pushed his arm away and glared at
Mark. "Talk about what? What more is there to say? April
is our daughter. We'll handle it from here."

Noelle and Mark exchanged an awkward look and
shrugged their shoulders.

"We've had one hell of a week. I just want to get some

sleep; that's all I meant."

Mark was a rotten liar. His face betrayed his feeble attempt at delaying the difficult, inevitable revelations to come. This only stoked Tommy and Stephanie's suspicions more.

Tommy's brow creased. "Sis? Is there something else?"

All eyes shifted to Noelle.

She looked at Tommy. During their childhood, he'd been a typical older brother. He rarely passed up an opportunity to annoy or tease her but was protective to a fault if some other kid dared to. But above all else, he was the rare type of brother who could decipher what his little sister was really thinking. Noelle would occasionally pull a fast one over on their parents, but Tommy always knew when she was not being honest. Much to his credit, he never ratted her out those times when she snuck out of the house late at night to see a boy. In return, she always leveled with Tommy.

Now he had looked her straight in the eyes and asked her if there was something else that she and Mark were not telling him.

Her shoulders slumped. "There's more. Things happened over in France that we haven't told you guys."

Noelle gestured toward the couch. Tommy and Stephanie looked at each other with a mixture of suspicion and trepidation. They linked arms, walked over to the couch, and sat down. Mark shuffled over and leaned against the arm of the couch.

She began. "You guys know about the charter flight Mark and I worked to Paris last week."

Tommy nodded.

"The customer who chartered our flight was Gerard Benoit."

Stephanie choked on her words as she raised her hand to her mouth. "Oh my god."

CHAPTER 7

"HE SAW AN ARTICLE IN the paper about the crash-landing of the Tech-Liner in the Azores a few months back," Mark explained.

"Every paper and news channel on the planet covered that story. They said your quick thinking in the cockpit saved all those passengers," Tommy said, visibly proud of his brother-in-law.

"I was just doing my job. Any other pilot would have done the same." Mark's cheeks blushed slightly at the praise.

"Don't pretend to be so modest, flyboy," Noelle teased. "Instructor pilots recreating the flight in the simulator still haven't been able to repeat what you pulled off."

Mark's hat size grew a few notches with her comment. He lifted his chin. "You didn't think I was going to let that SOB computer hacker onboard win, did you?"

"Not the Mark Smith I know," Noelle said.

"Unfortunately, some of the pictures of me in the papers showed Noelle in the background. With his resources, it didn't take Benoit long to track her down."

"He lied to our boss to manipulate the staffing on his charter flight just to get me back to France. That was his plan all along after he found me," Noelle said. "That bastard hadn't changed one bit since…" She paused. "Since I left him."

Tommy looked confused. "But why? Why was he so desperate to see you again?"

Mark smirked. "That pathetic old fool never got over Noelle leaving him. She broke his heart, and he never moved on from it. He actually thought he could win her back." There was a mixture of vengeance and victory in the tenor of his voice.

He was Noelle's true soul mate, not that jerk Benoit. Sparks had flown from the moment they'd met at the Alpha Airlines crew training center in Atlanta. He was there going through his initial checkout for the Boeing 737 in the incredibly realistic Level D flight simulator. Noelle had just been hired by the airline and was going through flight attendant training.

All it took for her was one look into Mark's alluring green eyes. She'd always preferred older—and theoretically more mature—men. Now this dashing airline captain had asked her to join him for lunch at his table in the employee cafeteria. It didn't take long for invitations to romantic dinners to follow. With his substantial salary, Mark was able to take her to the best restaurants in town. For a girl from a small town in Connecticut, Noelle couldn't help but be impressed by her debonair date.

She was fully aware of the reasons Mark's first marriage had ended, but as the familiar saying goes, love is blind. Within a year, they were married in a small ceremony at a picturesque winery overlooking Napa Valley. On the day they wed, Mark vowed to his bride that he had learned his lesson from his divorce and was going to be the trustworthy, loving husband she deserved.

On the job, they enjoyed occasionally working trips together as part of the same flight crew. The newlyweds toured the world on their days off. Taking weekend trips to Rome, London, and Madrid was easy for the two airline employees. With unlimited passes to fly standby on the flights of any airline, the hardest part was figuring out what city to visit next. They even joined in on the tradition of attaching a small padlock to the railing of the most picturesque bridge in each city they visited. All over the world, locks with the letters *M&N* etched inside a red heart symbolized their undying love for each other.

Mary came along a few years later, and Mark was the picture of a doting father. But old patterns of behavior were hard to shake. The damage inflicted from a dysfunctional upbringing by alcoholic parents proved even harder to move past. Years into the marriage, Mark thought that he had finally defeated his inner demons. That was until he foolishly let booze and a wandering eye ruin a good thing.

Noelle wasn't the only attractive flight attendant at Alpha Airlines. Long layovers alone in faraway cities provided ample opportunities for Mark to get to know some of them more intimately after a few too many drinks. Soon, rumors and gossip spread among the flight attendants faster than the jets they flew on.

Noelle had heard the rumors and had no intention of putting up with his layover trysts or his outrageous bar tabs. Despite numerous promises by Mark that he would change, he was unable to live up to them. She finally put her foot down and issued Mark an ultimatum. He blew the opportunity to make amends for his behavior by cracking a joke. That was the last straw. Noelle tossed him out. Their pride and stubbornness prevented any hope of working things out amicably.

Mary was devastated when her parents divorced. She pleaded with her parents to stay together to no avail.

Mark did the right thing and stayed involved in her life, always showing up for her tennis matches and school plays. He even moved into an apartment with other pilots to save money so he could foot the entire bill for Mary's undergrad and medical school tuition at Duke.

Until that fateful day when they were assigned to work together on the Tech-Liner flight, Mark and Noelle had rarely seen each other. Surviving a near-death experience like a crash-landing has a way of causing people to reevaluate the direction their lives are headed. Despite all that had happened, they decided to give their marriage another try. Mark and Noelle quit the airline after it wrongfully tried to pin the blame on Mark for the accident. They began working for a luxury jet charter company out of Teterboro Airport near New York City.

Then France happened.

CHAPTER 8

MARY AND APRIL CHARGED INTO the apartment. The angry looks on their faces told the parents that both women were spoiling for a fight.

"Why?" April demanded, as she glared at Noelle. She crossed her arms tightly across her chest and waited for what was an impossibly difficult answer to the simple one-word question.

Noelle reached out for April and started toward her.

Stephanie stepped in front of Noelle and cut her off.

"Sweetie, I know you are confused and hurting right now. I'm here for you, like I've always been." Stephanie tried to put her arm around April's shoulder.

April pushed her away. "Please, don't touch me." She put her hands up in front of her like stop signs. "I don't want anyone coming near me until I get answers."

"You deserve an explanation," Noelle said contritely. She gestured toward the couch. "Please sit down. We'll tell you everything."

April refused to move, her arms still tightly crossed.

"Please...sit," Noelle repeated.

April reached out and pulled Mary along by the hand, figuring there was strength in numbers. The two young women sat on the edge of the couch.

The foursome of parents gathered in front of them, in the same spot where they delivered the first bombshell earlier.

Noelle stepped forward and knelt in front of April,

gently taking her hand. Surprisingly, she let her take it and didn't pull away. "We should have…I should have told you sooner. I'm sorry you had to find out this way." Noelle turned back and gave Mark a scolding glare. "I would have done it a little more tactfully"—she looked back at April—"but there never seemed to be the perfect time to tell you."

"So, my whole life you lied to me," April said, tears welling up in her eyes. "And now you say you're sorry and think that all is forgiven?" She yanked her hands out of Noelle's grasp.

"There were so many times I wanted to tell you the truth. Instead, I watched you grow up, pretending to be your aunt. Every time you called Stephanie Mom, it felt like a knife was plunged into my heart. I desperately wanted you to call *me* Mom. I wanted to be the one to hug you and console you when someone hurt you." Tears rolled down Noelle's cheeks.

Stephanie grabbed a box of tissues and walked over to the couch. She handed it to April.

"No!" April slapped the box from Stephanie's hand. It tumbled across the apartment floor, slamming into the wall.

"April, please, she's trying to help," Tommy pleaded.

"Help me? How can you say that? My whole life you two have been part of this lie," she said, pointing an accusing finger at her parents.

Noelle spoke up. "I know it was a mistake to keep this from you, but I swear I thought it was best that you didn't know. I thought I was protecting you." She slumped down and sat on the floor. "Now I realize I was just protecting myself. From having to face up to the mistakes I'd made. From the guilt I felt." She buried her head in her hands.

April wheeled around to face Noelle. Her angry expression morphed into a puzzled look. "Guilt from what?"

CHAPTER 9

6 6 "TIMES WERE DIFFERENT BACK THEN," Noelle
explained. "I was young, unmarried, pregnant.
Adoption was the only practical option for me at the
time. I knew I couldn't raise you on my own, but I also
couldn't bear the idea of giving you up to some anonymous couple on the other side of the country. So…"

Tommy stepped forward. "Together, we decided to do
a closed adoption so no one would find out the details.
Mom and I would adopt you so you would stay here in
New York. It was the best way to make sure you remained
part of our extended family. We did it for you."

April plopped against the back of the couch. "This
doesn't make any sense. I don't believe any of you." She
pointed at Mark. "All you and Uncle Mark would have
had to do was get married. Then none of this would have
happened. My real parents would have raised me, and
there wouldn't have been any need for an adoption."

Mark stiffened up. "What?" He tucked his arms against
the sides of the crutches to keep them from falling. Mark
held his hands in the shape of a T. "Whoa, time out. I
think you are going in the wrong direction here. I just
found out about all this a week ago. I'm not your father."

"Then who is my real father?"

She looked up at her redheaded dad, Tommy. A perplexed expression flashed across her face. April titled her
head and squinted at him. Her jaw dropped.

"Oh my god!" April looked like she was going to

throw up.

Tommy's face was aghast. He raised both hands. "No, no, no. I'm not your biological father. Oh god, no. We adopted you, but not because of something like... *that*."

A shiver of relief shot through April's upper body. "Oh thank goodness."

Tommy looked over at Noelle. "We knew this day would eventually come, Sis. I just didn't imagine it would happen like this."

The time had come to divulge all the secrets, past and present. Only Mark and Noelle knew everything. In France, they had decided to spare Mary the shocking details to protect her from any more psychological trauma after her violent abduction. They hadn't had time after returning to confide in Tommy and Stephanie. Plus, the situation had gone so badly so quickly with April.

Noelle got up and walked over to Mark. They linked arms. "We have a lot to tell you. I think it would be best if everyone were sitting down first."

"You're being a little melodramatic, don't you think, Mom?" Mary chided. "I already told April about how you guys rescued me from that French guy's mansion after I was kidnapped."

Neither Mark nor Noelle responded.

Mary's comment hung in the air like a bad odor.

"Mom? Dad? What didn't you tell me?" Mary probed.

Mark nodded to Noelle to continue.

She swallowed hard. "April, the name of your biological father is Gerard Benoit. I had an affair with him when I was a model in Paris. That's how I got pregnant. When I found out he had lied to me and was married, I left him and came home. I stayed with Tommy and Stephanie until you were born, and that's when they adopted you."

April stood up and paced the apartment floor, trying to process the new information. "I don't understand. He's my real father, but all these years he never once tried to contact me. Never once tried to see me. Why would he do that?"

Noelle's head sagged. "I never told him I was pregnant. I just left."

"You lied to him, too? I never had a chance to have a relationship with my real father because of you?" April asked, her face reddening.

"You have to understand. I did it to protect you. He was not a nice man. I learned that the hard way. I thought you'd be better off without him in your life."

April raised her voice. "That should have been my decision, not yours!" Her pacing quickened as her anger increased. Suddenly, she stopped and spun around toward Noelle. "I don't believe my father could be so terrible that you wouldn't tell me about him. I want to meet him. I want to see what he looks like and hear his voice. Ask him if all of this is true." Her eyes narrowed as she glared at Noelle. "And I don't care if you think it's a good idea or not."

"I understand that you are angry with me. I was wrong to keep all of this from you all these years," Noelle said. "But you aren't going to meet him."

April had inherited more than just her mother's good looks. She also inherited her stubborn streak. "Just watch me," she replied. April started for the door.

"He's dead," Mark announced. Blunt and direct. Mark repeated himself in a more subdued voice. "You can't meet him; he's dead."

April froze in place with her hand on the doorknob. Her head felt like it was going to burst. That fateful day, revelation after revelation had shattered the reality she'd always believed.

Stephanie went over to her daughter and guided April back to the couch. "Mom is here for you, sweetie. Please, sit down." She sat on the couch and stroked April's hair as her daughter trembled. Stephanie glowered at Noelle.

"Look what you've done. You've hurt our daughter enough. Tommy, we're leaving."

Tommy nodded silently in agreement.

April looked up from the couch with tear-filled eyes. "How did he die? How did my father die?"

"Honey, we don't need to worry about that right now. You've been through a lot today. Why don't we go home and let you get some rest?" Stephanie suggested.

April shook her head. "No more secrets. I want to know. I *need* to know."

By this time, Noelle's heart was breaking from all the pain she had caused her daughter. She was unable to continue.

Mark stepped in to explain. "He was murdered. After he sent his bodyguard to kidnap Mary and bring her back to France, Benoit's man double-crossed him and murdered him right in front of us." Mark patted the bandage on his leg. "He winged me, but fortunately I was able to… well…take care of the bodyguard before he could get off a second shot. Luckily, Mary didn't have to witness any of that. We ushered her away from the room to prevent her from seeing the gruesome scene. She'd been through more than enough, so we decided not to tell her the rest of the…" Mark paused, unsure if he should be the one to tell April.

Noelle nodded her head, giving Mark permission to divulge the rest.

"Benoit was your father. What you don't know is, you are his only heir. He had no other children. You get his entire estate. April, you just inherited one billion dollars."

Stephanie fainted and fell face-first onto the floor.

CHAPTER 10

APRIL, MARY, AND TOMMY GAWKED at Mark with their mouths wide open. They tried to speak. Air moved past their vocal cords, but no words came out.

The three ignored Stephanie as she lay there passed out on the floor. There was a more important matter at hand.

Tommy clutched his chest. "Sis, is this true?"

Noelle nodded.

Mark went over to Stephanie and knelt next to her. He struggled to roll the hefty woman onto her back. Her long, hawkish nose had hit the floor first and was bleeding. Mark gestured toward the floor. "Hey, Tommy, a little help over here."

Tommy snapped out of the thick fog his mind was lost in. "Oh yeah...right. Sorry." He pulled out his handkerchief, sat her up, and pinched his wife's bleeding nose. After she was attended to, he turned to Mark. "I don't think I heard you right. Did you say one *million* dollars?"

Mark shook his head. "Nope, billion. With a B. As in the three-comma club. One billion dollars and some change."

With Mark's clarification on the staggering amount of money involved, Stephanie quickly came around.

She swatted Tommy's handkerchief away from her face. "Get that thing away from me. I'm fine. Help me up."

Tommy folded the blood-stained cloth into a small square and looked around for a safe place to dispose of it. Finding none, he reluctantly stuffed it back into his front pocket. With his help, Stephanie got up and took a seat on the couch next to April.

"I demand to know what the hell you are talking about, Mark," Stephanie barked. "How could April possibly have inherited that much money? You must have your facts screwed up. I don't believe it."

"It's true," Noelle said. "Gerard had no other children. He told me his prenups from his two failed marriages were rock solid. April is his only heir. Believe me; she gets it all."

Stephanie snorted out loud. "Believe *you!* Fat chance anyone will believe you after all the secrets you've been hiding." She pulled on Tommy's sleeve. "We need to hire a lawyer. We need to find out exactly what happened and what we need to do."

"Let's not worry about all that right now," Tommy replied. "April's world has been turned upside down today. Let's take her home so she can get a good night's sleep. We can talk about this tomorrow."

"Stop!" April yelled. "Everyone just *stop.* You're talking about me like I'm a child. I'm twenty-eight years old. I know better than anyone what's best for me."

Stephanie put her arm around April. "Of course you do, sweetie. Your dad and I just want to make sure—"

April pulled away. She stood up and spoke to the four parents in the room. "Do you have any idea how confusing and painful today has been for me? I find out that that I'm adopted and that my aunt is really my mother. Then I learn that this evil, horrible man is my father. That he was murdered by his own bodyguard before I could meet him. And then, after all the terrible things he did last week, you tell me I inherited one billion dollars from him. It's more shocking news than anyone should hear in a lifetime, let alone one day."

She walked over to the apartment door and pulled it open. Turning back, she said, "I don't want his money.

His ex-wives can go to war over it for all I care. I'm not taking one dime."

April Parker marched out and slammed the door.

CHAPTER 11

MARY DASHED OUT OF THE apartment to console her newfound big sister.

Stephanie jumped up from the couch and called out, "April, come back! Let's talk about this!"

Tommy stepped in front of his wife. "Let her go, Steph. She's got a lot to deal with right now. Let's all sit down and calmly discuss how to handle this."

Stephanie reached out pushed him aside. "She needs me. I have to—"

"I said sit *down!*" Tommy pointed back at the couch, his face bright red.

The shocked look on Stephanie's face was priceless. She'd been used to bullying Tommy, and everyone else in her life, and getting away with it.

He had finally had enough and put this foot down. "We…" he emphasized the word, "…will talk to April when I say so. Badgering her right now would only push her away when she needs us the most." With each passing second, Tommy's voice grew more forceful. "I said let her be, and that's final."

Noelle turned her head to the side and fought her facial muscles for control. She lost the battle. The sides of her mouth turned upward in a wide grin. Her pushy sister-in-law had finally been put in her place.

"Dammit, Tommy," Stephanie continued to argue, "that money is her rightful inheritance. Of course she should take it."

"I agree with April."

Everyone turned toward Mark.

"If she doesn't want the money, then it should be her decision and no one else's."

"Stay out of this, Smith," Stephanie ordered.

"That money is tainted. Duping Noelle into returning to France and kidnapping Mary was only the last thing that devious son of a bitch pulled in his life. Anyone who crossed him or challenged his enormous ego ended up ruined, if not dead. He was ruthless. Who knows who he destroyed to get the money she would inherit? It's dirty money. I agree with April. Screw it; put them in a cage and let his trophy wives fight over it."

"How noble of you to feel that way," Stephanie said, with a self-righteous smirk on her face. "You're not the one walking away from one billion dollars."

"Dammit, Stephanie, use your head. April is a good kid. Haven't you heard stories of the lottery winners whose lives were destroyed by striking it rich? This is like winning a hundred lotteries on the same day. Every lowlife and distant relative in her life will have their hands out demanding money. Not to mention complete strangers. She's too nice to say no."

"I won't let that happen. I'll be at April's side every step of the way helping her decide what to do with the money," Stephanie assured him.

Noelle spoke up. "How could you possibly know how to handle a billion dollars properly?"

"I know what I'm doing. I took bookkeeping courses by correspondence after I graduated from high school," she said in all seriousness.

Noelle laughed under her breath.

"Accounting is accounting, no matter how much money you're talking about." Stephanie crossed her arms and glared at Noelle. "And I suppose being a *stewardess*"—her voice dripped with disdain at Noelle's profession—"makes you a financial expert?"

Being a redhead, Noelle's fuse was never very long to start with. That contemptuous jab by her irritating sister-in-law had just put a torch to it.

Both husbands immediately realized it was time to break up this party and call it a day.

"Time to go, Steph," Tommy commanded, as he quickly lifted his wife to her feet.

Mark blocked Noelle's path to her sister-in-law. "Helluva good idea, Tommy." Before she could get in a verbal counterpunch of her own, Mark had spun Noelle around and was moving her involuntarily toward the bedroom door.

"We'll talk in a few days!" Tommy called out over his shoulder as he hustled Stephanie out of the apartment and closed the door.

Noelle tried to get around Mark. "That condescending little…"

"Easy, Rambo," he said, blocking her path with his arm, "she's gone. It's over."

"She doesn't care about April. All she cares about is getting her hands on—"

"I know what she's trying to do. Take a deep breath and try to relax. This might come as a surprise to you, but I'm incredibly good at reading people. It's like I have a third sense about them." Mark flashed a mischievous grin.

"It's *sixth sense*, you big dope." She tried, but failed, to muster up a convincing pout. "And stop making jokes." Noelle playfully whacked him on the arm. "I'm mad at her for the mean things she said."

"Okay you're right. What she said wasn't very nice."

Noelle hooked her arm through Mark's. "Thanks for taking my side."

He reached over and pulled her arm apart from his. "Hold on a minute. Let's get one thing straight. I'm not taking your side, or Tommy's, or Stephanie's in this. All three of you kept me in the dark about the adoption ever since I met you. Why should I trust any of you? What's best for April is my only concern here. I don't think she should take one cent of the bastard's money."

CHAPTER 12

APRIL PARKER'S TINY BEDROOM OVER-LOOKED a weed-infested courtyard. Broken beer bottles littered the crumbling asphalt. Buoyed by the warm wind, trash swirled around until it landed in the corners of the yard, adding to the existing piles.

April sat on her bed, hugging a well-worn teddy bear with patchy tan fur. Mary sat cross-legged on the floor, facing the bed.

"How could I possibly take the money from that psycho after what he did to you? What he did to your mom?" April asked. She shook her head in confusion. "I mean *our* mom." She clenched her teeth and let out a muffled scream of frustration, throwing the bear across the room. "I can't handle this." April dropped her head into her hands.

Mary got up and sat next to her sister. "I know it's confusing. There's no need to make any big decisions right now. Let all the crazy news you got today sink in first. Give it some time. Whatever you decide, I'll back you up."

April lifter her head. "You're always so calm and level-headed. Even when the world is going nuts around me, I know I can always count on you. You're going to make a great doctor." She turned and hugged her little sister. "Thanks."

Mary returned the hug. "You're welcome, Sis." Her eyes lit up. "Wow. Sister. My whole life I've wanted say that."

"Me, too," April said excitedly. "I always hated being an only child."

"You did? It's like you read my mind. We were thinking alike all these years and didn't even know it. That settles it. No matter how it happened, we were meant to be sisters."

April leaped off the bed and retrieved her teddy bear. "You're right. That settles it. Sisters for life." She dusted off the bear. "Since we're sisters now, does that means I can borrow that cute little black dress of yours?"

"You don't mean the one I got at Chanel last year, do you?"

"Yes. That short, tight one with the sequins along the neckline."

Mary drew in a breath through gritted teeth. "Um…I guess. Okay, sure. We're sisters. You can borrow my dress any time you like."

She got up and walked over to the desk. Mary aimlessly rearranged the Disney figurines on the desk, then looked down at the floor. "Sooo…inheriting a *BILLION* dollars. Is that ridiculous, or what?"

CHAPTER 13

"IT'S RIDICULOUS, ALL RIGHT." APRIL let out a long whistle. "I can't even imagine being that crazy rich."

"Not that you're going to take it. But what would you do with the money if you did?" Mary asked.

"I haven't even thought about that." She shrugged. "It doesn't matter. You're right. I'm not taking it."

Mary nodded. "That's cool. I wouldn't take it either. Like I said, it's your call. I'll back you up whatever you decide." Again, she toyed with the figurines. "But…"

"But what?"

"If you *did* decide to take your inheritance, you could afford to move out of your parents' apartment and get your own place. We could be roommates. We could finally get out of this crummy neighborhood and live anywhere we wanted with that kind of money. Even Park Avenue."

"Park Avenue? No, I couldn't picture myself rubbing elbows with the Rockefeller and Vanderbilt crowd. Too snooty."

"You could afford to go back to school and finish your nursing degree." Mary walked over and sat on the edge of the bed. "Think of all the brave, deserving troops you could help as a nurse at the VA. You could do a lot more than as a CNA, like you are now."

April got up and stared out the window. "I've always dreamed of being a real nurse. Not just an assistant cleaning out bedpans and changing dirty sheets all day long."

She turned back with a big smile. "After you become a doctor, I could work for you as your head nurse."

"I'd love that. Now you're thinking straight," Mary said, tapping the side of her head. "I know that money has a lot of terrible baggage attached to it, but think of all the good you could do with it. All the people you could help."

The sound of the apartment door opening was followed by Stephanie's grating voice. "Sweetie, it's Mom. Are you here?"

A few seconds later April's bedroom door opened.

"There you are." Stephanie rushed in and smothered her daughter in a hug. "I'm so glad you're okay. I was worried sick about you." She led April over to the bed and sat her down.

Tommy appeared in the doorway. "Hi, April." He walked over and took her hand. "Rough day, huh."

"Yeah, pretty rough," she replied, tears forming in her eyes. She cracked a smile as she dabbed at her blue eyes. "It's no big deal. I find out I'm adopted and inherited a billion dollars all the time. Just another day."

That drew a laugh from Tommy. "I'm glad to see your sense of humor is still intact. I have a feeling you're going to need it."

Stephanie looked at Mary. "I think it would be best if you leave. We'd like to be alone with our daughter."

"Oh…um…okay." Mary turned toward to leave.

"I want her to stay," April interjected. "We've been doing a lot of talking. Mary has been giving me some great advice." April looked sideways at Stephanie. "I trust *her.*"

"What have you been talking about, sweetie?" Stephanie asked, her eyes narrowing.

"Everything. All the crazy things that have happened today. That sort of thing."

"If you feel like talking, you know that I'm here for

you, right?" Stephanie said.

"There *is* something I want to talk to you about. Dad too. I want to talk about the money I'm supposed to inherit."

"Of course. That is, if you are up to it, I mean."

April took a deep breath. "I've made a decision."

The anticipation was killing Stephanie. "And?"

April shook her head. "It wouldn't be right for Noelle and Mark to be excluded from my announcement. They deserve to hear it at the same time as everyone else." She turned to Mary. "Would you please call your parents and ask them to come over?"

"Having Noelle come to our apartment right now might not be the best idea," Tommy warned. "Things got a little heated between your mother and…" He paused to rephrase. "Between Stephanie and Noelle before we left."

"You think I should wait a few days to tell everyone so they have time to cool off?" April asked Tommy.

"I'm fine," Stephanie interjected. She wagged her finger at Mary. "Call your folks and tell them to get over here."

Mary rolled her eyes. "Okay, relax. I'll call them." She walked out of the bedroom and into the kitchen to place the call.

When Noelle picked up, Mary explained the situation. "Hi, Mom. I'm at April's. We've been talking about everything, and she wants you guys to come over. She has an announcement she'd like to make, and April wants you guys to be here for it." Mary listened for a moment, then answered, "Yes, she's here." A few seconds later: "But it's really important. Can't you two just get along for one minute?" Changing her voice to a whisper, Mary turned her head to the side, shielding the phone with her hand. "It's about the money. April has decided what she is going to do with it."

Mary hung up and walked back into the bedroom. "They'll be here in ten minutes."

———————◆———————

The knock on the apartment door came eight minutes later. Tommy answered. Mark and Noelle hurried in.

Prudently, the two men stood between the feuding sisters-in-law as the group assembled in the small family room.

April stood facing the four parents. "It's important that everyone hear this at the same time. As jarring as today has been for me, I know I can't change what happened in the past. But I can control what I do about it. Mary and I talked about my inheritance. I fully understand it has a lot of bad baggage attached to it. I've come to a decision on what I'm going to do."

Everyone leaned forward with anticipation.

April stiffened up. "I'm not taking the money."

CHAPTER 14

"WAIT...WHAT?" MARY WAS IN SHOCK.
"Are you sure about this?" Tommy asked.

"But that money is rightfully yours," Stephanie said in a panic.

"I'm not finished," April said. "As much as it pains me to say this, I found out today I can't trust any of the parents in this room except one of you. He's the only person who hasn't been lying to me my whole life. I'm not going to accept my inheritance unless Uncle Mark agrees to help me manage it."

Mark's eyes opened wide. He pushed his fingertip into his chest. "Me? No, that's a bad idea," he warned.

"Uncle Mark might not be the best person for the job, sweetie," Tommy advised her.

"I know you are hurting and confused right now, but Tommy is right. Mark doesn't have the best track record with money," Noelle added.

"He blew all their money gambling," Stephanie said bluntly. "He's the last person you can trust with your inheritance."

"Thanks for the overwhelming vote of confidence, everyone," Mark huffed, his feelings bruised. He looked at his niece. "Look, you're a good kid, April. I don't want to see you get hurt. If you want my opinion, you should forget you ever heard of Gerard Benoit."

"It's too late for that," April said, glaring at Noelle.

"Seriously, you don't want me anywhere near your

money. Tommy has been the best parent you could possibly ask for growing up. Let him help you."

The absence of Stephanie's name in Mark's praise of April's upbringing stood out like an ogre at a tea party.

April refused to look at Tommy, effectively answering Mark's recommendation. She chewed on her bottom lip and paced the small room. After deliberating for a moment about the monumental decision, she stopped and announced, "I've made up my mind, and I'm not going to change it. I need a parent on my side I can trust."

Ouch.

"Either Uncle Mark helps me with my inheritance, or I'm not taking it."

Noelle shook her head in resignation and looked over at Mark. "It's your call. Do what you think is best."

"Of course he'll help you," Stephanie volunteered. "Right, Mark?"

Mark looked at April and sighed. "Have you even thought about what you are going to do with the money? Where you'd invest it?"

"I have," April said proudly. "I know exactly where to put it. I'm going to deposit the billion dollars into my credit union checking account."

CHAPTER 15

"YOUR CHECKING ACCOUNT? SERIOUSLY?" MARK closed his eyes and pinched the bridge of his nose. "I know I'm going to regret this." He opened them to see April eyeing him anxiously. "What the hell. Okay, kid, I'll help you."

"See, I told you Mark would do it," Stephanie declared.

"Thanks, Uncle Mark. Where do we start?"

"I don't have the slightest idea," he said truthfully. "I guess we need to go to France and collect your inheritance before we worry about anything else."

"Wait," Mary said, pulling out her phone and tapping on an app. "Before you get bogged down in all that, I want to tell the whole world I have a new big sister. An extremely rich big sister."

"No!" All four parents shouted out simultaneously, their eyes wide open.

"Absolutely do not tell anyone about April's inheritance," Stephanie said.

Mary rolled her eyes. "Parents. You're so stuck in the Stone Age. Do you know how many likes I would get from a video like that? It would go viral in minutes."

"That's exactly why you can't tell anyone," Mark said. "The last thing you want is the world knowing about April coming into a billion dollars. It's too dangerous."

"I can't tell anyone, either?" April questioned.

"No one!" the four parents again stated simultaneously.

Mary capitulated. "Fine." She handed her phone to

Mark. "I'll post the video on Instagram, but I won't mention the money."

With a confused look, he took the phone. "What is Instant Gram?"

"OMG! No, Dad, it's *Instagram*."

Noelle put her hand to her mouth and cleared her throat to keep from laughing. "Be nice to your father. You know how he is with technology."

"Never heard of it," Mark said.

"It's a way to send pictures and videos to everyone you know. I'll install the app on your phone. You'll love it."

"Don't bet on it."

Having qualified for membership in AARP many years ago, Mark had an ongoing love-hate relationship with gadgets. Despite having flown some of the most high-tech aircraft in the world, he still struggled with smartphones. Mark eventually gave up expecting his daughter to answer her phone when he called, so he'd learned to text. Trusting that an app knew the best route to get where he was driving was still a work in progress, though.

Mary exhaled in frustration. "Just take the video, please. After you're finished, I'll show you another high-tech invention. It's called fire."

"Never heard of it," Mark joked, intentionally tweaking his patronizing daughter.

After recording multiple takes of the new sibling-announcement video—the social media-obsessed girls felt the need for different poses—Mark sent the best one out for the entire world to see. Within fifteen minutes, ninety-seven of her closest friends had commented on it and shared the breaking news with their friends.

Mark got down to business. "Do you have a passport?" he asked April.

"No. I've never been out of the country before."

"Let's start there. It can take up to six weeks to get your

first passport. You'll need to get all your legal documents together first."

"Which documents?"

"I can help with that," Mary volunteered. She pulled her laptop out of its black bag and plugged it in. The computer clicked and whirred to life. A minute later, she had the answer. "The passport agency website says for your first one, you're required to submit two pass-port-size photos and a certified copy of your original birth certificate with a raised seal."

Tommy turned to Noelle. "Sis?"

"Don't look at me, I don't have it. Her birth certificate was included in the adoption paperwork you received. You guys have it."

"No, we don't," Stephanie insisted. "You have it."

"Knock off the arguing," Mark implored. "We have plenty of time to track it down. You three figure out where the birth certificate is. I'll take care of the pictures. After April gets her passport, we will fly to Paris and find out what she needs to do to claim her inheritance."

"Fly to Paris?" Mary shook her head. "Okay, Dad, his-tory lesson time. After they invented fire, they invented Google. Maybe you've heard about it?"

Noelle chuckled under her breath.

"You don't have to fly to Paris to get the information. I can search for the requirements for April to claim her inheritance right here," Mary explained, pointing at her laptop. She began tapping on the keyboard.

"Wow, Paris," April said excitedly. "The City of Lights. I've only seen pictures of it. I want to go to the top of the Eiffel Tower, tour the Louvre, get an espresso at a sidewalk café."

"Sure. We can do all that while we're there," Mark promised. "I know my way around Paris. I've been there many times on layovers."

"If you want haute couture, I know some great dress

shops you can check out while you're there," Noelle eagerly volunteered.

Mary held up a finger while examining the laptop screen. "Hold on. There's a small problem. With this much money on the line there are bound to be people lined up around the block trying to claim it." She slid her finger down the screen as she read. "The court in charge of large or contested inheritance cases in France is the *Tribunal de grande instance de Paris*. It says here it can take up to six months to settle an estate."

"April will have her passport long before that," Mark replied. "Besides, she's his only child. She gets the money."

"That's the problem," Mary said. "It says if there are any challenges to the legitimacy of lineage to a French citizen who died, all parties claiming to be the person's offspring must submit proof via a DNA test."

"I draw blood samples every day at the VA," April said. "I can get mine tested there."

"Passports are issued by the Department of State. That agency is slower and more bureaucratic than the DMV. Plus, the summer travel season is just around the corner. Everyone going out of the country on vacation will be applying for passports. It will be a miracle if April gets her passport in six weeks."

"But we have six months," Mark said.

"No, you don't." Mary continued reading the laptop screen. "It says the blood sample can only be taken by a doctor licensed in France. And, the sample must be submitted to the court for DNA testing within thirty days of the decedent's death. Failure to do both will result in permanent forfeiture of any claim to the inheritance. Gerard Benoit died one week ago."

CHAPTER 16

Twenty-three days until deadline

"SO, YOU'RE SAYING MY DAUGHTER is going to lose out on inheriting one billion dollars because the passport office is so damn incompetent it couldn't find its ass with both hands?" Stephanie grumbled, seething with anger. Fists balled up tight, the brash New Yorker declared, "Over my dead body. I'm going down there tomorrow and give them a piece of my—"

"Hold on, Steph," Tommy said. "Until we track down April's birth certificate, we are dead in the water. Rather than going down there tomorrow and getting yourself arrested, why don't you make yourself useful and go to the bank and see if it's in the safe deposit box?"

"Even if it is there, April only has three weeks left to get to France. Her passport will never be processed by then."

"She can pay extra for expedited processing," Mark proposed. "I had to do that once with my passport after it expired. The passport office will rush the application through in only two weeks."

"Oh thank God," Stephanie exclaimed. "How do we make that happen?"

"I'll check." Mary tapped on her keyboard. Thirty seconds later she had the answer. "April has to call a regional passport agency and schedule an appointment to apply in person for an expedited passport. The office is on Hudson Street in Manhattan. She needs: a completed application, locations and dates you intend to travel abroad, the required documents, and a fee of $170 dollars."

"That's going to be a problem," April said, cringing. "I don't get paid until the first, and I only have forty-two dollars in my checking account."

Mark chuckled. "Wouldn't that make a great headline. *The Broke Billionaire.*"

"For want of a nail, my kingdom was lost." Everyone turned toward Noelle when she uttered the obscure phrase.

"What are you talking about?" Stephanie asked.

"It's an old proverb about how something small can cause—"

"April doesn't need a nail; she needs a passport," Stephanie scolded.

Noelle just shook her head rather than try to explain. "Never mind."

"Don't worry about the money, sweetie. I'll pay for everything," Stephanie said.

April looked at Stephanie. "Thanks, M—" Before she completed her sentence, she paused and looked over at Noelle.

Her birth mother had a forlorn expression on her face. The words from earlier today came flooding back. Mixed emotions battled for her heart. April looked back at her mom. "Once I get my inheritance, I'll pay you back. Thanks…um…Stephanie."

CHAPTER 17

One week until deadline

"I GOT IT." APRIL BURST INTO the apartment waving the freshly minted blue US passport booklet in the air.

"Yes!" Stephanie exclaimed, pulling down a strong fist pump. "That's wonderful, darling."

April beamed with excitement. "I need to call Uncle Mark so he can make the airline reservations." She whipped out her iPhone from her back pocket.

"That's great, kid. Bring your passport over right away so I can book our flights." Mark clicked off then Googled the number for Air France reservations. He wrote the number down on a notepad then limped off to the bedroom, without the aid of his crutches. He went in search of his passport.

There was a loud knock on the apartment door. Noelle tossed the summer fashion edition of *Vogue* magazine aside and sprang up off the couch. She pulled the door open.

A large woman in a loud flower print dress stood in the hallway. She had one hand braced against the door frame, was partially bent at the waist, and was panting heavily.

Grinning from ear to ear, Noelle shouted, "Charlotte!

It's so good to see you!"

Charlotte had big hair, a big heart, and an even bigger personality. She waddled into the room, pulled a handkerchief out of her cleavage, and dabbed it at her sweaty brow. "Darlin', this place has *gotta* get an elevator, or else I'm fixin' to have an embolism." After taking a moment to catch her breath, Charlotte smothered Noelle in a hug. "Come here, you. I'm so sorry I haven't been able to come by any sooner. How you doin' after all that nonsense in France?"

Noelle's smile faded. "It's going to take time to move past it, of course. But every day is a little better than the last."

"How 'bout ol' gimpy? Still acting like that little scratch on his leg is a big deal?"

Noelle shook her head. "I thought you and Mark called a truce and agreed to be nice to each other."

Charlotte stuffed the hankie back down where it came from. "Well, I suppose I could cut him a *little* slack, seeing as how he did save my butt by getting our plane to dry land in the Azores." She flashed a big grin. "How about getting your best friend a Coke before I get all mushy and start saying nice things about the rascal."

Noelle waved Charlotte toward a chair in the kitchen while she retrieved a can from the refrigerator. She pulled the tab to open it and handed the can to Charlotte. "How's work going?"

"Thanks, darlin'." She took the can and guzzled down a mouthful. "Slow. Marty says he'd be able to book more charters with an extra pilot working. He bitches and complains constantly, asking when Mark is coming back."

Noelle pulled out a chair and sat across from her friend. "I made Mark promise he wouldn't fly until his leg was fully healed. The doctor said it'll be soon."

"Marty's not gonna be happy to hear that."

"Don't worry about Marty. He puts on a tough-guy

act, but inside he's really a soft pussy cat. Mark and I will never forget what he did for Mary."

"How's she doing? It had to be rough on her, getting kidnapped and all."

"She's handling it well considering what she went through. She's tougher than she thinks. When she goes back to med school in the fall, Mark and I think that will help take her mind off what happened."

Charlotte put down the can and turned serious. "Did you tell April yet?"

"A few weeks ago."

"How'd she take finding out she's adopted?"

"Not good," Noelle lamented. "She won't speak to me. She hates me for lying to her all these years."

"I'm sure she doesn't hate you, darlin'."

Her head slumped down. "I lost my mother to cancer when I was in high school. I was so confused and angry. I hated her for doing that to me. The time in my life when I needed a mother the most, I lost her forever. Now, I might lose *my* daughter forever."

Charlotte patted Noelle's hand. "Give her some time to sort things out. It's a big shock finding out you're adopted, at any age." Hoping to cheer her up, Charlotte diverted a bit. "Did I ever tell you ol' Bubba is adopted?"

Noelle lifted her head. "He is? How old was your husband when he found out?"

"Fourteen. Not that he remembers much about finding out. His old man drove him into town that night and got him drunk to mark the occasion."

"He got his fourteen-year-old son drunk?"

"Yep. Real Father of the Year material that old coot was."

Mark emerged from the bedroom with his passport in hand. "I found it." When he caught sight of Noelle's best friend, he mumbled, "Oh great." He quickly donned a phony smile. "Charlotte, always a treat to see you."

"Well, if it ain't Gimpy the Pilot."

Even though they'd called a truce, Charlotte delighted in tweaking Mark whenever she got the chance.

Her brow wrinkled as she pointed at the passport. "Going somewhere?"

Noelle leaned back out of Charlotte's peripheral vision. She held her index finger against her lips and shook her head side to side.

"As a matter of fact, I am," Mark said, ignoring the warning. "A place where they speak a strange foreign language. It's called Georgia."

His return volley in their verbal jousting, about her beloved home state, reddened Charlotte's plump cheeks.

"Careful, Mark. They like to shoot Yankees for sport down where I'm from. I'd sure hate to see you get shot in the leg again."

"All right, you two, be nice," Noelle implored, playing the peacemaker.

Mary walked out of her bedroom, reading the screen on her laptop. "You guys are not going to believe what is happening with Benoit's inheritance. His—"

"Mary, look who's here," Noelle quickly interrupted.

She looked up and squealed, "Auntie Charlotte!" Mary put the laptop down on the kitchen table and embraced her unofficial auntie.

"How's my little sweet pea? I'm so thankful you're back home safe and sound."

Mark slid over to the table and surreptitiously closed the laptop behind Charlotte's back.

Mary saw him do it and nodded in understanding. "I'm still having nightmares about what happened, but at least the bruises are gone."

Charlotte clamped a hand onto Mary's chin and nudged her head left and right, examining her skin. "They sure are. I don't see anything but your beautiful, smiling face." She feigned surprise. "Why, if I didn't know any better,

I'd say I was looking in a mirror right now, we look so much alike."

Mark burst out laughing.

Charlotte released Mary's chin and crossed her arms tightly across her chest. "Smith, you say one word, and it will be your last."

Mark wisely raised his hands in surrender and did not utter a single word that was sitting on the tip of his tongue.

April knocked once on the apartment door then let herself in. "Look what I've got," she said, waving her passport.

The Smith family gave April different body language clues on the need for secrecy about her upcoming trip.

Noelle waved her hand in front of her throat.

Mark shook his head.

Mary cleared her throat.

April got the message and stuffed the passport in her back pocket. "Hi, Charlotte. I didn't know you were going to be here. How are you?"

"I'm just fine, dear." Her eyes narrowed as she looked slowly around the room at each person. Pointing at April, Charlotte said, "Hmmm, what a coincidence. Looks like you are going to Georgia, too."

"Georgia?" April questioned.

Noelle reached out and ushered Charlotte toward the apartment door. "I'm so glad you stopped by. I hate to cut our visit short, but we're going to a movie. Let's do lunch soon." She pulled the door open and waited.

"And what movie would that be, dear?"

Noelle looked down at her shoes and searched for an answer. "Um…that new one with…with Kevin Bacon in it."

Charlotte gave her best friend a shallow hug. "You folks enjoy the movie. From the look of things around here, it should be quite the mystery tale."

Noelle clicked the door shut behind Charlotte after she left.

No one spoke until the heavy sound of Charlotte's footsteps in the hallway fell to a safe level.

Mark said, "Good job, everyone. We never talk about the inheritance in front of other people."

Mary opened her laptop and pointed at the screen. "We might not be talking openly about it, but everyone in France is. The media is going crazy trying to find out if Benoit had any children."

"As long as we're smart and keep our mouths shut, we should be fine. The only people over there who knew about April are dead," Mark said. "Until April files a formal claim to Benoit's estate with the court, she should remain anonymous."

"I hope you're right, Dad," Mary said. "Things are getting really nasty over there. The article says Benoit's sister, Josephine Benoit-Dechambeau, and both of his ex-wives are each claiming that they are the only rightful heir to his fortune. They've all hired powerful French law firms to dig up dirt on each other, trying to invalidate competing claims."

April wrung her hands. "I wish this was over already. I just want to go to Paris, get my inheritance, and get back home."

"Be careful what you wish for. I don't want to sound like the crusty old guy here, but money has a way of changing people. And not for the better," Mark cautioned.

"It won't change me," she replied confidently.

"It's not you I'm worried about."

CHAPTER 18

"LET'S GET BUSY," MARK COMMANDED, effort-lessly slipping back into his captain persona as he handed out everyone's marching orders. "Noelle, you speak French. Find the forms online the court requires to claim Benoit's inheritance and fill them out."

"It looks like that French degree I got from Yale wasn't a waste of money after all," Noelle bragged.

"Mary, track down a doctor in Paris who can take April's blood sample."

"Already done," Mary announced. "I called the medical school dean to ask for his help. He connected me with an old classmate from France who studied at Duke. His name is Dr. Adrien Boucher."

"The doctor's name is Boucher?" Noelle asked; her face distorted.

"Yes. Why?"

"*Boucher* means 'butcher' in French."

"Okay, well, that's a comforting omen," April moaned.

"Never mind that. I'll call Air France and book our flights," Mark said. "The deadline for submitting the claim is Friday of next week. How soon can you leave, April?"

"I can leave tomorrow. I used up the rest of my vacation time for the year and took off through next week to be safe. My boss wasn't very happy with me."

Mark smiled. "You won't need to worry about work *or* your boss after we get back. Your life will be a permanent vacation."

"Oh, I'm not quitting my job."

Her family members looked at April with skeptical expressions on their faces.

"I love working at the VA. My patients are so grateful that someone appreciates the sacrifices they made."

Mark felt a burst of pride swell up inside him toward his niece. From his time as a pilot in the Air Force, Mark knew firsthand what motivated members of the military to put their lives on the line for America. He had no intention of talking April out of quitting her job helping them in their time of need.

"I'll call Air France and book our flight for tomorrow," Mark said.

"Tomorrow isn't going to happen," Mary announced from the couch. She'd been tapping away on her laptop, researching flight options. "It looks like the summer rush has already started. Air France is the only airline with any available seats to Paris. And not until Wednesday— of next week. The flight departs Wednesday evening and arrives in Paris Thursday morning."

"Damn," Mark said, rubbing his chin, "that's cutting it close."

"You better book the flight now before it sells out," Mary suggested. "They aren't going to be cheap. Tickets are $1,200. Each. One-way."

"Ouch!" Mark looked at Noelle. "I don't have that kind of money. I haven't had a paycheck in almost a month."

"Don't worry, I'll take care of it," April said.

"You do realize you won't get your inheritance right away, don't you?" Mark warned.

April nodded. "I know. But I have this." She pulled out her mother's gleaming new American Express Platinum credit card. "She said I could use it for any expenses con- nected to getting my inheritance."

"How did Stephanie qualify for a platinum card?"

Mark asked suspiciously.

April just shrugged.

"Cool." Mary took the card. She booked two tickets from John F. Kennedy International Airport to Paris-Charles De Gaulle for her father and sister.

Mark looked up at hearing a knock on the door. He limped over and opened it.

"Hey, Mark! How's the leg, buddy?" Andy Wilson, one of Mark's roommates in the apartment he shared with other pilots, stood in the doorway.

Mark didn't let him in. "What are you doing here?"

"We're going on a date," Mary proclaimed. She closed her laptop and pulled herself up from the sagging, ratty couch.

Mark glared at Andy, his protective fatherly instincts on full display. "Is that a fact? I don't remember you asking me if you could date my daughter."

Mary stepped between the two men and ushered Andy into the apartment. She turned back and whispered, "Dad, be nice."

Andy had a satisfied look on his face as he glanced around the room at the furnishings. "Your new place is certainly coming together."

There were still some boxes to unpack after the hasty move and personal touches to be made before the new apartment would feel like home.

"How do you like the furniture I found for it?"

"Well…it's…certainly unique," Mary said, trying desperately to find something positive to say about the mismatched garage sale rejects he'd procured.

"I thought you'd like it." Andy turned his attention to Mark. "When I told Marty I was coming over here, he said to tell you to hurry up and get your sorry butt back to work."

"Is that right?"

"Well, those weren't his exact words. I cleaned them up

since there are ladies present."

"Good old Marty. Classy guy. Next time you see him, tell that Navy squid I'll be back soon."

"I'll see him tomorrow. I volunteered to fly charters for him on my days off from Jet Blue until you recovered. He gave me my first job flying jets, so I figured I'd help him out. Least I could do."

"Where are you flying?" Mark inquired.

"Fort Lauderdale, then—"

"All right," Mary interjected, as she grabbed Andy's arm, "before you two jet jocks spend the entire evening talking about flying, we'd better get going. What do you have in mind?"

"I thought we'd catch a movie. The latest sequel of the *Terminator* series looks tolerable," Andy said.

"I've got a better idea. The New York School of Interior Design is having an open house. We should stop by and check it out."

Andy shrugged. "Um…okay." Like a gentleman, he opened the door for Mary. The light bulb finally came on for Andy. "Oh wait. That was a hint, wasn't it?"

A guilty smirk spread across Mary's face. "Maybe."

CHAPTER 19

Forty-three hours until deadline

NOELLE PULLED THEIR RUSTED DODGE mini-van up to the curb on the departure level in front of Terminal 4 at JFK. The modern glass-and-steel structure was the airport's main gateway for international travel, accommodating a mind-bending twenty-one million passengers a year through its corridors.

Based on years of travel experience, Mark insisted they arrive three hours before takeoff to allow plenty of time to get through the long lines at the TSA security checkpoint. He jumped out and unloaded their bags from the back of the minivan. Mark had packed his worn, rolling black carry-on. April stuffed all she needed into a backpack.

Mark walked around to the driver's window. "Our flight leaves at six. I'll text you when we get there." He walked away.

Noticeably, there was no parting kiss.

Noelle rolled down the passenger window and waved at April. "Have a safe flight. I'll see you when you get back, sweetie."

April marched off and disappeared into the crowd without acknowledging the send-off from her mother.

Mark and April weaved in and out of the throng of people as they navigated the enormous terminal. Crossing the polished terrazzo floor felt like running an obstacle course. They dodged luggage trolleys, baby strollers, and passengers glued to their phone screens, oblivious to everyone around them.

Vacation-bound travelers represented every culture and nation. Terminal 4 resembled a United Nations family reunion every day of the year. Airliners sporting colorful liveries waited patiently at their gates to deliver travelers to their destination.

As he walked through the terminal, Mark looked over at an empty ticket counter. Despite the letters being removed months ago, it still had the ghost of the name *ALPHA AIRLINES* visible on the backdrop. He let out a heavy sigh. The crash of the Tech-Liner in the Azores had been the last straw for the financially teetering airline. It had declared bankruptcy within days of the tragedy.

After thirty-five years of dedicated service, Mark had been counting on his pension and company-paid health insurance once he retired. Now he had neither.

Luckily, he and Noelle had found jobs working for Luxury Jet Charters out of Teterboro Airport. It wasn't airline captain pay, but it paid the rent and Mark enjoyed flying ultra-wealthy passengers to exotic destinations. Free time to explore those destinations—on the passenger's dime—while waiting to return them back home was a nice perk, as well. It sure beat yet another layover in lovely downtown Detroit. The best part of all was not having to deal with the torturous experience that flying on the airlines had become.

Hundreds of impatient passengers were queued up at the TSA checkpoint. The pair took their place at the end of the line behind a family with four unruly kids. While the kids ran circles around their outnumbered parents, April ignored them and passed the time by scrolling through her iPhone screen. Mark looked over and read the sign mounted on the pole at the beginning of every TSA line: "Aviation Safety and Security are No joking

Matter. All Comments Will be Taken Seriously."

After inching forward in the line for an hour, Mark handed the overworked and underpaid TSA agent the two boarding passes he'd printed out at home.

"ID," the agent barked, not bothering to look up.

Mary handed the agent her new passport.

She compared it to the name on the boarding pass, scanned the bar code on the printout, and handed both back to April after receiving a confirmation beep and a green light from the scanner.

Mark handed the agent his passport. She checked that the names matched and scanned the boarding pass. The scanner let out a shrill warning tone accompanied by a red light. The agent looked up at Mark. She held his passport up in her line of sight, eyed the picture on his passport more carefully this time, then scanned the boarding pass again. The red light and shrill tone repeated.

After his boarding pass failed to scan successfully a second time, a TSA supervisor walked up beside the agent. She turned and whispered something in his ear. His eyes narrowed as he looked at Mark. "Sir, you need to step out of line and speak to a manager at the Air France ticket counter."

"What's the problem?" Mark asked.

"Step out of line, sir," the supervisor said sternly. He waved the line of passengers forward. "Next!"

Angry stares from the people in line behind him persuaded Mark to give up on debating the supervisor and go to the ticket counter for answers.

He and April lined up behind dozens of passengers waiting at the Air France ticket counter. Mark looked back over his shoulder. Two uniformed, and armed, Army soldiers were observing him while speaking into black walkie-talkies.

April noticed them also. "Uncle Mark, what's going on?"

"I don't know. But I'm damn sure going to find out."

As he looked around the terminal, Mark noticed a few passengers looking at him over the tops of their magazines and newspapers. Strangely, none of them seemed to be in any hurry to get to their flight. Mark assumed they were plainclothes undercover cops who stake out large airports watching for suspicious behavior.

When they finally reached the counter, he told the agent, "I need to talk to a manager."

"Is there a problem, Monsieur?" she replied.

"There's a problem with my boarding pass. It won't scan correctly at the TSA checkpoint. Our flight leaves soon, and I was told to talk to a manager."

"Let me have your boarding pass, *s'il vous plait.*" She took it and typed Mark's reservation number into her computer. When the information flashed up on the screen, she leaned forward and read it carefully. The agent stood up and scurried off to the back office without saying a word.

A minute later a thin, stern-looking man dressed in a stylish black suit came out of the office holding Mark's boarding pass. The agent trailed meekly behind him.

He stepped up to Mark. "Are you Monsieur Smith?

"Yes. What's going—"

"I'm sorry to tell you there is a problem. You will not be going on the flight to Paris."

"What the hell are you talking about? I've got a ticket right there," Mark said, pointing at his boarding pass. "There must be a mistake in your computer system. Check it again."

"There is no *mistake*, Monsieur," the manager declared with an offended tone.

"Screw this. I should have booked our flight with a US airline. We have to get to Paris tomorrow. Transfer our reservations to American Airlines, or United, or whoever your damned airline has a code-share agreement with."

"It will do you no good. You are not welcome in my country."

"Not welcome? I've been to France dozens of times over the years. I've never had a problem before. I'm not some damned *terrorist!*" he shouted in frustration.

Every person within earshot of Mark turned their heads on overhearing that explosive word. Fear radiated from their eyes. Parents tucked their children behind themselves out of an overabundance of caution.

Before that fateful September day in 2001, the last word you ever wanted to yell out in an airport was hijack. Now Mark had loudly uttered its threatening replacement.

"A terrorist, no, but you *are* on my country's Watch List." The manager turned the computer screen to face Mark and pointed at the starred and underlined French text. "By order of the Director General of the Police Nationale, you are barred from entering France."

Mark's head slumped. "Crap." He drew in a deep breath. "Is the name of the director general who issued the order Victor Arnoult?"

The manager spun the monitor back around and read the order. "Oui, Monsieur. It came from Victor Arnoult." He motioned for the soldiers to come to the ticket counter. "I'm afraid you must leave now."

The hulking soldiers had been hovering nearby as the conversation had gotten heated. They were outfitted in full battle gear, including M4 carbines and sidearms. A military presence had become a frightening but necessary addition to American airports since 9/11.

They walked up on either side of Mark. In a no-nonsense voice, the higher ranking of the two men said, "Sir, you will be leaving now. Come with us." He pointed at the front door to the terminal. The other soldier had his hand resting on his carbine.

"Uncle Mark, what's happening?" April said, her voice trembling.

"Now, sir," the soldier repeated.

"I'll explain later. Let's go."

Everyone in the terminal had their eyes glued on Mark as he was marched toward the door with two armed soldiers escorting him. Some passengers had their phones held at eye level, videoing the incident. April trailed behind. They exited the terminal building and stopped at the curb. The soldiers stood guard inside the sliding glass door to prevent his reentry.

Now, the normally packed sidewalk was conspicuously empty around the pair. Only the undercover cops were within fifty feet of Mark and April. None of them were reading.

Mark took out his phone and tapped the speed-dial listing for Noelle.

CHAPTER 20

Thirty-nine hours until deadline

"THAT VINDICTIVE SON OF A bitch." Mark's cheeks were crimson as he paced around their small apartment.

Noelle, Mary, and April sat around the kitchen table with desperate expressions.

"He did say you were no longer welcome in his country after he finished questioning you. Looks like Director Arnoult followed through on his warning," Noelle said.

"Arnoult knows I didn't murder Benoit. His bodyguard murdered him," Mark responded.

"Of course he knows that. But Arnoult said he spent years building a tax evasion case against Gerard Benoit. He was robbed of the chance to make Benoit do the perp walk in front of the cameras like he'd planned. A highly publicized conviction like that could have been his ticket to become the official occupant of the Élysée Palace. Men with grand political ambitions like becoming the president of France don't just shrug and walk away when their opportunity to steal the spotlight is denied them. They exact revenge on anyone who gets in their way. Unfortunately, as an American, you make an easy scapegoat for him. He can bar you from entering France as long as he is director general."

"What about my inheritance? I need it to go back to nursing school," April pleaded.

The look of disappointment on April's face hurt Mark worse than being shot. "I'm sorry, kid."

"Sorry? Tell that to the soldiers who need my help. I was going to buy my parents a new condo and get them out of this crappy neighborhood. Because of you, none of that will ever happen."

Mark sat down at the kitchen table, taking the weight off his leg. "I know I promised I'd help you, but I can't even enter the country. I'd be arrested the moment I stepped off the plane." He reached toward April's side of the table. "Just because I can't go doesn't mean you can't. I'll find you another flight somehow, and you can petition the court yourself for your inheritance."

She pulled away and threw her hands up in frustration. "How can I do that? I don't speak French. I have no idea what I need to do with the court. I've never even gotten a parking ticket. The lawyers for Benoit's sister and ex-wives will be there, just waiting for me to miss dotting an I or crossing a T."

Mary cleared her throat. "I have a little bit of good news. I've been following this case on the internet. All the frivolous claims from the crackpots who always pop up in these situations have been thrown out. And Benoit's ex-wives have been ruled ineligible from receiving his inheritance by the court. The sister's legal team was able to find the prenup agreements he forced them to sign. His sister, Josephine, is the only one left claiming the money. She's alleging her brother told her she would get the money when he died."

"What about a will? A guy with that much money must have created a will." Mark said.

"There's no will. For some reason, men with colossal egos never seem to think they're going to die. Crazy, huh?" Mary said, shaking her head.

Noelle tried to see the silver lining. "That settles it then. As long as you submit a blood sample before the deadline, then you should get the money."

April ignored her.

"Josephine Benoit-Dechambeau is no one to be taken lightly. She's a multimillionaire in her own right," Mary warned. "Until your money is safely in your account…"

Mark rolled his eyes at the thought of that much money sitting in a checking account.

Everyone at the table saw his doubtful gesture.

"Or *wherever* it should go," Mary said loudly, for dramatic effect. "We need to be very careful when claiming the money and not make any mistakes."

With so much on her mind, April failed to notice the seemingly insignificant two-letter word Mary included in her last sentence.

We.

CHAPTER 21

" APRIL, YOU'RE GOING TO PARIS, and you will get your inheritance," Mark declared with confidence. "Mary, keep looking for open seats. Check every airline again."

He noticed the scene playing on the muted TV. The president was speaking at a campaign rally. "I'll call the damned president of the United States to intervene if I have to."

"He's a little busy right now trying to get reelected. I got this." Mary opened her laptop and began clicking away.

April pulled herself up from the kitchen table and cast her eyes downward. "I think I made a big mistake." She moved to the side and slid her chair back under the table. "I should have listened to my parents." April's eyes moistened. She looked across the table. "I think it was a mistake trusting you, Uncle Mark." April started for the door.

The sadness in her voice and the disappointment written on her face wounded Mark deep down inside. At that moment, he told himself he'd do whatever it took to do right by his niece.

Mark jumped up. "Please, I can fix this." He stepped between April and the door. "Give me until tomorrow morning. I *will* find a way to get you to Paris before the deadline. I promise."

April shook her head. "I'm leaving."

"I don't blame you for feeling like I let you down."

Mark swallowed hard. "Hear me out. I know you're not going to like this idea, but the best option is for Noelle to go with you to Paris. We still need to find seats, but she's the best choice."

"Absolutely not," April exclaimed. "I'd rather miss out on my inheritance than go anywhere with her."

Noelle dropped her head into her hands. Her shoulders jerked as she sobbed at the hurtful comment.

Mary reached over and lightly patted her mother's shoulder, hoping to lessen her pain. She turned toward April. "I'm not taking sides here; I'm really not. But my dad is right. Mom is your only option if you hope to get your inheritance. Won't you at least consider it?"

April opened the door. Her head drooped down. "I'm going to go ask my real mother for help." She walked out.

Despite Mark closing the door gently, the sound of the latch engaging echoed loudly in the small apartment.

Mark went to Noelle's side. "She's upset. She didn't mean what she said."

Noelle lifted her head out of her hands and wiped the tears from her eyes. "She's right. I'm not her real mom. I was around for the birthday parties and the fun stuff, but I wasn't the person who stayed up all night with her when she had the flu. I wasn't there for her when her first love broke her heart. She went to Stephanie for consolation, not me."

Mark pulled his chair over next to Noelle's and sat down at the kitchen table. "She'll come around. It's early. Don't give up yet."

"If she doesn't get her inheritance, all of her dreams will be crushed. April will never speak to me again if that happens."

"I'm not going to let it. I promised April I would get her to Paris, and I will."

Mary closed her laptop. "It's too late to get out on a flight tonight. All the flights to Europe have already left.

Why don't we sleep on it and see if we can come up with any new ideas tomorrow?"

Noelle forced a weak smile at her daughter's youthful optimism. "I'm sure we'll think of something in the morning." Her words lacked much conviction.

As they headed to their bedrooms to get some much-needed rest, Noelle paused at the light switch for the room. She slowly shook her head side to side then turned out the lights.

CHAPTER 22

Twenty-six hours until deadline

MARK AND NOELLE EMERGED FROM their bedroom at 7 a.m., bleary-eyed and exhausted after tossing and turning most of the night. Their mood was as dreary as the old, faded furniture.

Mary was seated at the kitchen table with her laptop open.

"How long have you been awake?" Mark asked her.

"A few hours," Mary said, yawning and rubbing sleep from her eyes. "I've been trying to find flights with open seats, but there's just nothing available. I even looked for flights to Paris that connected first in London, Rome, Frankfurt, or any other nearby city."

"Good thinking. I'm impressed," Mark said.

"What did you expect? I *was* raised by two airline employees," she teased. "I'm a pro at this. We traveled everywhere on standby when I was a kid. You need to think outside the box sometimes if you hope to get where you're going. Do you remember that trip to Prague over spring break? It took two days, four connecting flights, and a train just to get there."

The memories of being able to show their daughter so much of the world brought a smile to Noelle's face.

Mark cocked his head. He brought his hand to his mouth and tapped his lips with the tip of his index finger. "I have an idea." He rushed over to the kitchen table and spun Mary's laptop around to face him. Mark began tapping on the keys. "I'm gonna need everyone's help to pull this off."

———◆———

Eighteen hours until deadline

April wandered into the kitchen to talk to Stephanie. "Need any help making dinner, Mom?"

"Sure, sweetie. I'm making your favorite dish tonight, chicken spiedini." Stephanie put her arm around April's sagging shoulders. "I'm sorry about Paris. If I'd known Mark was going to screw up your only chance to get there, I would have gotten a passport and taken you myself."

April was too distraught to give the comment any consideration. She lost interest in food and wandered out of the kitchen. She flopped down on the couch, stabbed at the TV remote, and cycled through channels looking for anything other than a fake reality dating show. The last thing she needed to hear was a bunch of actress wannabes cry about not getting a rose when she was about to lose out on one billion dollars.

There was a loud knock at the door. April tossed the remote aside and went to the door. She opened it to find Mark and Mary standing there with huge grins on their faces.

"Are you still packed?" Mark asked.

"What's the point? It's too late," April moaned.

"I don't have time to explain; we have to hurry. Pack up your stuff; we're headed to the airport," Mark said breathlessly.

"Mary, what's going on?" April asked, wide eyed.

"I can't tell you. I'm sworn to secrecy. I'll help you pack." Mary hustled April off toward her bedroom.

———◆———

Mark blasted his horn at the traffic on the Grand Central Parkway as it slowed to a snail's pace at the exit to LaGuardia Airport.

April watched the airport pass by out her window.

Once Mark passed the airport exit, he floored it to the maximum speed the snarled NYC traffic would allow—a maddening thirty miles per hour. Yankee Stadium passed off to their right twenty minutes later. After crossing the Hudson River, traffic began to thin out. An hour after leaving April's apartment, they pulled into the parking lot of Luxury Jet Charters.

CHAPTER 23

THE THREE BURST THROUGH THE front door of the opulently decorated charter company headquarters. Italian marble floors, Swarovski crystal chandeliers, and the latest business magazines neatly laid out on carved oak tables greeted them. The type of clientele that could afford to charter a jet expected nothing less.

Marty Dawson, owner of the company, came around the corner chomping on an unlit cigar. He was dressed in an ill-fitting thirty-year-old suit that hadn't gotten any bigger as Marty put on a few pounds. The hair on his balding head was the only thing thinner than when he first bought the suit. "Hey, Air Farce, what are you doing here? I thought your leg was still healing."

"I missed your handsome mug, you old squid. I thought I'd stop by for a visit," Mark answered.

Despite being decades past leaving their respective military branches, interservice rivalry still burned fiercely in both men.

"Before you two drop down on the floor and start arm wrestling," Mary interjected, "let me get to the real reason why we're here." She pulled a bag of homemade chocolate chip cookies out of her purse. "These are for you. Your favorite."

Marty eyed the three suspiciously. "You drove all this way to give me cookies?"

"I have another reason for coming," Mary admitted. She took in a deep breath. "I'm here to thank you for

helping save my life. If it wasn't for your kindness in letting my folks borrow your plane to rescue me, I'd be
dead." She teared up as she hugged the gruff retired Navy
man. "Thank you."

Marty was caught flatfooted by her heartfelt comment.
"Of course. Glad to do it. I have a daughter of my own.
I'd move heaven and earth to help her if she was in dan-
ger."

"I didn't know you have a daughter. What's her name?"
Mary asked, mock surprise in her voice.

"Her name is April," Marty said, beaming ear to ear.

"April? What a small world. I'd like you to meet someone, Mr. Dawson." Mary waved her big sister forward.
"What happened over in France was terrible, but a wonderful thing came from it. I learned that I have a sister.
Marty, meet April Parker."

April reached out and eagerly shook his hand. "It's very
nice to meet you, sir."

Marty's eyes narrowed as he pulled his cigar from his
mouth and returned the handshake. "Nice to meet you,
April." His BS radar began to pick up a faint signal.
"Hmmm, what a coincidence, you havin' the same first
name as my daughter."

Mark jumped in to divert the conversation. "So, how's
business, Marty?"

"Crappy," he huffed. "The market is down big time
this year. My Wall Street clients who normally wouldn't
think twice about flying to their second homes for the
weekend are staying in town."

"Sorry to hear that. I'm sure business will pick up
soon." Mark shifted his weight back and forth on the
polished floor. "Um…I have a big favor to ask you."

"Make it quick; I need to get back to work."

"I need to borrow your Gulfstream again." Blunt and
direct.

CHAPTER 24

"I'M IN NO MOOD FOR jokes, Air Farce," Marty grumbled.

"I'm not joking, Marty. I need to get April to Europe as soon as possible, and you're the only option I have left."

Marty gnawed on his unlit cigar as he considered Mark's outrageous request. "How long do you need it for?"

Mark was expecting a different response. "I…um…no more than three days. So, I can borrow it?"

Marty paused for a moment then nodded his head. "Sure, you can borrow my jet. The cookies ought to cover my cost for the use of the plane. Just bring it back with a full tank."

"Really?" Mary asked, flabbergasted by his generosity.

"He's being sarcastic," Mark pointed out to his gullible daughter.

"I knew that," Mary muttered unconvincingly.

"You know I wouldn't ask you for a huge favor like this if it wasn't extremely important," Mark said.

Marty smirked and said, "Did someone else in your family get kidnapped that you need to go rescue?"

"No," Mark replied.

"Then what's so important that you think I would even consider letting you borrow my Gulfstream again?"

Mark glanced over at April. "She is. I gave her my word I would help her." He looked back at Marty. "I can't tell you why I need the plane, but it's important."

Marty took in deep, measured breaths as he paced back

and forth. He stopped and said, "Look, I'm happy that you and Noelle got Mary back safely, but I was out a lot of money for those flights to France and back. I can't afford to toss you the keys to my plane every time there's a problem. Besides, you need a copilot, and you're not cleared to fly yet. The FAA would shut me down in a New York minute if I let you fly."

Mark pulled a piece of paper out of his back pocket, unfolded it, and handed it to Marty. "I saw my doctor this morning. I'm cleared to fly." He slapped the area on his leg that the bullet had passed through to prove his leg was healed. "Good as new." Mark marshaled up all his inner strength to keep the intense pain he was feeling from registering on his face.

Andy Wilson walked in the front door. "Sorry I'm late. The traffic in the Lincoln Tunnel was ridiculous." He was carrying his black leather flight bag and a suitcase.

Mary walked over and gave him a peck on the cheek. "Thanks for helping us."

"Where are we going, Mark?" Andy asked.

Marty's eyes narrowed as he took in the scene.

"I'm still working on Marty, but why don't you get started checking the weather reports for Western Europe?" Mark said confidently.

"Still working on Marty? Okay. Good luck with that." Andy disappeared into the hangar.

"I see what's going on here," Marty sniffed. "You've thought of everything, haven't you, Air Farce? Well hear this. I ain't running a damned charity. I got bills to pay. It costs $9,000 an hour to charter my Gulfstream. Between this trip and the last one, I'd be out over $150,000. You and Noelle could both work for free for six months and not make up that kind of money. Now get outta here and leave me alone. I have work to do finding *paying* customers. The answer is no."

"I'll pay for it."

Everyone turned toward April.

"Both trips. You won't be out a dime," she declared.

"*Riiight.* How in the world could a kid like you afford to charter a Gulfstream?" Marty scoffed.

"I can afford it," April responded. "I'm a billionaire."

Mark and Mary cringed inside when April let the secret slip out.

Marty rolled his eyes. "*You* are a billionaire?"

"Yep."

"What a coincidence. Can I tell you a little secret?"

"Sure," April said.

"I'm a billionaire, too. I just bust my ass every day trying to keep this operation afloat because I get bored sailing my yacht to my private island over and over."

April crossed her arms and exhaled loudly. "You're being sarcastic again, aren't you?"

"Ya think?" Marty pointed his thumb toward the door. "Hit the bricks. I've got work to do. The answer is still no."

Mark's and Mary's shoulders wilted as they turned to leave.

"Maybe this will change your mind." April pulled out her mother's American Express Platinum card.

He looked at it very closely. This type of elite credit card was the standard form of payment in his line of business.

He snatched the card out of her hand. The owner of Luxury Jet Charters held it up to the light beaming down from the two-thousand-dollar chandelier overhead. Marty smiled and nodded. "It's a pleasure doing business with you, Ms. Parker. I'll have my guys get your jet ready for your trip and pulled out of the hangar right away."

CHAPTER 25

MARTY WALKED AWAY WHISTLING A cheer-ful rendition of the Navy fight song, "Anchors Aweigh."

April looked at the two coconspirators in this secret plan. "Why didn't you guys tell me?"

"I knew it was a long shot that Marty would actually say yes. I figured the less you knew, the less upset you'd be if it didn't work," Mark explained.

"Our plan never would have worked if you didn't think of using Stephanie's credit card," Mary said. "Good move."

"About your top-secret plan. I'm confused. As soon as we land in Paris you're going to be arrested, Uncle Mark. That's not much of a plan," April said.

"We're not flying to Paris."

Confusion blanketed April's face.

"We're flying to Brussels," Mark announced.

"Belgium?" April shook her head. "Now you've completely lost me."

"I'll explain in a second." He turned to Mary. "Go tell Andy to work up a flight plan to Brussels. I'll fill April in."

"Got it," Mary replied. She dashed off down a hallway toward the door leading to the hangar.

"It took a lot to orchestrate everything, but I think my plan will work," Mark said. "Brussels is the closest major city to Paris. I'll drop you off at the airport, then you'll go into town and take the high-speed train from Brussels directly to Paris. It goes three hundred kilometers per hour so you should arrive at the Paris Nord Station no later than noon. That gives you three hours to get to the courthouse before the deadline. I've arranged for someone to help you with the court proceedings. The doctor will meet both of you at the courthouse to take your blood sample."

April looked away, avoiding eye contact with Mark. She slowly shook her head side to side. "I'm sorry you went to so much trouble," she said, looking up at him.

The air went out of Mark's lungs. "Won't you at least consider giving my plan a chance? I think it could work."

April smiled. "I think it's a great plan. I'm sorry you went to so much trouble after I said such mean things to you." She went over to Mark and gave him a big hug. "I'll never doubt you again. You have my complete trust from now on."

CHAPTER 26

"THANKS FOR YOUR VOTE OF confidence, but we have a long way to go before this is all over. Let's not count your chickens before they're hatched," Mark replied.

A confused looked flashed across April's face. "Chickens before they're hatched?"

Mark chuckled at the inevitable gaps in understanding that have plagued different generations throughout all human history. "Google it," he suggested.

April pulled out her iPhone.

"I didn't mean now. You'll have plenty of time for that later. Go grab our bags from the car, and I'll help Andy with the flight planning."

———◆———

An hour later Mark, Mary, Andy, and April stood on the tarmac under a warm June sun. The airport hummed with activity. Impressive business jets of every type came and went, transporting captains of industry, and their trophy wives, to important meetings.

Pulled across the tarmac by a tug, the Gulfstream rolled up in front of them and came to a stop. A worker opened a small access door on the side of the plane and pressed a switch. The front door popped opened, followed by the boarding stairs mechanically unfurling until they were fully extended. The stairway provided a welcoming pathway to extravagance. The ground crew disconnected the tow bar from the nose gear and drove away.

The Gulfstream 500 stood tall and majestic on its long, sturdy landing gear. Considered the top-of-the-line aircraft in the business world, there were few ways to get around that were more luxurious than cruising in a Gulfstream. The gleaming jet was the ultimate status symbol for the rich and powerful.

"I'll do the walk-around," Andy said. He walked up to the jet and began a meticulous inspection of every inch on the outside of the plane.

April acted like a kid on Christmas morning. "Can I go on board?" she asked excitedly.

"You can do whatever you like; you're paying the bill," Mark joked.

April scooped her backpack up off the concrete and sprinted up the stairs into the jet.

Like 99.99 percent of the general population, she'd never been inside a forty-five-million-dollar business jet. Entering it for the first time took her breath away. The opulent cabin was stunning. It was appointed with twelve gold-trimmed, buttery-soft leather seats, a full-size divan that turned into a bed, plush silk carpet, a wood-paneled credenza along the wall with a bouquet of fresh flowers on top, and a bathroom in the rear that a normal-size person could stand upright in.

April spread her arms and plopped down into one of the seats, melting into the soft, leather-covered cushions. The wide grin on her face said it all.

———◆———

Andy finished his inspection of the plane and walked up to Mary.

"Thanks again for helping us out on such short notice. I owe you one," Mary said, with a twinkle in her eye.

"I intend to collect on that when I get back." Andy

leaned in to give her a kiss.

"All right, Romeo, time to go." Mark step between the two and broke up the amorous occasion. "Go get the cockpit ready. I'll be there in a minute," Mark ordered.

"Yes sir, Captain sir," Andy replied, along with a rigid salute.

The two young people held eye contact until Andy disappeared into the cockpit.

Mary turned and scolded her dad. "Go easy on him; he's a good guy."

"Now what kind of father would I be if I didn't give every guy who thought he was good enough for my daughter a hard time?"

"I see your point. God forbid I would end up marrying a *pilot*," April said, sarcasm dripping from her words.

———————

Sixteen hours until deadline

The sleek jet lifted off the runway at Teterboro Airport and headed northeast to join its planned route across the Atlantic Ocean.

After the Gulfstream 500 leveled off at forty-one thousand feet, Mark turned on the autopilot and got up out of his seat. "I'll be back," he told Andy in his best Arnold Schwarzenegger impersonation.

"Never heard that one before," Andy teased.

"Just don't get us lost, smart-ass. Been there, done that, on the Tech-Liner. I don't want to go through that again."

Mark actually liked Andy, but he wasn't about to let him know it.

"Where are we?" April asked as Mark came through the cabin.

"We're about to cross the border into Canada." He swept his hand across the impressive cabin. "Not a bad way to get from A to B, don't you think?"

"I'll say." She straightened her legs out and hit nothing but air. "No bruised kneecaps from the seat in front of me suddenly reclining. No battling over the armrest."

"You should see the cockpit." Mark's eyes lit up. "GPS approaches for every airport in the world are loaded into the FMS. The plane has CAT 3 autoland capability and EVS—"

"Auto what?" April asked, confusion evident on her face.

"Oh right. It's pilot speak for cool, high-tech equipment on modern jets that pilots salivate over. With that type of equipment onboard I can land in any type weather."

"Whatever." April stretched out in her seat and sighed loudly. "All I know is I sure could get used to traveling like this."

Mark looked down at his wristwatch. "In a few hours you'll be able to do just that."

"I still can't get my head around the fact that I'm about to inherit one *billion* dollars." April shook her head in disbelief.

"You have no idea how much money you are about to come in to. With a billion dollars you could buy your own Gulfstream, your own private airport to fly it from, and mansions on almost every continent to fly it to. And you'd still have over nine hundred million dollars left. Just the interest alone on that amount of money could easily bring in fifty million dollars a year. Every year."

"Damn." April blushed slightly at using that word. "Just think of all the veterans I could help. I could buy wheelchairs, cover the cost for the latest-generation prosthetics…I could even build an entire wing on a hospital dedicated to helping the heroes who sacrificed for our freedom. None of that would be possible if it wasn't for you. How can I ever repay you?"

"You can stay true to who you are and don't let the

money change you. That's how you can repay me," Mark replied. He walked over to the galley. "Are you hungry? An assortment of gourmet food and drinks comes standard with all charter flights. Help yourself to whatever you find. Have you checked out the bathroom yet?"

"Is it as nice as the rest of the plane?" April asked.

"Better. Go look."

April hurried to the rear of the cabin and pulled the bathroom door open.

Noelle Parker looked out from the small space with an anxious look on her face.

CHAPTER 27

APRIL'S JAW DROPPED. SHE REPEATEDLY blinked her eyes, as if doing so would make Noelle magically disappear. When that didn't happen, April turned and stomped up the aisle. "How dare you trick me like that, Uncle Mark. Turn this plane around. I want to go back to New York City right now."

"Calm down; let me explain," he said, hands up in a defensive position.

"I'm the one paying for this flight, and I demand that you turn this plane around right now."

Mark crossed his arms and stood his ground. "That's not going to happen until you hear me out. Unless of course you know how to fly a Gulfstream and want to take over the controls yourself."

Noelle walked up the aisle and gingerly approached April. "We did trick you; you're right. But don't blame Mark. It was my idea."

"Well, that figures," April said as she glared at Noelle.

"If you'd just let us explain, I think you'll realize why we did it," Noelle said.

"Five minutes. Give us five minutes to tell you why. If you don't like what you hear, I will turn the plane around and go straight back to New York," Mark said. He held up a three-finger salute. "Scout's honor."

April plopped down in a seat, clamped her arms across her chest, and glared straight ahead without responding.

Noelle took the seat directly across the aisle. "I'm the

person Mark mentioned helping you at the courthouse in Paris. We knew you wouldn't get on the plane if he told you."

Mark sat on the armrest of the seat in front of April. "With your generous heart, you are going to do so much good with that money. But if you don't get your inheritance first, you can't help anybody. Working with Noelle is the only option you have if you hope to build that hospital wing you talked about."

The scowl on April's face softened slightly. Despite how angry she felt at the moment, she knew they were right. She pointed back at the bathroom. "How did you get in the…"

"You can thank Andy for that," Mark said. "He drove Noelle to the airport, then snuck her in the back door of the hangar while we kept Marty occupied."

"So, he wasn't really checking the weather in Europe like you asked him to do?" April asked, the light bulb coming on about the masterful job of deception everyone involved had pulled off.

"Nope. I can pull up all the weather information I need in ten seconds on the internet." Mark was finally able to boast about his tech skills to a millennial, and he had no intention of letting the opportunity pass him by. He paused for a moment to enjoy the small victory, then stood up. "That's all we have to say. It's your call now. Do we turn back or keep going to Brussels?"

CHAPTER 28

APRIL SAT SILENTLY AND PONDERED all that she had heard. Much more time would have to pass, and heartaches mended, before she could consider putting her trust in Noelle again. Believing someone after learning they had given you up for adoption, then lied about it your entire life, was asking a lot so soon.

April stood up and faced Noelle. "Just because I've decided to go to Paris with you doesn't mean I forgive you." She marched up the aisle toward the front of the aircraft and claimed the seat farthest from Noelle.

"Should I go talk to her?" Noelle asked Mark.

"Give her some space," Mark said. He looked at her with his intense green eyes. "To be honest with you, I feel the same way about *us*." Mark went back into the cockpit and closed the door.

———◆———

Halfway across the Atlantic Ocean, Andy came out of the cockpit to grab some food from the galley. He saw the two women separated by the length of the cabin. He wisely avoided asking any questions about the situation when he spoke to April. "We have about three hours to go before we land in Brussels. Have you had a chance to try this fantastic food?"

April looked up from her magazine with an annoyed expression and didn't answer.

Andy took the hint. He returned his focus to his stomach and began pulling open galley drawers. The savory aroma of expensive foods filled the cabin. He loaded up a plate with smoked salmon, pasta primavera, and a bunch of grapes. He yanked a juicy grape off the stem and popped it into his mouth. "Mary never filled me in on the details. What's so important that you have to get to Europe in such a hurry?"

April tossed her magazine aside, frustrated by the chatty copilot. "None of your business," she replied curtly. She looked at Andy and raised an eyebrow. "So, how long have you two been dating?"

"Um...a few weeks now. Why?"

"What are your intentions? Are you seeing anyone else besides Mary?"

"I don't see how that is any of your..."

"Do you have a college degree?"

Andy put his plate down on the counter. "I know you care about Mary, but you're not her mother. We're both adults."

April was about to continue the interrogation when a sudden look of revelation washed across her face. Her head dropped as she shook it side to side. "I'm sorry, Andy, you're right. What goes on between you and Mary is none of my business."

Not knowing what just happened, and far from being able to understand the complexities of females, Andy decided to go back to the safety of the cockpit. "Um... okay. See you in Brussels." He quickly left with his plate of food.

April turned and looked back at Noelle. She let out a deep sigh then walked back and sat across the aisle from Noelle. "Can we talk?"

"Of course."

"I think I'm beginning to understand."

"Understand what?"

"The extra effort you always put in making sure my birthday presents were really cool. The hint of sadness in your smile when you looked at me. The way you always grilled me about my choices in boyfriends." She rolled her eyes. "Especially that. Now it all makes sense."

Noelle pointed toward the galley. "I overheard your conversation with Andy. It's okay. That's what a person does when they care about someone deeply." She gave April her best *I told you so* look. "Even if they don't want to hear it."

"I know what you mean. Mary can sure be hardheaded at times," April said with a self-deprecating laugh.

Noelle smiled. "I believe that's something my daughter inherited from me."

"I believe she did," April replied, returning the smile.

Noelle reached across the aisle and took April's hand.

April continued, her eyes misting up. "What you did really hurt me. It's going to take some time for us to develop a relationship. I hope you understand."

"Of course I do, sweetie. You take all the time you need. Mark and I will support you however we can until you feel more comfortable."

"Thanks, Mom."

CHAPTER 29

MOTHER AND DAUGHTER EMBRACED. THEY talked and cried out buckets of pent-up emotions. April stayed in the seat closest to Noelle for the rest of the flight.

"I hope I'm not prying, but are you and Uncle Mark going to get remarried?" April asked during a lull in their conversation.

For reasons she could never quite understand, Noelle had kept her wedding ring on her left hand all these years. Even after the divorce, she couldn't bear to remove it. The simple act of taking it off represented a finality and a sense of failure that she couldn't accept. Noelle spun the wedding ring in circles around her finger as she looked at the locked cockpit door. "There's a lot of hurt there from what I've done. It's going to take time to fix the damage."

"I'm sure it will all work out eventually." April's face had a puzzled look. "So, if you guys do get remarried, will Mark be my uncle, my dad, or my stepdad? Everything is so confusing right now."

Noelle chuckled. "I don't have the slightest idea to be honest with you. Let's cross that bridge when we come to it, okay?"

Eight hours until deadline

The Gulfstream 500 arrived in the Brussels airport airspace to gray skies and a cold, steady drizzle.

Andy checked in. "Brussels tower, Gulfstream Three-Two-Two-Lima-Juliet requesting an approach for a full-stop landing."

The controller's response crackled over the radio. "*Goedemorgen* Gulfstream Three-Two-Two-Lima-Juliet. Approach clearance denied. The weather on the field is zero-zero due to fog. Enter a holding pattern at your current position."

Andy blew out an exasperated sigh at the prospect of flying circles in the sky after such a long flight. He keyed the mic. "How long can we expect to hold?"

"Our meteorologist believes the fog should lift in approximately two hours."

Mark looked at the fuel gauge and shook his head. "Tell him we don't have enough gas to hold that long."

"Tower, we are unable to hold for two hours due to low fuel."

"Understood. All airports in Northern Europe are closed at this time due to the fog. Your best option is to head south. You are cleared direct to Lima Foxtrot Papa Golf airport. Climb to flight level two two zero."

With his left hand, Andy began punching the airport identifier code into the navigation computer. Acutely aware of their fuel state, Andy quickly responded, "Roger. Proceeding direct to Lima Foxtrot Papa Golf airport at this time. Climb to—"

Mark pressed his mic switch, cutting Andy off. "Standby, Brussels tower."

Andy threw up his hands with a perturbed expression on his face. "Mark, we don't have time to waste. We need to divert."

Mark resisted the urge to roll his eyes. In a rare moment

of patience he explained his decision not to divert. "Lima Foxtrot Papa Golf is the code for Charles de Gaulle airport."

Andy had a deer in the headlights look on his face.

"It's north of Paris. As in Paris, France."

The embarrassed look that blanketed the young pilots' face was only exceeded by his wholly unconvincing meek response as he sunk down in his seat. "I knew that."

This time Mark did roll his eyes. "Sure you did, kid." He reached out for the mic switch on the control yoke. "Brussels tower, we have the equipment onboard to execute an approach in zero-zero conditions. Requesting approach clearance."

"Why didn't you notify me of this before?" the annoyed controller crossly responded.

Mark leaned back in his seat and folded his arms across his chest, sending a clear message he had no intention of bailing Andy out.

Andy cleared his throat. He reluctantly keyed his mic. "Sorry for the confusion, tower. Are we cleared for the approach?"

Despite the thick fog blanketing the airport, Mark greased the landing on runway two-five Right then turned onto the taxiway. The jet taxied slowly through the dense mist. The glare from its bright landing lights reflected off the fog and into the pilot's eyes. The journey across the fog-shrouded airport proved more harrowing than the low visibility landing. After safely reaching the ramp, Mark brought the jet to a stop.

Ramp workers assigned to care for the plane during its stay quickly chocked the main landing gear as the two Pratt & Whitney PW800 turbofans wound down.

Mark unlatched the door and pressed an electric switch on the side wall. The door opened, and the stairs went through their mechanical gyrations until fully extended.

A worker wearing coveralls and a bright yellow safety

vest trotted up the stairs holding out his hand. "No one is allowed off the aircraft until cleared by customs."

"We are in a very big hurry. How long will it be until customs arrives?"

"Customs has been called. They will arrive as soon as possible," the worker said with an annoyed voice. "You must stay on the plane."

"I heard you the first time." He shooed the worker away. "Top off the tanks with Jet-A fuel and let me know when the customs officer arrives."

The worker left in a huff without responding.

"We don't have time to wait. We need to leave now," April said.

"I understand. But when it comes to customs, we can't risk violating the rules. When you arrive in a foreign country, until you've cleared customs, you are in no-man's-land. You aren't legally in *any* country. They can make your life miserable for as long as they want, and there's nothing you can do about it. If you hope to get to the courthouse before the deadline, our only option is to wait," Mark said. "Grab some food. It's going to be a long day."

———◆———

An hour later, the customs official finally boarded the aircraft. In less than a minute, he had stamped everyone's passports and left.

Looking at Noelle and April, Mark said, "This is as far as I go. You're on your own now. Take the airport train to downtown. Get off at the Brussels Midi Station. Then take the Thalys high-speed train directly to the Paris Nord Station. Make sure you get tickets for the high-speed train; otherwise, you'll stop at every station along the way. The doctor's fee has already been paid. He agreed to meet you outside the courtroom and then draw April's blood in front of the judge. Any questions?"

"Very impressive, flyboy. You've thought of every-thing," Noelle said. She turned to April. "Let's go get your inheritance."

"Text me and keep me updated!" Mark yelled out as the two women hurried across the tarmac. "We'll be waiting for you right here when you get back!" They disappeared into the fog.

———◆———

Noelle and April boarded the bullet train to Paris at the Midi Station and settled into their seats. After cruising across the Atlantic Ocean in regal style, the coach-class seats on the train were a big step down in comfort. There certainly wasn't going to be any poached salmon offered to them on this leg of the trip.

April and Noelle didn't mind. They had a mission to complete, and the intense looks on their faces showed it.

With its highly raked nose and hot rod-red paint scheme, the train looked like a fighter jet on rails. It pulled out of the station exactly on time. A few minutes later the train was up to its top speed, cruising at three hundred kilometers per hour. The ride was so smooth it felt like they were floating on air. The cabin was so quiet they could hear the couple five rows ahead whisper-ing about their romantic plans after reaching their hotel overlooking the Seine.

The sleek train roared past quaint French villages en route so rapidly that they were nothing more than a blur. One hour and twenty-two minutes later, the train came to a stop at the busy Paris Nord Station. Noelle and April scooped up their luggage and rushed outside to find a taxi.

———◆———

Three hours until deadline

A taxi driver stood on the sidewalk holding up a piece of paper with the name *PARKER* scrawled on it in large letters. The middle-aged man was short and stocky with slicked back black hair. An ugly scar angled across his left cheek. Despite being summer, he wore a black leather jacket in the hopes that he would appear stylish. Even in the open air the driver reeked of cigarette smoke.

"I'm Parker," Noelle said loudly, waving for his attention as they approached the driver.

He crumpled up the sign and tossed it into a nearby trash can. "Welcome to Paris, Mademoiselle and Madame," the driver said in decent English. His weak smile displayed his crooked, tobacco stained teeth.

"We are going to—"

"The Judicial Campus of Paris in Batignolles," he said, finishing her sentence.

Noelle looked confused. "How did you know that?"

"I spoke to your husband, Madame."

Noelle nodded her head in admiration. "He really did think of everything."

"Come with me." He walked up to a dented and rusting black Citroën taxi and opened the trunk. Without offering to help load their luggage, the driver got behind the wheel and waited.

April and Noelle heaved their luggage into the trunk then got in on opposite sides in the back seat.

"Your husband said you have business with the Tribunal de grande instance de Paris. Something about an exceptionally large inheritance."

"Mark told you that?" Noelle was surprised that he would tell a stranger why they were in Paris after admonishing everyone to keep mum.

"Oui, Madame."

The tires squealed as the driver jerked away from the

curb and headed north. Noelle and April dug their fingernails into their armrests to keep from being jostled around. They quickly located their seat belts and latched them.

April leaned forward and said, "Sir, I work at a hospital. I see automobile accident victims almost every day. I think it would be best if you put on your seat belt."

"Typical bossy American," the driver scoffed. "Always telling everyone else what to do."

He continued driving wildly without securing his seat belt.

"That was rude," April said under her breath as she sat back.

Noelle leaned over and whispered to April, "Welcome to France."

She pulled out her phone and tapped out a text message to update Mark: "In the cab, headed to the courthouse."

As they wound through the charming Tenth Arrondissement, April pressed her nose against the side window, taking in the stark contrasts between the City of Lights and the City That Never Sleeps. She beamed with excitement at the wonders of Paris.

Perched high atop Montmartre, the impressive Sacré-Coeur basilica came into view. Visitors who climbed the steep path up to the white Romano-Byzantine-style church were rewarded with one of the most magnificent, panoramic views of the capital city.

"Beautiful, isn't it?" Noelle said as she pointed at the basilica. "I lived in this neighborhood when I was a model." The initial excitement she felt at sharing her knowledge of the area faded away, replaced by remorse at ever having come to this city.

The driver continued north at a reckless speed. When he failed to turn west on the Boulevard Périphérique (the roadway that rings Paris and led to the judicial campus), Noelle said, "Monsieur, you missed the turn."

"I know the city well, Madame. You insult me," he snarled. "The traffic on the 'Périph' is no good at this time of day. It will be much faster this way."

Decades had passed since Noelle lived in Paris. She shrugged and sat back, leaving the driving to the cabbie.

Every time she glanced at the rearview mirror, Noelle noticed the driver leering at her and her daughter with his beady eyes.

"Monsieur Parker is a lucky man to have such beautiful women in his life," he said with a creepy laugh.

Every muscle in Noelle's body tensed up.

She tried to act nonchalant as she pulled out her phone and texted April: "Something's wrong. Don't speak, only text me."

She waited anxiously for the urgent electronic message to work its way through thousands of miles of network cables before it ended up on the phone only two feet away from her. Finally, April's phone let out a snippet of a Taylor Swift song—her message notification tone.

April pulled her face away from the window and retrieved her phone. When she read the message, her head snapped to the right. Noelle subtly shook her head side to side, warning April not to speak.

The clue Noelle heard that had tipped her off something was terribly wrong: The driver had called Mark, Mr. Parker.

CHAPTER 30

NOELLE LEANED FORWARD. "MONSIEUR, WE will need the phone number to call a taxi to return to the train station after we finish our business. Do you have a business card with your company dispatch phone number on it?"

The driver pretended to fish around the dashboard and the glove compartment searching for a card. Coming up empty-handed, he said, "I have no card."

"Check behind the sun visor," Noelle suggested. "Maybe there's one up there."

The driver grunted loudly to signal his irritation then reached over and folded down the passenger-side sun visor. A small stack of cards was held in place under an elastic band. The license information and a photo of the owner of the taxi were also mounted on the visor. The driver slowly folded the sun visor back up against the ceiling without pulling out a card.

He shook his head in frustration. "You couldn't just go easily."

The picture attached to the sun visor was that of a skinny, young African male. Unfortunately for the real owner of the taxi, he went to work today not realizing it would be his last.

With his left hand, the driver whipped out a Ruger LCP pistol from under his jacket and pointed it at Noelle and April.

April let out a terrified scream.

Noelle reached over and grabbed her trembling hands. "It's okay, sweetie. Don't panic." Noelle's protective instincts kicked in. Despite the danger she faced, Noelle shouted, "You're scaring her! Put that gun down!"

"Shut up!" he barked, spittle flying from his mouth.

The ruthless look in the driver's eyes convinced Noelle to pick her battles more wisely. They were alive, and she intended to keep it that way.

She put her hands up in a show of submission. "Okay, okay. Please calm down."

"Give me your phones," he growled.

Noelle collected both phones and tossed them up to the front seat.

The driver opened his window, scooped up the phones, and threw them out onto the road. Their only possible connection to help shattered into pieces as the phones tumbled across the road. The electric door locks clicked, the stems now hidden and inaccessible.

Trapped and terrified, Noelle and April held each other tightly.

The driver continued north out of the city. Slowly, the urban sprawl of Paris gave way to open fields and sparse, rolling countryside. On any other day, Noelle would have described the view as beautiful.

Noelle memorized every road sign that passed by to keep her bearings. The traffic on the road thinned out until no other cars were in sight.

After the driver had calmed down, she got up some courage. "My ex-husband never contacted you, did he?"

The driver looked surprised. "Ex-husband? But you are wearing a wedding ring. I assumed you were married. That's why I decided to try mentioning your husband when we met. To gain your trust." With an obviously misplaced feeling of superiority, he jeered, "Any man who would let a beautiful woman like you get away is a fool."

"But your sign…" April looked confused. "How could you have known we would be at the train station? How did you know my last name?"

"Shut up. You ask too many questions." He brandished his pistol in their direction to emphasize his control over their fate.

Noelle ignored his order. "What are you going to do to us?"

"What I was paid to do," the driver responded coldly. Using the rearview mirror, his creepy eyes looked April up and down. "But that doesn't mean I can't have a little fun first."

"Please. Let us go," April said, her quivering voice barely above a whisper.

The drive just laughed.

She covered her face with her hands and began sobbing.

Hatred for the animal in the front seat burned like the sun in Noelle. She could barely keep her anger from erupting. Not wanting to give him any excuse to begin shooting, she managed to contain her fury.

As a flight attendant for thirty years, dealing with every type of personality imaginable, Noelle had become a student of human nature by default. She decided to try to get the driver to slip up and provide clues to explain their deadly predicament. On a hunch, Noelle played to the warped sense of accomplishment criminals have when they succeed. "Josephine will be very pleased with how cunning you were to lure us into the taxi."

She stared intently at his face in the rearview mirror. For the briefest of moments, a perverted sense of pride showed on his face. The man quickly erased it. His cold-blooded expression returned.

Benoit's only sister, Josephine Benoit-Dechambeau, second in line to inherit his fortune after April, was behind this. Being a multimillionaire wasn't enough for her. She wanted it all—regardless of how she got it.

"How much is Josephine paying you?" Noelle asked.

"I don't know what you are speaking of, Madame."

"I can pay you," April offered. "More than she can. If you let us go, I will inherit the estate, not her. I'll give you double—no, triple—what she is paying you to do this terrible thing."

"You could offer me all of the money. It wouldn't matter. I wouldn't take it," the driver said, true fear palpable in his voice.

"Do you have any idea how much money is involved here? You'd be a fool not to take the money and let us go," Noelle said, hoping to use his greed against the driver.

"I know exactly how much money is in the estate." The driver turned to address Noelle and April. The expression on his face had switched from cocky predator to terrified prey. "It wouldn't matter if you gave me all of it. That bitch would find me."

"But how?" Noelle questioned. "With that kind of money, you could disappear."

Looking directly at April, he spelled it out for them. "She found you, didn't she?"

CHAPTER 31

THE KILLER TURNED BACK AND continued driving north at a breakneck speed. Figuring the information would go to their graves, he filled in the details as he drove. Looking back at April in the mirror, he said, "She didn't even know you existed until your new little sister was dumb enough to put that video of the two of you on the internet. With millions of Euros and the connections she has, it was only a matter of time before enough pieces of the puzzle came together to connect the dots. Your cell phone has been tracked ever since. When she saw that you were headed for Europe, I got the call."

"You make it all sound so normal, what you do for a living," Noelle snapped.

He turned and glared at her. "I do the job, I collect my fee, and I live the rest of my life not having to constantly look over my shoulder for someone like me. It's as simple as that."

"You sick son of a bitch. You talk about what you're doing like it's no different than getting paid after mowing your neighbor's grass." Unable to hold back any more of the emotional trauma welling up inside her, Noelle repeatedly kicked the back of the driver's seat like an annoying kid on an airplane. April quickly joined in.

The killer snatched his gun off the front seat with his left hand and aimed it back at Noelle. "I'll kill you both right now if you don't knock it off!"

Without thinking, Noelle grabbed his wrist and pulled.

A deafening roar rang out.

The back window shattered.

April pressed herself into the door as far from the gun as possible. She closed her eyes and covered her ears.

With their survival at stake, Noelle pulled his wrist with every ounce of strength she had.

The killer's body twisted while he fought for control of his gun, involuntarily pulling the steering wheel to the right. The Citroën swerved off the pavement and struck a metal post holding a road sign, just inside the car's right headlight.

The killer's body catapulted forward, his face slamming into the steering wheel from the impact.

Noelle and April grabbed their armrests just as the inertia reels on their seat belt shoulder straps locked tight.

The off-center impact sent the car into a violent clockwise spin. The tires screeched across the asphalt as the car rotated 360 degrees.

April kept shrieking, "Oh my god! Oh my god!"

CHAPTER 32

THE WOUNDED CAR CAME TO a stop in the middle of the desolate road. The engine purred along at idle like nothing had happened—a testament to the car's sturdy construction.

The driver's airbag had deployed then deflated. But without the aid of his seat belt, the true meaning of the sticker on the dash labeling airbags as only Supplemental Restraint Systems became obvious. The killer slumped forward against the steering wheel. He was unconscious and bleeding profusely from a large gash on his forehead.

Noelle reached over to April. "Are you okay?"

She continued to scream. "Oh my god!"

Noelle reverted to her flight attendant training. Even after the worst crash, flight attendants were expected to stay calm. Failure to do so could result in passengers needlessly dying when they could have been saved by calm but forceful instructions on how to swiftly get out of the plane.

"It's over, sweetie. You're safe now. Mom is here. Look at me, April. Mom is here. You're safe."

April slowly regained control of her emotions as she sat in the backseat of the idling vehicle. Her breathing slowed down to only a frantic pace.

"Are you hurt?" Noelle asked.

April looked down. She examined her hands and legs. Nothing seemed broken. She put her hand to her face and felt around. When she pulled it away from her nose there was blood on her hand. April pinched her nose and said, in an unintentional comically nasally voice, "I think I'm okay."

Both women chuckled at such a silly, humorous occurrence taking place in the middle of the deadly chaos that had just transpired.

They unbuckled and slowly climbed out of the car to assess the situation. Every muscle hurt.

The driver moaned in pain against the steering wheel as he regained consciousness. April ignored her bloody nose and opened his door to examine the driver. She gently laid him back in his seat. Blood cascaded down his face.

"Get a shirt from my backpack," she instructed Noelle.

Noelle quickly retrieved a shirt and handed it to April.

She put it in the palm of the driver's hand and raised it up to his forehead. "Press this against your head. We have to stop the bleeding." She turned to Noelle. "Help me get him out of the car. He's in shock. We need to lay him down."

The two maneuvered his upper body out the open door then pulled him out of the car. The driver screamed in agony as they tugged on him. His right tibia had shattered from the impact with the lower console. They dragged his body off the road and laid him down on the dirt shoulder.

"We need to get him medical help," April said, looking up at Noelle.

"What?" Noelle asked, incredulously. "He was going to murder us. Who knows what god-awful things he was going to do to you first? He's going to get what's coming to him." Noelle raced back to the car and retrieved the Ruger pistol. She stormed back toward the driver, blood-lust in her eyes.

"No! Don't!" April yelled out.

CHAPTER 33

NOELLE ANGLED THE PISTOL DOWNWARD at the hit man and fired off round after round.

His body flinched with each bullet hitting the dirt around him, spraying up dust and rocks.

"Stop! Please stop!" he begged. His previous bravado now replaced by abject fear.

Noelle continued firing until the clip was empty. She threw the gun as far as she could into the weeds.

After doing an admirable job keeping her composure during the terrifying ordeal, Noelle's emotional dam finally broke.

"How does it feel!" she screamed in his face. "How does it feel to fear for your life?" She stomped away and slumped down against the front tire of the car, sobbing.

April came over and, in a reversal of roles, hugged her mother until she calmed down. After a few minutes had passed, April pulled back and looked at Noelle. "I knew you couldn't do it."

Noelle wiped at her tears. "I wanted him dead. For what he did to us. He doesn't deserve to live."

"He'll get what's coming to him. But neither of us could ever look ourselves in the mirror again if his blood was on *our* hands."

Noelle nodded. "You're right." She hugged April. After she had calmed down, Noelle looked over at the killer and tilted her head. An odd smile spread across her face. "I have an idea." She got up. "Find his phone."

April searched the car while Noelle checked the driver's pockets.

"Found it." Noelle held up the phone. She waved April over. "Help me prop him up against that tree over there."

The two pulled the man over to a nearby tree and sat him in an upright position against the trunk.

Noelle held the phone in front of his face. "You are going to do a video confession telling us everything you know about Josephine and her plan."

"Go to hell," the man said defiantly.

"Let me explain something to you. Your injuries from the accident aren't life threatening, but you know as well as I do, you're already a dead man. After Josephine finds out you failed, even if you *could* run and hide, which is going to be a little challenging in your current state"—Noelle pointed at his shattered tibia—"she's going to find you."

His defiant expression softened slightly.

"I'm offering you the chance to take her down. Make her pay for what she did to you."

You could almost hear the wheels spinning in his feeble brain.

Noelle leaned closer. "For once in your life you get to call the shots. You finally get revenge on this lousy world for everything it's done to you."

Her carefully chosen words struck a nerve.

The hit man pushed down on the dirt with both hands and pulled himself up a little straighter against the trunk. "Start the video, Madame."

———◆———

One hour until deadline

With the confession complete, Noelle pocketed the phone. "You don't mind if we borrow your car, do you?"

The man looked up with surprise. "You can't leave me

here. I'm gravely injured. I must get to a hospital."

"Once we are safely back in Paris, I will call an ambulance to come get you. Don't go anywhere," Noelle snickered. She walked off and got into the driver's seat.

Before joining her mother in the car, April leaned down toward the man. "Next time, wear your seat belt."

———————◆———————

Thirty minutes before the deadline

Noelle re-joined the roadway ringing Paris and headed west toward the judicial campus. After a few minutes, their speed slowed to a crawl. The famously bad Parisian traffic threatened to prevent them from arriving before the deadline. Noelle weaved between the cars as they crept along, looking for an opening. Suddenly, flashing blue lights filled the view in the rearview mirror. The classic two-tone warble of a French police car followed immediately after.

April looked back over her shoulder. "Oh no."

It was no wonder they were being stopped. The back window of the sedan had been blown out by the gunshot. The right-front area of the grill was smashed. The airbag had deployed. And there were traces of blood on the steering wheel.

Noelle carefully pulled over onto the shoulder and stopped. The policeman got out of his compact white-and-blue vehicle and walked toward them.

Noelle whispered to April, "Put your head down in your lap and don't look up."

The officer stood cautiously at the driver's window and quizzed Noelle in French about the damage to the car. She responded in perfect French, occasionally pointing over at April.

He gave out a knowing laugh, tipped his hat, and said, "*Au revoir*, Madame," before walking away.

Noelle made sure to use her turn signal as she pulled back onto the roadway.

April lifted her head as they drove off. "How did you get the policeman to let us go? What did you say?"

"I blamed the damage to the car on you."

"Me?"

"I told him you just got fired from your job, then you found out your boyfriend was cheating on you, and on top of all that, it was that time of the month for you. That's when you unwisely decided to go for a drive."

"He bought that explanation?"

"He said he has five teenage daughters and completely understood why the car looks the way it does."

CHAPTER 34

Fifteen minutes until deadline

THE BEAT-UP CITROËN TAXICAB SCREECHED
to a halt in front of the towering glass-and-steel judicial building. Noelle and April sprinted to the entrance.
They scanned the directory board hanging on the wall
inside the entrance until they found the courtroom for
the Tribunal de grande instance. Fourth floor, courtroom
4C.

After riding up to the fourth floor in what seemed like
the world's slowest and smallest elevator, the pair dashed
down the hallway toward the courtroom.

As they got closer, they noticed a horde of reporters and cameramen prowling the hallway. Not allowed
inside the courtroom during proceedings, they waited
anxiously outside for the deadline to expire.

"Damned vultures," Noelle said. "Don't look at them,"
she warned April, "just keep walking."

The two weaved through the pack of reporters unmo-
lested. In fact, they went completely unnoticed.

Once past the mob, Noelle turned to April with a
quizzical look on her face. "They don't know about you
yet." Disbelief was evident in her voice.

"Thank goodness," April replied. "Let's get this over
with."

Noelle looked with concern at her daughter's face. She
touched the area just above April's lips. "There's still some

blood from your bloody nose. You can't show up in court looking like that. Go to the restroom and clean it off. I'll wait here for you. And make it quick."

April hurried off to find a restroom. She entered the lavatory and examined her lip in the bathroom mirror. She easily wiped away the small spot of blood with just a tissue. Three minutes later, April returned looking more presentable. "How do I look?"

"Better," Noelle said. "Let's find the doctor."

Pacing nearby, with a decidedly annoyed look on his face, was a tall, thin gentleman with meticulously groomed gray hair. Wire rim spectacles framed his eyes. A woman in a nurse uniform sat on a bench against the wall.

"Dr. Boucher?" Noelle asked as they approached the man.

"Oui," he responded. "Are you Mademoiselle Parker?" he asked, pointing at April.

"Yes. Thank you so much for helping us," she replied.

"You are late. I've been here for hours."

Noelle ignored his gruff admonishment. She was certain he would have been much more understanding if he had known what they went through to get to the courtroom before the deadline. "We apologize for being late. I see you brought your nurse." Noelle moved toward the door, trying to speed the good doctor along. "Shall we go into the courtroom now?"

The doctor nodded his head sideways away from his nurse. In a hushed voice, he said, "May I have a word in private?"

"Of course. But please hurry," Noelle said.

After the three had gotten out of earshot of the nurse, Dr. Boucher said, "While I was waiting, I sat in on the proceedings. A remarkably interesting case, indeed. My fee for appearing in court and drawing the blood sample is no longer five hundred euros. It is now fifty thousand euros."

"What? That's extortion," April said, stating the obvious.

"It is a mere pittance for someone about to be as rich as you, mademoiselle." He pulled out his gold-plated pocket watch. "The deadline is in five minutes. What is your answer?"

CHAPTER 35

THE CONNIVING DOCTOR HELD ALL the cards, and he knew it. He waited for an answer.

"You bastard," Noelle hissed.

"I don't care. I just want to get this over with. I'll pay what you're asking," April said reluctantly.

"And I want my fee announced by you on the record before I will draw the sample."

April shook her head in disgust. "Whatever. Let's go."

The doctor waved his nurse forward. She picked up his black bag and fell in step behind the doctor.

Noelle pushed open the tall wooden doors leading into the courtroom. Mother and daughter entered the Tribunal de grande instance.

A bailiff guarding the entrance extended his arm and stopped them. "*Affaires officielles seulement.*"

"But we *do* have official business with the court," Noelle responded. She raised her voice. "My daughter is here to claim her inheritance."

Every head in the room snapped around. Snickers could be heard from the crowd, certain another crackpot was trying to get their hands on the fortune.

The judge looked down at his wristwatch. He waved the pair forward. "*Avancez.*"

The bailiff lowered his arm and escorted the women up to the bench.

"Thank you for hearing us out, Your Honor," Noelle said. "My name is Noelle Parker. My daughter, April

Parker, is the rightful heir to Monsieur Benoit's estate. As you will soon see, there will be no doubt to that fact. I am here to represent her. My daughter does not speak French. If the court would indulge us so that she can adequately present her case and fully understand everything in this important matter, I request that the proceedings take place in English."

The judge leaned forward; his eyes narrowed. "Madame, for you to come to France and expect me to conduct business in my courtroom in English is the height of hubris. Obviously, you must be an *American*." Disdain dripped from his voice as he guessed Noelle's country of origin.

"Yes, Your Honor, you are correct. I am an American. Your willingness to consider my extraordinary request speaks highly of your commitment to fairness toward everyone who comes before you seeking justice."

Noelle's response was crafted from her keen understanding of people. She'd learned when dealing with arrogant, egotistical men, nothing worked better than flattery. Especially when it came from an attractive woman.

"In the interest of justice, I will consider your request." With a self-satisfied look, the judge addressed the table where Josephine Benoit-Dechambeau and her army of high-priced lawyers were seated. "Are there any objections to conducting the proceedings in English from this point forward?"

The senior partner of the prestigious law firm that bore his name leaned over and conferred with his client. He straightened up and replied, "No, Your Honor. We believe we have an irrefutable case and look forward to your ruling confirming that."

The judge bristled at the thought of being blamed by the American media for robbing an innocent girl of her inheritance. He made a strategic decision. "Very well. Both parties are in agreement. Who am I to deny the request?" The judge directed Noelle and April to an empty table next to Benoit-Dechambeau's. "Be seated."

As Noelle walked past her, she said, "I know it's been a long time, Josephine, but you seemed surprised to see me. Why is that?"

Josephine Benoit-Dechambeau glared at Noelle behind her expensive Cartier Panthère glasses. She wore a mink stole wrapped loosely around her boney shoulders. A large string of pearls hung from her neck. Her long, claw-like fingernails were painted a deep red color. The garish layers of makeup plastered on her gaunt face left the impression she couldn't afford a descent mirror. Rather than respond to Noelle, she whipped around and barked orders into the ear of her assistant, shielding her voice with her hand. The assistant rushed from the courtroom.

After reaching their table, Noelle addressed the court. "Your Honor, thirty years ago I came to Paris a naïve and trusting person. Homesick and alone, I foolishly engaged in a relationship with Gerard Benoit, despite the differences in our ages. His sister, Josephine"—she pointed at the scowling woman—"tried numerous times to break us apart. Apparently, his being seen with an American, from a middle-class family no less, was an embarrassment to the Benoit family name. When I found out he was married and had lied to me the entire time we were together, I went back home in shame, a bitter and jaded shell of my former cheerful self. Seven months later, I gave birth to a beautiful baby girl." She looked over at April and smiled the type of warm, loving smile only a mother can express.

She held up the paperwork she'd filled out. Addressing the judge, she said, "My daughter, April Parker, is the only offspring of Monsieur Gerard Benoit. Under French law, she alone is entitled to his estate."

Pandemonium erupted in the gallery. Reporters who had been masquerading as spectators rushed out to break the explosive news to their colleagues.

Lawyers across the aisle went into a panic. Law books and file folders flew open. Urgent, hushed conversations broke out between the attorneys.

Josephine's face went even more pasty white. She jumped up and yelled, "This is an obvious fraud! I've never seen this woman before in my life! I demand that these charlatans be expelled from the courtroom immediately!"

The judge pounded his gavel. "Sit down, Madame Dechambeau! How dare you dictate to me how I will run my courtroom. You are not to address this court unless I have called on you. If you have anything to say, you will relay it through your counsel. Do you understand?"

Not used to being told when she could speak, she continued her tirade. "I will not stand for this outrage! I am the rightful heir to the estate of my beloved brother, not her!"

"Your outbursts will not be tolerated in my courtroom! Madame Dechambeau, I find you in contempt of court," the judge bellowed from his perch. "One more word from you, and I will throw out your claim to the estate. Do I make myself clear?"

One word away from losing the largest client fee in the law firm's history, every lawyer at her table stepped in, trying to calm down the overly entitled millionaire. Eventually, they succeeded in getting her to sit down and stay silent for the remainder of the proceedings.

Noelle continued. "My daughter is prepared to submit a blood sample for DNA testing to prove the paternity of Gerard Benoit. Our doctor"—she pointed at Boucher—"is present and ready to draw the sample."

Dr. Boucher crossed his arms and remained seated, projecting a reluctance to get involved.

"For the record," Noelle said through gritted teeth, "we are very grateful that the good doctor has taken time out of his busy schedule to assist us today and have agreed to pay him fifty thousand euros for his expertise."

A smug look of victory crossed the doctor's face.

The judge shook his head, fully aware of what just happened but powerless to intervene. "Dr. Boucher come forward and present your credentials to the bailiff. Madame Parker, hand your paperwork to him as well."

The bailiff took the documents and presented them to the judge. He put on his reading glasses and scanned them thoroughly. "Everything looks in order."

The lead attorney for Josephine stood up. "Your Honor, may we take a look at the documents?"

The judge handed them to his bailiff, who delivered them to the lawyer. Each person on his team immediately took individual pages of the documents and began poring over them.

Twenty minutes later, the lead attorney reluctantly announced, "The paperwork appears to be correct."

"Draw the blood sample," the judge instructed Dr. Boucher.

The doctor opened his small black leather bag and took out items necessary to draw a sample. He began by securing a rubber tube around April's upper arm, creating a tourniquet. Next, he tapped the crevice of her elbow, identifying a large, easily accessible vein. He sterilized the area with an alcohol wipe. Without warning, he jabbed the needle into her arm.

It had been years since the doctor had drawn blood. Without regular practice, his technique had grown very rough.

April winced in pain. At that precise moment, her determination to be gentler when *she* drew blood from her patients vastly increased.

Slowly, the deep-red fluid that would prove paternity

oozed into the tube. He removed the tourniquet as the tube filled. The doctor yanked the needle out of April's arm and covered the puncture with a small pad of gauze, securing it with a Band-Aid. He carefully handed over the tube containing the answer to the true rightful heir to the huge fortune. The bailiff handed the tube off to a government lab technician who'd been summoned while the paperwork was being reviewed.

"Bailiff, escort the sample to the lab. Do not let it out of your sight. This court will reconvene Monday morning to announce the results."

The senior partner quickly stood. "Your Honor, if I may. The court already has a DNA sample from Monsieur Benoit. Due to the large amount of money in question, I humbly ask that you have this new sample analyzed and compared immediately so as to not burden Your Honor with any more duties involving this case over a well-deserved break this weekend."

The judge had no desire to be preoccupied with this case until Monday morning. He had hoped to enjoy the weekend away from his overbearing, shrill wife while pampering his mistress at his country cottage. He asked the lab technician, "How quickly can you have the results?"

The lab geek's eyes lit up at the opportunity to boast about his skills. "We use the latest 3500 Series Genetic Analyzer. Performing the Sanger sequencing methodology, it has a 99.9 percent accuracy—"

"How long?" he asked impatiently.

"Less than an hour, Your Honor."

"Bring the results directly to me when you get them. No one else is to see the results."

"Yes, Your Honor."

"Off with you." The judge waved the lab tech away. "The court will wait for the results of the test to prove conclusively the validity of the claims of April Parker as to the paternity of Gerard Benoit."

———◆———

As promised, the judge had the results of the paternity test in less than one hour.

The piece of paper he held in his hands was worth one billion dollars.

The judge carefully scanned the test results, reading it twice to insure he made no mistakes in interpreting the finding.

He laid it down in front of himself and drew in a deep breath.

"This court finds that April Parker is the sole heir to the estate of Gerard Benoit."

CHAPTER 36

THE GALLERY ERUPTED.
The judge banged his gavel to quiet the crowd. "There will be order in my court!" Once the uproar had died down, he continued. "Due to the large amount of money involved, as required by your country's USA Patriot Act, Mademoiselle Parker, the inheritance must be transferred to the United States Treasury Department for proper vetting before being released to you." He took off his reading glasses and looked directly at April. With a sympathetic voice, he said, "I do not envy you, young lady. May God watch over you." The judge pounded his gavel one final time. "This court is adjourned."

As mother and daughter rose to leave, Josephine stormed over to their table. She thrust her boney finger toward April—the tip of it resembling a razor-sharp claw dipped in blood. Spittle flew from her pursed lips as she screamed the venomous words. "No one does this to me. Enjoy your victory, you illegitimate bastard child. You won't live long enough to spend any of my money."

Noelle stood toe-to-toe with Josephine. She bared her protective mama bear instincts as well as her teeth, slapping away the woman's hand. "Get the hell away from my daughter, you bitch."

Suddenly, a horde of reporters and cameramen burst through the doors to the courtroom. They rushed up the aisle. Noelle and April prepared to be overwhelmed by the approaching mob.

Instead, they surrounded Josephine.

"Madame Dechambeau is it true you hired an assassin to murder the American to prevent her from getting your brother's money?" a reporter shouted.

Reporters pushed and shoved each other trying to get closer while they yelled out similar questions.

She held up her hand to shield her eyes from the unflinching glare of the lights mounted on cameras. "Get out of my way, trash," she squealed. She tried to force her way through the mob without any luck.

The judge pounded his gavel so hard the head broke off the handle. "Order! I will have order in my courtroom! Clear the room, bailiff."

A female reporter pulled a cell phone out of her purse. "Wait, Your Honor. You must hear this." She tapped the screen.

The bruised and bloody face of the taxi driver appeared. The confession of the killer hired to murder Noelle and April began playing on his phone.

"Josephine Benoit-Dechambeau hired me to kill Mademoiselle Parker in order to steal the money from her brother's estate."

Josephine turned to her army of lawyers. "Stop that! I order you to stop that!" she shrieked, her eyes bulging in their sockets.

The senior partner bolted out of his seat. Like a rat abandoning a sinking ship, he shouted, "I am shocked and appalled at what I am hearing, Your Honor! My firm had absolutely no knowledge of this. Having issued your ruling on the case we were hired for, my firm no longer represents Josephine Benoit-Dechambeau in any capacity on any other matter."

A pleased expression spread across the judge's face. "Monsieur, your firm is hereby released from representing your client. Thank you for your time." He pointed at the now-frantic woman. "Bailiff, take Madame Josephine

Benoit-Dechambeau into custody."

"Now we are adjourned."

CHAPTER 37

NOELLE AND APRIL SLIPPED THROUGH the scrum of reporters unnoticed while they were occupied getting the story of their careers. The two dashed out of the courtroom, flew down four stories of steps in the fire stairwell, and out of the building.

A line of taxicabs waited along the curb for workers to pour out of the building at the end of the day then whisk them to their favorite brasserie after a long week.

Mother and daughter collected their belongings from the trunk of the damaged Citroën and went up to the first taxi in line.

Through the open passenger window, Noelle said, "Train station, *s'il vous plait.*"

Before getting in the taxi, April folded down the passenger side sun visor. The picture on the license was a perfect match to the man sitting in the driver's seat.

On the way to the station, safely away from the madness in the courtroom, April looked suspiciously over at Noelle. "How did the reporters get his cell phone with the confession on it?"

Noelle winked at her daughter. "Let's go home, sweetie."

———◆———

With the Gulfstream safely cruising westward on autopilot, Mark sat in the cabin across from Noelle and April. He shook his head. "You two had one hell of a day."

"Thanks to Mom, everything worked out okay," April said.

"I'd say things worked out better than just okay," Mark replied.

April let out a low whistle. "Watch out. Don't mess with Noelle Parker when she gets mad."

"Trust me, I know what you mean," Mark said, speaking from experience. "Good job." He leaned across the aisle and gave Noelle a peck on the cheek.

"*Okay*, that's my cue to go. I'll leave you two kids alone," April said, smiling at the prospect of Mark and Noelle reconciling. "I'm going to grab some sleep."

She went to the rear of the cabin, removed her shoes, and slid under the down-filled blanket covering the divan, which had been converted into a double bed.

Noelle looked at her ex-husband. His thick head of hair was a lot more salt than pepper these days. The wrinkles on his face were visible even when he wasn't squinting. But there was no denying he was still a handsome man.

Mark's looks weren't what sealed the deal for her many years ago when he proposed. With her stunning good looks, getting hit on by vain pretty boys was an almost daily occurrence for Noelle. Mark was different. Sure, he was cocky. He was a pilot after all. But his self-confidence wasn't based on his appearance. It had been earned the hard way. He had excelled as an Air Force pilot, flown every airplane Alpha Airlines had, and had achieved the position of chief pilot of one of the largest airlines in the world.

Noelle's mind wandered as she reminisced about her favorite picture of them. It was a framed photo that sat on the coffee table in her old apartment. The faded picture had been taken early in their marriage in front of the Colosseum in Rome. Mark and Noelle had their arms wrapped around each other, radiating love and optimism for their future.

"What happened to us?" Noelle asked wistfully.

Mark plopped his head back against the headrest and stared up at the ceiling. "I don't know. Life happened, I guess." He got up and started for the cockpit. Before opening the door, Mark turned back toward Noelle. "That's not true."

"What's not true?"

"It wasn't life. I'm what happened to us." He looked at the floor. "It was me. It's taken me far too long to figure that out." His eyes moistened. "I almost lost you today. I don't know what I would do without you. I should have been there to protect you and April from that savage. It's my fault."

"Don't be so hard on yourself. No one could have known that Josephine was *that* desperate to get the money," Noelle countered.

"The things some people are willing to do for money is unbelievable." He looked back at April peacefully nestled under the blanket. "This is going to be just the beginning of the problems that money will cause. We need to be there for her."

Noelle got out of her seat and strolled up to Mark. She wrapped her arms around his broad shoulders and gave him a flirtatious smile. The same smile that had worked wonders for her in the past when she wanted something. "You said *we*. We do make a pretty good team if I do say so myself. Does that mean you'll give us another chance?"

Mark knew exactly what she was doing. He was no slouch himself in countering her attempts at manipulating him. "My leg is fine now. You've taken care of me long enough. I can get back to flying charters for Marty. It might be best if I move out and get my own place. Give me some time to think about our future."

"Move out?" Noelle switched to plan B. A fabricated pout formed on her pretty face. "I won't hear of it. You are staying, and we are going to work things out between us. That's final." The pout morphed into a scowl. "You don't want to make me mad, do you?"

She won. As tough as Mark was, he could never resist Noelle's wily ways of getting to his heart. "No, ma'am. I've seen what happens when you get mad. I'll stay." He saluted her. "You're the boss."

Noelle rolled her eyes. "Yeah, right. That will be the day. Go back to the cockpit and do your pilot stuff, fly-boy." She gave him a playful pat on the butt.

Mark cupped his hand in the small of her back and pulled Noelle close. His hand slid lower as he planted a passionate kiss on her lips.

April had been spying on them. She raised her head. "Ewww. Get a room, people."

CHAPTER 38

THE HOT SUMMER DAY HAD faded into a muggy, unpleasant night. The temperature on the ramp at Teterboro Airport hovered near eighty-five degrees, the humidity still oppressive.

After the wheels were chocked, Marty Dawson activated the switch on the outside of his Gulfstream 500. The door opened, and the stairs unfurled. He waved the serious-looking man standing next to him up the stairs. A minute later, the US Customs and Border Protection agent descended the stairs and went on his way.

April was the first person to deplane. Marty rushed up to her and vigorously shook her hand. "Ms. Parker, it's so good to see you again. How was your trip? Can I help you with your bag?"

Mark was right behind her. "You're in a friendlier mood than the last time we saw you, Marty. Let me guess. You heard about why April needed to get to Europe so quickly?"

"Who hasn't!" he exclaimed. "It's on every news channel. The media has dubbed her the world's most eligible bachelorette."

Mark rubbed the back of his neck. "Crap. So much for anonymity."

Marty continued sucking up to April. "Anytime you need to fly somewhere, Ms. Parker, just give your old buddy Marty a call. Any time day or night."

Mary screeched to a stop next to the plane in the rundown family minivan. Her parents waited on the tarmac with open arms.

She jumped out of the car and rushed up to April, hugging her tightly. "OMG, thank goodness you're safe. I've been texting you for the last two days. Why haven't you answered me?"

"Long story," April replied, returning the hug.

Mark and Noelle joined in the embrace, making it a group hug.

Mary put an end to the tender moment. "Your parents are worried sick about you, April. I promised them we'd drive you straight home. I want to hear every detail on the way."

The sisters went off to the car and jumped in the back seat, talking nonstop.

Mark and Noelle approached Marty. Temporarily at a loss for words to express her gratitude for everything he had done for their family, Noelle simply embraced him.

Mark reached out his hand. "Marty, I don't care what everyone else says about you, in my book you're a hell of a guy."

"You're not half-bad yourself. As far as Air Farce pukes go, of course." He returned the handshake. Returning to his tough-guy persona, Marty said, "If you two really wanna thank me, you can get your butts back to work."

"You gotta deal, ya old squid," Mark said with a smirk. "Call us when you get your next charter booking. It's about time our lives got back to normal."

◆

Mark pulled the minivan up to the curb in front of April's building. A mob of reporters and cameramen suddenly surrounded the vehicle. Like a pack of hyenas ready to pounce, they clawed at the windows trying to get a sound bite. The salivating reporters shouted out a cacophony of questions about April's newfound wealth.

An opening appeared as Tommy pushed his way through the throng up to April's door.

"Let me pass!" he yelled. "There will be no interviews of my daughter tonight!"

He yanked open her door and intentionally slammed it against the knees of nearby reporters. Tommy put his arm around April's shoulders and hustled her off, disappearing into the crowd. Once safely inside the foyer, Tommy forced the door closed in the reporters' faces.

Understandably shaken, April asked, "How did they know I was coming?"

"They didn't. The press has been camped out here all day."

Stephanie rushed up to her the instant April walked into their apartment. "I've been worried sick about you, sweetie. Are you okay?"

The terrifying events of the last few days finally overwhelmed April. She broke down crying. "It was so scary. This horrible woman sent a hit man to kill Noelle and me so she would get the money. Then this unscrupulous doctor demanded fifty thousand euros to take my blood sample with only five minutes left before the deadline to claim my inheritance."

"But you did get it, right? The money. The court awarded you your inheritance, didn't it?"

"Yes, it did. One billion dollars."

"Let's not make her relive every detail tonight," Tommy said. "There'll be plenty of time for that later. We're just glad you're back home safely." Tommy kissed her on the forehead. "It's late. Are you tired?"

"I'm exhausted," April answered.

The temperature in the small apartment was even more unbearable than outside. The windows were open, hoping to catch a breeze. The relentless din of the streets of Queens intruded into their conversation. Frustrated drivers stuck in traffic could be heard honking their horns while mothers yelled out apartment windows at their oblivious children.

"The air conditioning in the apartment is on the fritz again," Tommy said. "I'll get the fan and set it up in your bedroom so you can get a good night's rest."

April opened her backpack and pulled out Stephanie's credit card. Handing it over, she said, "I kind of melted your credit card. I had to pay some really big expenses to get my inheritance."

"It doesn't matter, as long as you're safe."

"It sure came in handy." She tilted her head. "I gotta ask. How did you qualify for a platinum card on a secretary's salary?"

Stephanie stumbled over her words as she concocted an answer. "Well...I might have *accidentally* shifted some decimal places to the right a few times when I applied online."

"Isn't that dishonest?" April asked.

True to form, Stephanie justified her deceit. "It's their fault for sending me the card, not mine for using it. But it doesn't matter. With your inheritance, you can pay me back with no problem."

"Of course. As soon as I get my money, I'll pay you back."

"I know you will. I trust you. No rush." Stephanie bit her lower lip. "Um...about how much did you charge on my card?"

"Almost a quarter of a million dollars."

Stephanie's eyes opened wide. "Holy..."

"You're not mad, are you?"

Stephanie swallowed hard. "No, sweetie, I'm not mad."

Tommy came out of the bedroom. "Okay, the fan is on. Your bedroom should start cooling down now."

———◆———

Mentally and physically drained from the ordeal she'd

gone through, April Parker slept fourteen hours straight.

She emerged from her bedroom the next day yawning and rubbing her blurry eyes. "What time is it?" April asked in a groggy voice.

Tommy looked up from the TV where he was watching the president board Air Force One for a trip to Europe. "Well, if it isn't sleeping beauty," her dad teased. "Half the day is already over. Any big plans today for the world's most eligible bachelorette?"

"Not funny, Dad. I'm the same person I was before I left for Paris."

"Tommy, leave the poor girl alone," Stephanie said. "Can I get you something to eat?"

April turned away from the kitchen with an urgent look on her face. "I don't have time for that right now. There's something more important I need to do. It's been over a day now without my phone." Completely serious about the supposedly essential electronic appendage, she said, "How did people survive before cell phones?"

Tommy answered, "Easy. We spent our days painting pictures to each other on cave walls."

April groaned and rolled her eyes. "Please, no more dad jokes. They're *sooo* lame."

Tommy just chuckled.

"Can you go with me to the Verizon store, Dad?"

"Sure. While we're there, let's set you up with your own account. I think you can afford it now."

April dashed off to her bedroom, emerging five minutes later wearing a tight white tank top, cutoff blue jean shorts, and pink canvas Chuck Taylors. She looked out the apartment window at the sidewalk below. The pack of reporters was still there, milling around. When they saw her, they shouted questions her way.

She pulled back from the window and let out an exasperated growl. "How long are these people going to hang around outside our building?"

"I'm afraid you're going to attract attention wherever you go from now on because of the money," Tommy said. "Let's go out the back door of the building and through the alley so we avoid those jackals."

Tommy and April exited the building into the grimy and dimly lit alley. The putrid stench of rotting garbage caused April to pinch her nose to block the foul smell.

They came face to face with two seedy-looking guys sharing a forty-ounce bottle of malt liquor. Tattoos identifying their gang affiliation covered their arms like sleeves. Each had more than one teardrop tattooed below their right eyes.

"Hey, Parker, lookin' fine, chica," the taller one said between swigs.

"You know these punks?" Tommy asked.

"Unfortunately. It's Juan and Chico. I went to high school with them. They were expelled for fighting. They're in the El Salvadorian gang that's always causing trouble in the neighborhood."

"Let's go back in the building." Tommy turned around and blocked their view of his daughter.

He reached out.

The stout metal door they had just come through had no doorknob on the outside.

As designed, it prevented unauthorized entry by people who didn't live in the building. The only escape from the alley was straight ahead.

Tommy wrapped his arm around April's shoulder and led her up the alley. "Just ignore them. Keep walking."

"Yo, Parker, is it really true you inherited a billion dollars?" Juan asked with a slurred voice.

Tommy wheeled around, the fury of a protective father evident on his face. "Back off!"

The two thugs laughed like drunken hyenas.

Tommy and April turned and continued up the alley.

Chico taunted Tommy. "Chill, *hombre*, we just wanna

talk to your daughter." When he ignored him, Chico yelled out, "Hey, I'm talking to you!"

Tommy and April reached the end of the alley, returning to safety.

In a chilling voice, Chico screamed, "I know where you live, bitch!"

CHAPTER 39

Monday morning

TOMMY AND STEPHANIE WERE IN their bedroom getting dressed for work when an authoritative knock came at the apartment door. April walked over, checked the peephole, then swung it open.

A tall gentleman with wisps of white hair accenting his neatly trimmed sideburns stood in the hallway. "Is this the Parker residence?" he asked in a cultured New England accent.

"Yes." April turned toward her parents' bedroom and yelled, "The guy is here to fix the A/C!"

The man looked down at his five-thousand-dollar Armani suit and let out a polite chuckle. "I'm afraid there's been a misunderstanding. Allow me to introduce myself. I'm Lowell Huntington III."

The blank look on April's face told him she had no idea who he was.

"Ah of course. I understand. We've never met," he mumbled diplomatically. "I'm the CEO of JP Goldman, the largest investment bank on Wall Street."

"Um…okay. That's nice. Are you here to see my parents?" April asked.

"I'm here to see you." He pulled a large, colorful bouquet of flowers out from behind his back. "These are for you, April. Do you mind if I come in?"

Tommy and Stephanie came out of their bedroom,

ready to put in another day's work.

Stephanie saw April inhaling the fragrant smell of the flowers. She glared suspiciously at Huntington. "Who the hell are you?"

"Good morning, madam. You must be Mrs. Parker. You certainly do look lovely. I'm Lowell Huntington III, the CEO of JP Goldman. I stopped by to speak to April. May I come in?"

The dollars signs were practically visible in Stephanie's eyes. "Yes, of course, Mr. Huntington. Please come in." She turned excitedly to Tommy. "Dear, this is—"

"I heard. What brings you here this morning, Mr. Huntington?" Tommy asked, mistrust evident in his voice.

"My firm was pleased to learn that a New Yorker, and such a wonderful person, had prevailed in that nasty battle over her inheritance in France. In the hope that April considers my firm when looking for a trusted custodian to manage her inheritance, I've brought her a small gift."

"Look, Dad, he brought me flowers." She held out the bouquet.

Huntington pulled out a set of car keys. "Actually, this is our gift." He gestured toward the window. "Come look."

April hurried over to the window. Parked at the curb was a midlife crisis red Maserati GranTurismo. Two armed guards flanked the $150,000 luxury sports car to prevent curious onlookers from touching it. A huge silk bow adorned the hood.

"I hope you like it," Huntington said, handing the keys to April.

April's eyes narrowed as she scooped the keys from his hand. "You're giving me that car?"

"Yes."

"For free?"

"For free. No strings attached."

"Why?" She extended the pronunciation of the word, sure that this was some sort of scam.

"You have a lot of decisions to make now that you have your inheritance. We'd like to help you navigate the confusing times ahead. The only thing my firm asks is that you consider us when deciding whom to trust with your money. Your choices moving forward are extremely important. We'd hate to see you make costly mistakes."

Completely overwhelmed, April turned to her parents. "Mom? Dad? A little help, please."

Tommy threw up his hands. "I'm an insurance salesman. Your mother is a secretary. This is so far out of our league it's not funny. I don't have any idea what you should do."

"Perfectly understandable, Mr. and Mrs. Parker. I appreciate your reluctance to make any decisions right now. If you'd like, I can sit down and explain how our firm helps people like your daughter."

Stephanie rushed over to the kitchen table and dusted off the seat of a chair with her hand. "We would love to hear what you have to say, Mr. Huntington. Please, have a seat."

April furrowed her brow. "Hold on a second. I'm going to call Uncle Mark and ask him to come over. He should be here before I make any decisions."

Stephanie excused herself from their guest and pulled April aside. In a firm but low voice, she cautioned her. "That idiot almost cost you your inheritance. We don't need him here messing up this opportunity."

April crossed her arms and glared at Stephanie. "That *idiot* is the only reason I even got to France. Without his help, I wouldn't have gotten a dime. I'm calling him."

Ten minutes later, Mark walked into the apartment.

CHAPTER 40

MARK CROSSED HIS ARMS AND leaned back in
his chair. Sitting directly across from Huntington,
he said, "I'm listening."

Huntington forced a smile, knowing that keeping
Mark on his good side could seal the deal for his firm.
"Thanks for coming on such short notice, Mark. April is
lucky to have someone as savvy about finances as you in
her corner. Like her parents, I'm sure you only have her
best interests in mind. I won't forget your willingness to
hear me out."

The bribe implicit in his last comment didn't go
unnoticed by Mark. "Every firm on Wall Street will be
salivating to get their hands on my niece's money. Why
should she go with yours?" he asked rudely, hoping to
rile the man.

Huntington hadn't risen to the rank of CEO of a mul-
tibillion-dollar firm by being easily rattled. "That's a very
good question, sir," he calmly replied. "As I mentioned,
JP Goldman is the largest investment bank on Wall Street.
That gives us unprecedented influence and expertise
when it comes to managing April's six hundred million
dollars."

Stephanie held up a finger. "Wait. She inherited one
billion dollars, not six hundred million. You have your
numbers wrong."

"You are correct, madam. April did inherit one billion
dollars. Before France released the money to our Trea-

sury Department, it assessed their outrageous inheritance tax." Huntington's oversized ego led him to snap, "So you see, my numbers are *not* wrong."

"Those bastards took 40 percent of my daughter's money! That's robbery!" Stephanie bellowed.

"No, madam, that's socialism," Huntington quipped, understandably partial to the market-based economic system in the US that had made him an extraordinarily rich man. "Of course, six hundred million dollars is nothing to be unhappy about."

"You mentioned the Treasury Department," Mark said. "Why did it get involved?"

"The Uniting and Strengthening America by Providing Appropriate Tools Required to Intercept and Obstruct Terrorism Act of 2001 was enacted—"

"Excuse me. The what?" Mark interrupted.

Only a bureaucracy hopelessly enamored with itself could have come up with such a ridiculous title and acronym for a government program.

"I'm sorry," Huntington said, "that title is industry jargon for the USA PATRIOT Act. It was enacted after 9/11 to stop money laundering and the funding of terrorists. All financial institutions are bound by its regulations before opening a new account."

"So, you do realize April doesn't actually have the money yet. She can't commit to anything until after the review is finished."

"I'm glad you brought that up, Mark. This situation is a perfect example of the benefits of going with my firm. I called the secretary of the Treasury this morning before I stopped by. We were fraternity brothers at Harvard. As a personal favor, he assured me he would see to it that the vetting process is expedited. It should be done in no more than three weeks."

"Three weeks?" Stephanie questioned. "What is my daughter supposed to live on while the government has her money tied up with red tape?"

Mark held back a laugh. The implied claim of poverty by Stephanie was absurd.

"I think I can help there as well," Huntington said. "My firm would be happy to offer April a small bridge loan on very favorable terms while she waits for the review to be completed."

"How much money are you willing to loan my daughter?" Stephanie asked.

"One hundred million dollars."

CHAPTER 41

"YOU'VE GOT TO BE KIDDING me." April's face went white at the enormity of the amount Huntington had just casually offered to loan her.

He smiled. "I know it's going to take some time to get used to, April, but you now live in a completely different universe than what you are accustomed to. To help you with these crucial decisions, you might consider giving power of attorney to someone you trust implicitly."

Of course, he was referring to his firm.

"To make the transition to managing your new net worth easier, we would be happy to set up a family office on your behalf."

Stephanie jumped in. "We plan on moving out of this cracker box-size apartment soon, but until we do, there really isn't any extra space to set up an office, Mr. Huntington."

Huntington let out a snide laugh. "Not a home office, madam, a family office. It means a dedicated staff of professional investment advisors, accountants, and lawyers who exclusively manage the funds of our ultra-wealthy clients."

Huntington stood to leave. Being a shrewd businessman, he handed Mark—not April—his business card. "If I can be of any assistance while you think about my offer, I am at your beck and call 24/7. It was a pleasure meeting all of you." He turned to April. "Enjoy your beautiful new car, young lady."

After the Wall Street power broker left, April looked ghostly pale. She supported her drooping head in her hands and moaned, "I think I'm going to throw up."

The mind-boggling amounts of money being casually bandied about had made her nauseated. She rushed to the kitchen sink and upchucked her breakfast.

After splashing cold water on her face, April looked up from the sink. "That man just gave me a Maserati. A friggin' Maserati! *And* he wants to loan me one hundred million dollars!"

Tommy supported April, easing her back over to the table. "Sit down before you faint."

"What should I do?" April said, terrified by the weight of the decisions she had to make.

"Take the loan, of course," Stephanie replied.

"All right, everybody, calm down. Take a breath," Mark said.

"What do you think I should do, Uncle Mark?"

"I say don't rush into anything. There's plenty of time to think things through before you have to make any big decisions."

"But I don't *want* to make any big decisions. What if I mess them up? Will you help me?"

Mark stepped back. "I fly airplanes; I don't manage huge fortunes. What about your parents?"

Tommy and Stephanie had surprised looks on their faces.

"Us?" Tommy questioned, looking around the apartment as if Mark was referring to someone else.

April shook her head. "No offense, Mom and Dad, but you said it yourself. You are so far out of your league when it comes to this kind of money it's not funny." She turned to Mark. "I know I can trust you. I'll give *you* power of attorney. That way, you can help me make decisions about investing my inheritance."

Mark had a pained look on his face as he shook his

head. "I don't think so, kid. That's a lot of responsibility. Your parents will back me up on this; being responsible with money is not exactly my strong suit."

April looked at Mark with her pretty blues eyes. In her sweetest voice, accompanied with a full-on pout, she whined, "*Please*, Uncle Mark. I can't do this myself."

It turned out April had inherited more from Noelle than her looks. She'd learned what to say—and how to say it—to get men to throw common sense out the window.

———◆———

Two weeks later

Noelle sat at the kitchen table in their drab apartment, hunched over a mounting stack of bills. Mark walked out of the bedroom as he pocketed his cell phone.

"Who was that?" Noelle asked.

"Marty. He finally has a trip for us. It's an out-and-back to Kansas City tomorrow."

"On the Fourth of July? But we had plans to take the girls on a picnic then watch fireworks."

"Do you want me to call him back and turn down the charter?" Mark asked.

Noelle picked up the bills and sighed. "No, we can't afford to turn down any flights. With business so slow, who knows when we might get another one. We're behind on our rent, and these bills aren't going to pay themselves."

"I'm sure the girls will understand."

Mary and April walked in the apartment weighed down with bags from Macy's, Louis Vuitton, and Saks Fifth Avenue. They collapsed on the tattered couch after their long day of shopping.

"Mom, you *have* to see this cute outfit I got," Mary said, beaming with excitement. She pulled a sequined silk blouse and matching short skirt out of the Saks bag.

Mary stood and held them up against her body. "What do you think?"

Noelle grimaced. "I think they look very expensive. How can you afford that?"

"Oh, I didn't buy them. April did. Wasn't that generous of her?" Mary gave her big sister a big hug. "Thanks, Sis. You're the best."

"That was very...generous." Noelle hesitated as she carefully thought out her next comment. "April, I don't want this to sound ungrateful. But ever since you chose to go with Mr. Huntington's firm and take out the bridge loan, you've...well...don't you think you've been getting kind of carried away with your spending?"

"Not at all. I enjoy being able to spend my money on the people I care about." April dug down into one of the bags and came up with a small robin's egg-blue box. "I didn't want you to feel left out, Mom, so I got you a little something."

Noelle immediately recognized the distinctive blue color of the box from her modeling days. Her eyes lit up. "You bought me something from Tiffany?"

She handed the box to Noelle. "Open it."

Noelle eagerly accepted the box and untied the silk ribbon around it. Inside was a pair of platinum earrings in the shape of flowers. They were encrusted with sparkling diamonds.

"They're stunning," Noelle gushed. She removed the earrings from the box and walked over to the hallway mirror. Turning her head side to side, Noelle admired the dazzling jewelry as she held them up to her ears. "I love them. What do you think, Mark?"

Ignoring Noelle as she modeled her expensive new trinkets, Mark said, "I think Noelle is right. Your spending is out of control, April. I agreed to help you manage your money. You can start being more responsible with it and returning those earrings and the clothes."

Noelle's big smile melted away at hearing Mark's advice. She knew he was right. But she felt as disappointed as a kid who just had her balloon popped by the mall Santa after telling her he wasn't real.

"Your accountant came by earlier," Mark continued. "He said you haven't returned any of his calls. He left this." Mark picked up a spreadsheet off the kitchen table and read from it. "Since you got the loan you've: paid Stephanie's credit card bill off, bought a handicapped-accessible van and motorized wheelchair for one of your patients at the VA, purchased a condo overlooking Central Park, and racked up huge bills on these shopping trips you keep going on. It's got to stop."

April bit her bottom lip. "My accountant didn't tell you what I got you, did he?"

"What are you talking about?"

"Wait until you see this, Dad," Mary said excitedly. Turning to April, she said, "Show him."

April pulled out her iPhone and tapped on the screen, bringing up a photo. "Uncle Mark, you more than anyone, have been responsible for me getting my inheritance. Without your help, none of this would have happened. I can never repay you for everything you've done for me. But I hope this small token of my appreciation will come close." She turned her phone around and showed Mark the photo on the screen.

His jaw dropped. "You bought me a Gulfstream jet?"

CHAPTER 42

IN CONTRAST TO NOELLE'S DISAPPOINTED expression, Mark's face resembled a kid who just got the Christmas present of his wildest dreams. He leaned forward to examine the small screen. "Is that the new G700?"

"It sure is," April replied. "The salesman said it has all the latest cool technology a pilot could want." She pointed at the photo. "Check out the tail number."

Mark looked closely at the screen trying to make out the small characters on the tail. They had been Photoshopped onto the generic photo of the plane. With his eyesight not being as sharp as it once was, Mark spread his fingers apart on the screen to enlarge the photo. The tail number was N711MS.

"Seven eleven Mike Sierra," Mark read with astonishment, using the code words from the phonetic alphabet assigned to the matching letters on the tail number. "Mike Sierra. Mark Smith."

"I guess this means I'm keeping the earrings then, right, flyboy?" Noelle said sarcastically.

A five-thousand-dollar pair of earrings was pocket change compared to a seventy-five-million-dollar jet.

"I can't possibly accept…" Mark muttered, too stunned to formulate a complete sentence. "How could I…how could I ever afford the fuel for a jet like that, let alone pay to hangar it and insure it?"

"That's all taken care of, Uncle Mark. Don't worry

about it. I put a deposit down yesterday for a position on the production line. The salesman said your plane should be completed in about four months." April looked nervously at her uncle. "Well, what do you think? Do you like it?"

Mark had never felt so conflicted in his life. Before him was an opportunity to own the most prized possession he could dream of as a pilot—at no cost. On the other hand, less than one minute ago he had reprimanded April for her reckless spending.

"You don't have to answer right now," April said. "I know it's a big shock. Let it sink in. If you think it's too much money to spend, I can cancel the order with Gulfstream." She hooked her arm with Mary's. "We have to run. I'm meeting my interior decorator to go over the fabrics I want the custom-made furniture covered in."

The two young women quickly headed for the door. Mary looked back and said, "Sorry, but we have to cancel for the picnic tomorrow. We met these two cute guys at Times Square, and they invited us to their parents' beach house. I hope you don't mind."

A disappointed look filled Noelle's face.

"It's okay," Mark said. "We have a trip tomorrow, anyway. But I want to talk more when we get back about your spending, April."

"Sure, Uncle Mark. Gotta run. Bye."

With a better offer from strangers who obviously ranked higher than spending the holiday with their dull parents, the sisters left.

Mark and Noelle walked into their bedroom to pack a few essential items to take on their trip tomorrow. They'd been flying long enough to know that if you don't bring along an overnight bag on an out-and-back trip, providence would virtually guarantee that something would go wrong with the plane and leave you stranded with no clean change of clothes.

Noelle turned her head when she heard a knock at the apartment door. She left the bedroom and opened the door, expecting to see her daughters returning to grab their beach clothes.

Instead, two stern-looking men dressed in suits straight off the rack from JC Penny stood in the hallway. The older of the two said, "I'm Special Agent Reed. This is my partner, Special Agent Powell. We're investigators with the Treasury Department."

Both men reached inside their suit jackets and pulled out leather cases holding impressive gold Treasury Department badges with an eagle perched on top.

"My partner and I have been assigned the case of April Parker and the money she inherited from France," Reed said.

"You just missed her. April left a few minutes ago. I can call her." Noelle pulled her cell phone out of her pocket. "Maybe she can come back if she hasn't gone too far."

"We're not here to speak to April Parker," agent Reed said. "We'd like to speak to Mark Smith and Noelle Parker. Are you Noelle, ma'am?"

Noelle's eyes narrowed as she examined the agents more closely. "What's this about?"

"So, you *are* Noelle Parker?" he said, ignoring her question. "Is Mark Smith here?"

Noelle called out over her right shoulder. "Mark. Come out here. Now."

He came out of the bedroom and walked up next to Noelle.

The agents flashed their badges and repeated their introductions for Mark. "We'd like to speak to you both," agent Reed said. "May we come in?"

"Why don't you gentlemen tell us why you're here before I decide whether to let you in our home?" Mark replied.

Agent Reed wasn't amused by Mark's reticence to

allow him in. Intentionally raising his voice, he said, "If you'd prefer to discuss the six-hundred-million-dollar inheritance April Parker is slated to receive out here in the hallway where all your neighbors can hear, fine with me."

Neighbors cracked open their apartment doors and peeked out to see what the commotion was.

Mark glared at the agents. "Real nice." He opened the apartment door wide. "I'm Mark Smith. This is Noelle Parker. Get in here before the whole world knows about the money." He pointed at the kitchen table. "Have a seat."

The agents settled into chairs at the table and handed out their business cards.

"We are investigators with the Financial Crimes and Enforcement Network," Agent Powell said. "FinCen is the intelligence arm of the Treasury Department tasked with supporting the Bank Secrecy Act. Our bureau investigates banking transactions for any connections to money laundering or the financing of terrorism."

After that complicated explanation of their roles at Treasury, it became obvious why the two men looked more like accountants than cops.

Agent Reed took over. "Our job is to certify that large banking transactions have no suspicious origins or any connections to criminal activity before the funds can be released. The Treasury Department is concerned with some troubling discoveries my partner and I have come up with during our investigation. At this point in time, I'm advising my superiors that the money April Parker is set to receive should be confiscated by the government and deposited into the general fund."

CHAPTER 43

M ARK BOLTED FROM HIS CHAIR. "What the hell are you talking about? April is the last person on earth who'd be involved in any criminal activity."

"As I said, we are here to speak to you and Noelle Parker, not April." Reed sat back in his chair and watched his targets squirm.

Noelle grabbed Mark's arm, pulling him back down into his chair. "But we're not getting the money; April is. Why would you be investigating us?"

Agent Powell pulled a manila folder from his brief-case and opened it on the table. "It's our job to follow the money trail and see where it leads." He pointed to a report the men had written. "During our investiga-tion, we learned that the money in question came from Gerard Benoit. We were shocked to learn that Mr. Benoit had quite an unscrupulous past. The French government found evidence of involvement with drug smuggling, embezzlement of funds from his businesses, tax evasion, and billions of dollars laundered through offshore bank accounts." Powell closed the folder. "You had an affair with Benoit, Ms. Parker. You bore his child. What exactly was your involvement with these illegal activities?"

Mark balled up both fists. "You son of a bitch!"

Only Noelle reaching across and forcibly holding him back kept Mark from going to jail for assaulting a federal officer.

"That was thirty years ago," he shouted. "If you two had

done a *thorough* investigation, you'd know that. Noelle had nothing to do with any of that. Besides, the French government already confiscated billions of dollars from Benoit's estate that they determined was the result of illegal activity. The money April is getting is clean."

Reed leaned forward and glared at Mark. "We did conduct a *thorough* investigation, Smith. That's why we wanted to talk to you. It seems you had a problem at JFK recently. We learned you were denied access through the security screening checkpoint by the TSA. We also have video surveillance footage from the airport showing you getting into a verbal altercation with the manager at the Air France ticket counter. You were filmed being escorted out of the terminal by armed soldiers. They overheard you yell out the word *terrorist*."

Noelle's eyes opened wide as she looked at Mark. "You said that? In an airport?"

Mark held up both hands. "Hold on…wait…this is not what it seems. Okay, I did say the word…"

"Terrorist," Reed volunteered for Mark.

"Yes…terrorist."

The two agents whipped out their note pads and started scribbling in them.

"But the only reason I said it was because I was furious about not being allowed into France. The director general of the Police Nationale hates my guts. He still thinks I murdered Benoit."

Agent Reed's head snapped up. "Did you say murder?"

Mark couldn't have dug a bigger hole for himself if he'd been using an earth mover.

With the interview rapidly spiraling out of control, Noelle jumped in. "Time out, everyone. Let's back up here before you fine public servants get the wrong impression. I'm sure if you check with your counterparts in the Ministry of the Treasury in France, you'll find that every penny that April is getting has been thoroughly vetted. You gentlemen don't really believe that after the terrible terrorist incidents in Nice, Paris, Lyon, and other cities, that officials there would release any of that money if they had any suspicion that there might be a connection to terrorists, do you?"

Agents Powell and Reed fell silent. They each turned to the other hoping one would come up with an answer to Noelle's brilliant observation.

Looking for a way to finish the interview quickly, Reed said, "One final question. Have either of you, or will you in the future, receive anything of value from the money April Parker would receive *if* the release of funds is approved?" Agent Reed looked down at his note pad, avoiding eye contact. "If so, the information you've provided today might be viewed as unreliable or a conflict of interest."

Noelle glanced over at the box from Tiffany. Mark cleared his throat and fidgeted in his chair.

Reed looked up from his notepad. "Well?"

Just as Noelle was about to speak, Mark put his hand on top of hers. "Let's talk about conflict of interest. Correct me if I'm wrong, Agents, but doesn't the Treasury have a bounty system in place for its investigators? Employees who solve large financial crimes that result in a windfall for the government can get as much as thirty percentage of the amount involved. Right?"

Now Reed and Powell shifted uncomfortably in their seats.

"If, on the off chance you two gentlemen were the ones credited with April losing out on collecting her inheritance, you'd stand to profit handsomely, correct?"

Reed and Powell declined to respond to Mark's damming observation.

"Of course I'm not implying you fine public servants would ever risk losing your jobs by ignoring certain facts or even bending the regulations a little." Mark turned to

Noelle. "Help me out here. What was the name of the fraternity brother that Lowell Huntington, the CEO of JP Goldman, mentioned? He was going to do Lowell a personal favor and expedite the vetting of April's fortune so it could be invested in his firm."

Noelle tapped her fingertip on her lips. "Let me see. I remember his close friend had a government job doing something. What was it?" Her face lit up. "I remember now. He's the secretary of the Treasury."

Reed and Powell scooped up their files, shoved them into their briefcases, and stood to leave.

"Thanks for your time today," agent Reed said. "I'll be sure to contact the Ministry of the Treasury before we file our final report. Good day."

CHAPTER 44

LOOKING SHARP IN THEIR LUXURY Jet Charters uniforms, Mark and Noelle walked into the building, glad to escape the heat of the July day. And money issues.

"Well, I'll be damned. Look who's here!" Charlotte called out from the lobby. "The Three Musketeers are back together and ready to ride again."

Mark sighed and muttered under his breath, "Great, just what I didn't need."

"What are you doing here?" Noelle asked as she hugged her best friend.

"I'm working the charter to KC with you guys. We're taking a bunch of fat cat donors to the president's rally. Marty wanted to impress them by assigning his two best flight attendants to pamper them." She sneered at Mark. "Looks like all the *good* pilots were busy."

"Am I going to have to put the two of you in the corner for a time-out?" Noelle joked.

Charlotte let out a hearty laugh. "I'm just ribbing him. Don't mean nothin' by it. Mark knows I think the world of him. Besides, we're flying over land today, so even if he runs out of gas again, we won't have to ditch."

With the frightening memories of their near-death experience on the Tech-Liner flight somewhat faded, the gallows humor typical among crews in the airline industry was back.

Mark shook his head and walked off toward the flight planning room, not interested in getting in an insult war with Charlotte. "You're welcome for saving your butt, by the way," he called out over his shoulder before entering the room, not completely above a little immature tit-for-tat.

"Hey, Mark," Andy Wilson said, as Mark entered the flight planning room, "I'm your copilot today. I've already finished all the flight planning for you."

Mark suspected Andy's eagerness to please him had more to do with his interest in Mark's daughter than to be an accommodating copilot.

"Thanks. How's the weather?" Mark responded, grateful for the assistance regardless of the motivation.

"It's going to be hotter than hell in KC today. One hundred eight degrees. Other than that, no thunderstorms are forecast."

Marty Dawson entered the room. He patted Mark on the back. "Hello, Mark. Thanks so much for flying this trip to Kansas City. I really appreciate you giving up your holiday to help me out. You guys should be back in time to catch the fireworks."

Andy's sucking up was nothing compared to the Jekyll-and-Hyde reversal in behavior from the normally gruff Navy man.

"How's that lovely niece of yours?"

The real reason for the cordial treatment from Marty became obvious.

"April is fine. She asked me to tell you again how grateful she was for letting her charter your jet on such short notice. Anytime another family emergency comes up, she is certain you'd be happy to let me borrow it again." Now he was just messing with the owner.

Marty quickly changed the subject. "There's been a last-minute passenger added to the flight. The Speaker of the House is in town. He's going with you to babysit the president's five biggest donors at the rally. These guys could become regular customers, so don't screw up,

Air…" Marty caught himself. "I know you will impress them with your flying skills, Mark." Marty almost choked verbalizing the compliment.

"See, Andy," Mark said to his copilot, "I told you the old squid has a heart hiding somewhere in that stumpy little body of his." Mark took full advantage of the opportunity to get in a few jabs at his cantankerous boss, knowing he wouldn't retaliate and risk losing potential charter bookings from his rich niece.

Andy rolled his eyes at the two grown men acting like squabbling children.

Marty had reached his limit of politeness. He gnawed on his unlit cigar, biting it in half. "Arrivals will be shut down at three o'clock for the arrival of Air Force One in KC. You two clowns need to stop flapping your jaws and get your butts in gear so you don't miss the cutoff. Now get outta here." He stomped out of the flight planning room.

Mark and Andy walked out of the building as five black limousines pulled away from the Gulfstream. The pampering of the five men, whose fortunes easily eclipsed April's, had already begun as Noelle and Charlotte catered to their every demand inside the plane.

Andy did the external inspection as Mark stood on the tarmac admiring the jet. Knowing he might be the owner of one of these sleek planes soon gave Mark a completely different perspective. It was like buying a new car then suddenly spotting that model everywhere, when before you never noticed them.

Andy walked up to Mark. "Preflight inspection is done. Let's get going before the field in Kansas City closes."

Mark didn't hear a word Andy said.

Andy snapped his fingers in front of Mark's face. "Earth to Mark. Anybody home?"

Mark just smiled, knowing how ecstatic Andy would be if he were the potential recipient of such a beautiful plane. "Let's go to KC," Mark replied.

Andy entered the cockpit while Mark turned right to go into the cabin and greet his passengers. "Hello, folks, I'm Mark Smith. I'll be your captain today on the flight to Kansas City," he announced.

The tycoons didn't even bother looking up from their *Wall Street Journals*. To them, Mark was no more than a chauffeur of a faster vehicle. Certainly someone beneath themselves to engage in idle small talk with. Mark took the hint and went to the cockpit.

Noelle poured a glass of Cristal for one of her passengers. When she turned to go back to the galley, he grabbed her arm. "Why don't you leave the bottle with me, sweetie."

Charlotte and the other passengers saw him grab Noelle. An explosive silence enveloped the cabin.

Noelle calmly looked down at the chubby hand restraining her arm. Her gaze lifted. She looked directly at the brazen passenger. "Sir, as a flight attendant, I've been trained to engage in close-quarters combat with terrorists, fight fires at thirty-five thousand feet, identify bombs, give CPR, and administer first aid. If you don't remove your hand from my arm right now, you'll leave me no choice but to use some of that training."

The other passengers snickered behind their newspapers.

The passenger wisely removed his hand.

Attempting to save face and demonstrate he wasn't intimidated by Noelle, he grumbled, "When are we leaving? I don't want to be late."

"As soon as the Speaker arrives, we'll be on our way."

Accustomed to bought-and-paid-for politicians waiting on him, not the other way around, he barked, "If that jackass doesn't get here in the next five minutes, he can walk to Kansas City."

Noelle went back to the galley, not bothering to

respond.

Charlotte whispered in her ear. "If that backside of a mule gives you any more guff, ol' Charlotte will set him straight."

Noelle chuckled. "That's what I'm afraid of. I've had enough drama lately. Let's just get through today without any incidents."

CHAPTER 45

MARK DRUMMED HIS FINGERS ON the glareshield in the cockpit. He repeatedly looked over at the gate to the tarmac. VIP or not, he'd waited long enough for the tardy passenger. He turned to Andy. "Crank them up."

When projected flight time was added to the current time in Kansas City, indicating that they would arrive precisely at three o'clock, Mark had directed Andy to start both engines. Once they were running, Mark requested taxi clearance from the tower.

Just as taxi clearance was approved, a black limo screeched up to the boarding stairs. A flustered congressional aide jumped out and opened the back door. He assisted Speaker of the House Wilber Clayton from the car. A large, disheveled man, Clayton had the red, swollen nose typical of a heavy drinker. His aide helped him navigate the flat, smooth path to the plane and up the stairs.

"Sorry we're late," the aide said while he propped up Clayton. "The Speaker was up late last night working on very important legislation."

Charlotte caught a whiff of the leader of the House of Representatives as he stumbled by. Under her breath she muttered, "Dang sure that wasn't the only thing he was workin' on last night."

The door was quickly closed, and Mark taxied out to the runway. The aide led his boss to the seat nearest the bathroom, having been through this type of situa-

tion more than once before. Speaker Clayton passed out
before the plane lifted off.

Mark turned west after departing Teterboro Airport
and accelerated the Gulfstream to its maximum speed of
Mach .925.

———◆———

The ground crew at Joint Base Andrews pulled away
the boarding stairs from Air Force One. All movement on
the airport was shut down until the VC-25A was safely
underway. Armed Humvees escorted the highly modi-
fied 747 from the ramp to the end of the runway. The
jumbo jet, with its distinctive blue, white, and gold paint
scheme, lumbered off the runway, defying gravity once
again. It slowly turned west, passing over the epicenter of
government for the United States.

Air Force One was cleared on a direct course to the
Kansas City downtown airport. Air traffic controllers
gave the flying Oval Office a clear path to its destination,
keeping all other traffic a minimum of five miles from it.

President Jack Kincaid enjoyed a gourmet lunch in his
private suite in the front of Air Force One. Kincaid was a
casting director's dream. He looked presidential in every
way. His boyish good looks, tall stature, and full head of
hair with just the right amount of gray projected wisdom
and competence. He was born with a natural charisma
and magnetism that no amount of high-society upbringing could hope to duplicate.

Eldest son of Sen. Alfred Kincaid and grandson of the
notorious Missouri governor Joseph "Tuffy" Kincaid,
Jack was anointed to carry on the family political dynasty.

He'd learned the game of politics well from his grandfather and father. Rather than spurn journalists, Kincaid
let them believe they were part of his inner circle by
regularly inviting them to parties at the family compound. Puff pieces downplaying the family's seamy past

and exaggerating its accomplishments were the predicable result.

Jack had been given the nickname "Boy Scout" by the press because of his supposedly strait-laced personality. The nickname stuck and was even used by the Secret Service as the president's code name.

After finishing lunch, he got to work. Sitting across the desk from the president was his chief of staff, "Dirty Harry" Wilcox. Wilcox was a veteran of the rough-and-tumble world of New York politics. Kincaid's father had strategically chosen Wilcox to be his son's chief of staff during his early days as a legislator back in his home state of Missouri. He'd calculated that having Wilcox on Jack's staff would help overcome the inherent bias among East Coast power brokers against flyover country candidates when his son made the move into national politics. Wilcox had been willing to go to any length to get his boss elected, had been wildly successful at his job, and was very well paid for it.

First Lady Sarah Whitcomb-Kincaid, only daughter of the Greenwich, Connecticut, Whitcombs, sat at her husband's side. She was his fiercest advocate and could play the Washington game better than most career politicians.

When they first met at a cocktail party years ago, she had rebuffed every advance from the junior congressman. Sarah had recently graduated from Brown University and was an aide for the powerful Senator Cornwall from Connecticut. Jack had taken six years to get a political science degree from Western Missouri State College— the only school he could get into with his subpar GPA. Shortly after Jack had been elected to his first term in the Senate, Sarah had a sudden change of heart, and the two had been inseparable ever since.

The first lady's PR team had done yeoman's work since she changed her address to 1600 Pennsylvania Avenue, trying to convince the public she was warm and likable.

Despite calling in favors to get friendly interviews on daytime TV shows, she still had an unfavorable rating. Even staged photo ops with sick children in hospitals hadn't worked.

Wilcox briefed his boss. "Mr. President, Sergio Rodriguez stopped by my office again yesterday. The vice president is furious about the stories in the papers. He's demanding that you publicly reaffirm your support for him as your running mate."

Before Kincaid could respond, the first lady said, "If I ever find out who leaked our plan to dump him from the ticket before running for a second term, they'll wish they were never born."

President Kincaid leaned back in his overstuffed leather chair. "You'd think the son of a bitch would be grateful I picked him to be my running mate the first time. If he'd keep his political ambitions in check and learn to play ball, he could become president after my second term." Kincaid shook his head. "God help the country if that ever happens." He tossed his pen onto the desk. "It's too late to make a change now. Besides, we need every Latino vote we can get. Tell him privately I'm proud to be on the ticket with him again. That will have to do. No public announcement. It wouldn't look presidential."

"Yes, sir." Wilcox paused for a moment before bringing up the next subject. "About your poll numbers, Mr. President. You and I have been butting heads for the past year over your legislative priorities. You're getting killed in the polls every time you take a stand on one of the divisive political issues. I recommend in the strongest possible terms you lie low and do nothing politically controversial until after the election."

Kincaid's normally unflappable demeanor suddenly changed. "Do nothing? My base will think I'm just another power-hungry politician willing to sell his soul to get reelected. I've been saying for months we need to do something big, something bold, if there is any chance of turning my abysmal poll numbers around before Election Day. And what do you come up with? A rally in my hometown for a bunch of cow-town hicks on the Fourth of July."

"Jack's right," Sarah said from the president's side.

Throughout the years, there had been no love lost between Sarah and Harry as they vied for supremacy in influencing the most powerful man in the world.

"Hell, even I could have come up with a better idea to get our base energized," she continued. "With campaign funds drying up, we can't afford to saturate the networks with TV ads 24/7 anymore. We need money. Now. Against my better advice, my husband kept you on as his chief of staff, Wilcox. Now his lapse in judgment could cost him a second term."

Wilcox bristled at her blatant attempt to undermine him. "Madam First Lady, if your husband doesn't stop flirting with every third-rail issue out there, he won't *see* a second term." Wilcox turned to his boss. "Jack, we go way back. I've stuck with you since your dad hired me to watch your back in the state legislature. I know what it takes to get reelected, but you're making my job impossible. Trust me when I tell you you're making a mistake."

President Kincaid stroked his chin as he pondered the advice from his longtime advisor. "Maybe you're right." Kincaid stood up and paced behind his desk. "Maybe I am making a mistake." He glared at Wilcox. "My mistake was assuming you would do your job and get me reelected. After we return to Washington, I'm going to officially announce a shakeup in my administration."

Kincaid leaned forward and planted his fists on his desk. "One more thing. When I'm conducting the people's business, don't ever call me Jack again. It's Mr. President." He stood straight, jutted out his chin, and dismissed his aide. "That will be all, Harry."

CHAPTER 46

THE AIRPORT IN KANSAS CITY swarmed with uniformed and undercover cops. As instructed from their nervous superiors, they went over every detail for a third time before the president's arrival.

The former main airport for TWA during the prop era was conveniently located just across the Missouri River from the smattering of skyscrapers that made up downtown. With its short runway considered only marginally safe for jets, commercial airline operations had relocated many decades ago to a sprawling airport situated among cornfields miles north of the city center.

A conference room located next to a hangar floor was packed full of leaders from numerous law enforcement agencies. They were tasked with the grave responsibility of protecting the president during his campaign rally. The room served as the command center for all aspects of the event. Rows of monitors lined the walls, displaying feeds from dozens of surveillance cameras. Communication techs manned banks of phones and radios.

The Secret Service, FBI, Missouri state troopers, and officers with the Kansas City Police Department were just a few of the organizations present. Clad in bulletproof vests and toting high-powered weapons, while of course sporting the requisite dark sunglasses, there was enough testosterone in the room to float a boat.

The lead agent from the Kansas City Secret Service office stood and reviewed the preparations. "Secret Service is the lead agency for this operation. Everything goes through me and my team. Counter Assault Team snipers are set up on rooftops around the airport that have a clear line of fire at the crowd. Radio call sign is Hawkeye. Drones are airborne now and will remain up during the event with IR and video camera downlinks to the command center." He leaned forward and planted his hands on the table. "We intercepted online chatter recently discussing a terrorist cell arriving in a Midwest town. Our analysts haven't been able to verify what town or what organizations might be involved. Tell your people to be alert for anyone in the crowd appearing to communicate with other random spectators."

The agent requested an update from the heads of each organization. "KCPD, where are you at with your preparations?"

The chief of police cleared his throat and tried to sound as tough and professional as the federal boys. "Every manhole cover within a mile radius of the airport has been welded shut. Our teams of bomb-sniffing dogs swept the area yesterday and just finished repeating the sweep as we speak. Every gate in the perimeter fence has been secured with a high-strength padlock. The only entry point for the public is at the east side of the ramp. That allows us to easily funnel everyone through the security screening checkpoint. It's kinda like herding cattle for you big city folks." He pulled out a handkerchief and wiped the perspiration from his brow. "Sorry about the heat wave, fellas. Welcome to the Show Me State in July."

"FBI, you're up."

A man in a dark suit leaned forward in his chair. "All leaves and vacations in our office were canceled to ensure maximum manning for the event. Agents spent the week paying a visit to all the nuts in the area on the Class Three list. They were politely *encouraged* to avoid the rally." He couldn't help getting in a little jab at the straitlaced Secret

Service and the recent scandals it had faced. "The whore-houses in town have been shut down for the duration, so your people wouldn't be distracted."

The Secret Service lead agent almost leaped across the table. He wanted to smack the smarmy grin off the FBI agent's face after his affront to his agency. But he wisely kept his anger in check. Another publicity nightmare was the last thing he needed to bring down on the Secret Service if he ever wanted to be promoted to the big show in DC. He took a sharp breath. "State troopers, you're next."

The burly trooper stood to give his report. His flat, stiff brimmed campaign-style hat was firmly affixed to his shaved head. "Unfortunately, our manning at the airport is a little thinner than I prefer. This being the Fourth of July, locals feel it's their God-given right to set off fireworks despite the law banning them. Every time we hear a bomb bursting in air, two of our people get pulled away from their post to go check it out and make sure it's not gunfire."

"Thank you, Francis Scott Key, for that enlightening report," the lead agent said mockingly. He closed the file folder lying on the table and stood up. "The gate opens in five minutes. Get your people in place. All cell phone signals in the area have been jammed to prevent remote detonation of explosive devices, so call the command center on your radio if anything out of the ordinary happens." As the attendees stood to leave, the lead agent barked, "No president, especially Missouri's favorite son, has ever had so much as a scratch while visiting my city. Do your jobs and keep it that way."

CHAPTER 47

A S THE CHASTENED CHIEF OF staff rose to leave after being so rudely dismissed by his boss, there was a knock at the door. Wilcox flung the door open and stomped out, brushing aside the person waiting outside.

Dirk Miller, lead agent for President Kincaid's presidential protective detail, stood back to let Harry Wilcox pass. The PPD was exclusively tasked with protecting the president, or POTUS, as they called him. Miller looked like a former NFL linebacker. His broad shoulders, thick neck, and high-and-tight haircut complemented his disarmingly good looks. The stern expression on his face left no doubt he was all business, though.

Agent Miller poked his head in the office. "Mr. President, is this a good time for your arrival briefing?"

Kincaid waved him in. "As good a time as any. Come in, Dirk."

Miller walked over to the chair in front of the desk but did not take a seat. He looked over at Sarah and nodded his head. "Madam First Lady, it's a pleasure to see you again."

Sarah Kincaid stood and smoothed out the creases in her dress. She smiled. "Agent Miller, I expect you to take good care of my husband during the rally today."

"I'll protect him with my life, ma'am."

Sarah squeezed through the small opening between the desk and agent Miller as she made her way to the door. "I'll leave you boys alone." She closed the door behind her.

Miller stood at attention in front of the president. Kincaid gave him a dismissive wave. "At ease, son. Take a seat."

He relaxed and sat down in the comfortable leather chair.

Kincaid kicked his feet up on his desk, looked his personal bodyguard in the eyes, and asked, "Why, Agent Miller?"

Miller's back stiffened up. "Sir?"

"You said you'd protect me with your life. Not to sound ungrateful, but why would you be willing to leave that beautiful wife of yours a widow and your adorable kids fatherless for a guy like me? With your meteoric rise through the ranks of Special Operations Command, then Delta Force, and now my bodyguard after only five years with the Secret Service, an ambitious guy like you could write your own check in this town. With your impressive background, wealthy clients would be lining up to hire you as their bodyguard."

He downplayed his excitement at the prospect of cashing in on his skills. "Maybe someday, sir. Right now, I've got more important duties." Miller shifted uneasily in the chair. "May I speak candidly, sir?"

"Of course, Agent Miller."

"As an agent, I know I'm not supposed to have any political or personal opinions about my protectee. Nothing I see or hear on the job will ever be shared with anyone. But…"

Kincaid narrowed his eyes. "But what?"

"Sir, you are the first president in my lifetime to have the balls to stand up for what you believe in. Even when it's not beneficial to you politically. I admire that in a man, sir. This great country of ours would be a hell of a lot better off if there were more honorable men like you leading it." He looked around as if they were being spied upon. In a whisper, he said, "I hope you kick the ass of that flake from California during the election in November."

Kincaid had been in politics long enough to know when someone was kissing his backside, hoping to somehow benefit from it in the future. He held his cards close to his vest and said, "With loyal supporters like you on my side, how could I not win in November? Let's get to the arrival briefing."

"Yes, sir. I will deplane first to oversee the preparations to make an immediate takeoff in case of emergency. Once that's done, I'll give the all-clear on the radio for you to disembark. The rally will take place on the ramp at the airport, so you will walk from Air Force One to the stage. The mayor and governor will give their usual welcome speeches, then you will speak. After you've finished, there will be a few minutes available for interviews and pictures with the press. When you want to leave, give me the sign. I'll tell the press that you are running behind schedule and escort you directly back to Air Force One. The temperature during your speech will be 108 degrees with light winds." Miller looked at his watch. "We land in forty-five minutes. Any questions, Mr. President?"

———————◆———————

The congressman's aide was perched in the cockpit jump seat, trying to impress the two career pilots with his minimal flying experience. "I've logged almost twenty-five hours of flight time since I got my private pilot's license. I'd sure like to get my hands on a hot jet like this. Looks pretty easy to fly."

Mark didn't bother to look back at the novice pilot as he sniffed. "Yeah, thirty-five years at this job helps make it look that way."

Mark began his approach to the airport.

Andy keyed the mic switch on his control yoke and called the tower through his headset microphone.

"Downtown Tower, Gulfstream Three-Two-Two-Lima-Juliet ten miles to the east for a full-stop landing."

The controller replied in a hesitant, apologetic voice. "Gulfstream Three-Two-Two-Lima-Juliet, the field closes to all traffic at fifteen hundred hours local time for inbound VIP traffic. I calculate your arrival time to be fifteen zero one hours. Landing clearance denied. Divert to an alternate airport. Sorry about that."

"Seriously? One friggin' minute late." Mark shook his head and turned to the aide. "Thanks to your boss showing up late, the president's fat cat donors won't be going to the rally today."

The aide let out a sarcastic laugh. "You boys might know airplanes, but you don't know shit about politics. Hand me the microphone."

Mark and Andy looked at each other with confused expressions.

Mark shrugged. "Sure. Go right ahead."

Andy pulled the hand mic from its clip on the dashboard and handed it back to the aide, stretching the spiral cord attached to it to the limit.

The aide leaned back in the jump seat and pressed the transmit button on the side of the microphone. "Tower, this is Benjamin Cohen, senior aide to Congressman Wilber Clayton, Speaker of the House of Representatives. The Speaker is on board and would be extremely disappointed if he missed the rally for his close friend, President Kincaid. You tell that Secret Service agent in the tower standing next to you that unless he wants to be reassigned guarding sheep in North Dakota in the winter, he'd better recalculate our arrival time. Understood?"

The radio fell silent.

The brash aide was about to press the transmit button again when the radio came to life.

"Gulfstream Three-Two-Two-Lima-Juliet, you are cleared to land on runway one. Turn left off the runway and park on the west ramp."

"Roger, cleared to land runway one," Andy responded into his headset mic. He turned and nodded. "Impressive."

The aide handed the microphone back to Andy. "Yeah, thirty-five years working inside the Beltway can make it look that way." He left the cockpit with a smirk on his face.

Mark touched down on the short runway then applied maximum braking. The two Rolls Royce jet engines howled as the thrust from the engines was reversed and directed forward. He slowed the jet down to a safe taxi speed by the end of the runway and pulled off onto the west ramp. He rolled to a stop in front of a large hangar and shut down the engines. All other aircraft on the field had been tucked away inside hangars by order of the Secret Service.

Ramp workers rushed up to chock the landing gear. Nearby, an idling stretch limousine was parked on the tarmac.

Charlotte opened the door and extended the stairs down to the tarmac. Sweltering, damp air poured into the plane. "Sweet Jesus. It's hot enough out there to make the devil sweat," she groaned.

The wealthy passengers gulped down the last of their drinks and headed for the exit. Speaker Clayton wobbled as he attempted to stand. He clasped his hand over his mouth and ran for the bathroom. Once locked inside, the sound of repeated retching could be heard by everyone on board. His aide hovered outside the bathroom door, eager to render any needed assistance.

Noelle searched the galley for club soda to offer the hungover Speaker.

A short, rotund passenger pulled his cigar out of his mouth and barked, "Screw him. We're late as it is because of that buffoon. Leave him behind."

None of the passengers objected to abandoning their host. They descended the steps to the ramp and were taken away in the limo to the rally.

Mark walked up to a ramp worker and said, "We're leaving immediately after the rally. Top off the fuel tanks so we won't have to delay our departure."

The ramp worker shook his head. "No can do, Captain. Secret Service has the fuel truck locked down. No one gets gas until Air Force One has been refueled."

Mark went back into the Gulfstream, seeking refuge from the heat. "Crank up the APU," he instructed Andy. "We're hanging out on the plane until our passengers get back."

The copilot started the auxiliary power unit located in the tail of the aircraft and selected the lowest temperature setting possible on the overhead control panel. The small jet engine gulped fuel from the tanks as it struggled to operate the air conditioning system at its maximum capacity.

On the east side of the field, the last of the crowd made its way through the security checkpoint. A large tent had been set up containing walk-through metal detectors, explosives-sniffing dogs, and cameras. The single-file line served as the perfect hunting ground for the cameras connected to the NSA facial-recognition program. Luckily for the president, the program recognized one known terrorists in the crowd. He was discretely escorted out of line for additional screening. He did not return.

The large crowd was a mixture of true believers who supported anything President Kincaid did, curious locals, and parents who dragged their kids along for the rare opportunity to see a sitting president in person—albeit from a distance and from behind steel barriers. After waiting in the blazing sun for hours, the enthusiasm of the crowd had wilted away like the parched grass.

Rookie Secret Service agent Steve Zimmerman sat

slumped down in the passenger seat of the fuel truck with his dirty shoes plopped up on the dash. Sweat streamed down his face and drenched his standard-issue dark suit. New to the job, he hadn't yet learned that performing mundane, yet vital, tasks made up 99 percent of his chosen career.

"Doesn't this hunk of junk have air conditioning?" he grumbled.

"Yeah, it does, slick," the driver said, rolling his eyes. "I just enjoy roasting like a pig out here, so I don't turn it on."

Agent Zimmerman popped another stick of mint-flavored nicotine gum into his mouth. "I should be up front guarding the stage. I didn't join this dammed outfit to babysit some pump jockey all day."

The driver snapped his head around. "No offense taken, pal."

"This sucks." Zimmerman hopped out of the truck and stuck a Marlboro cigarette between his lips.

When the agent pulled out his lighter, the startled driver yelled, "Hey, Einstein, you're standing next to fifty thousand gallons of jet fuel. Ya mind?"

Zimmerman flipped off the driver then went behind the truck, out of sight. He flicked his Bic and took a big draw on his cigarette.

CHAPTER 48

A IR FORCE ONE WAS FIFTY miles from the field, in a descent for the arrival and landing. Off the right wing, a Lockheed Martin F-22 stealth fighter flew protective cover for the massive plane. At first glance, the fighter appeared to lack any weapons to fight back with if attacked. The awesome firepower that the F-22 was capable of unleashing was hidden inside the fuselage, rather than dangling from bulky exterior pylons. This was done to maintain its low, stealthy radar cross-section. An RCS reportedly the size of a marble.

The Raptor pilot keyed his mic, calling the pilots of the 747. "Ten minutes out, boys. If any planes approach showing hostile intent, don't wet yourselves. I'll save your asses."

Viewing themselves as God's gift to aviation, the inflated egos of most fighter pilots wouldn't let them pass up an opportunity to taunt pilots they judged to be inferior. Like those flying the lumbering Air Force One.

Before the aircraft commander could stop his copilot, the right-seater fired off a return barb over the radio. "Gee thanks, Voodoo Two-One. Too bad you're strapped into an ejection seat with an oxygen mask covering your ugly mug. I'd have the chef whip up an extra plate of linguine. Feel free to come by after we land and help yourself to any leftover scraps you find."

The fighter jock reached for the radio button on his control stick to tell the copilot where he could stick his linguine. He wisely thought better of it. Trading insults over the radio on a high-profile flight like this was a sure way to go viral on the internet because some aviation geek listening on a scanner recorded the transmissions. Careers had been ruined by just such a thing recently.

As Kansas City came into view, the president picked up the phone on his desk and called the cockpit. "Hey, Paul, do me a favor. Don't land right away. Fly low and slow one time around the city. I wouldn't want to deprive the good folks in town the chance to see their favorite son returning home now, would I?" As expected, Kincaid heard the answer he was looking for. "Great, thanks, Paul."

The first lady nodded in approval. "Excellent idea, Jack. Everyone with a phone will be posting videos on Facebook of Air Force One flying over their heads before we even touch down."

———◆———

The aircraft commander hung up the handset and looked at the copilot. "Wonderful. The boss wants to make it easier for the bad guys to take shots at us. Activate self-defense measures now."

The copilot reached up and flipped switches on the overhead panel. "Wide-spectrum radar jamming— activated. Infrared jammers—activated. Flares and chaff—armed."

The commander shook his head in disgust. "Let's put on a damned show."

CHAPTER 49

WITH THE RISKY FLYOVER OF the city safely completed, the 747 sailed over the dike separating the Missouri River from the airport and planted itself onto the short runway. The aircraft commander stomped on the brakes while commanding, "Maximum reverse thrust."

The copilot yanked all four throttles aft to the idle stop, lifted them, then pulled back. The General Electric CF6 engines howled as they redirected thrust forward to help decelerate the behemoth. With the plane rapidly approaching the end of the runway, the copilot joined his boss on the brake pedals.

With only fifty feet to spare, the plane taxied off the short runway. The colonel in the left seat exhaled a heavy sigh of relief, acutely aware that a runway overrun incident would have certainly derailed his plans to make one-star general next year.

Air Force One taxied slowly toward the southeast corner of the airport, aiming for the red carpet rolled out on the concrete. The F-22 fighter coasted by on the runway after landing, then parked on the north end, out of view of the crowd.

As soon as the jumbo jet came to a stop, carefully choreographed actions commenced. A ring of armed Secret Service agents surrounded the plane. Mobile stairs rolled up to the front door.

The built-in stairs from the secondary entrance behind

the left wing descended from the belly until coming to rest on the ramp. Agent Miller was the first person off the plane. He paused, scanning the ramp for threats. Satisfied it was safe, he moved quickly to supervise the preparations. Walking by the main landing gear, he noticed an acrid smell and smoke rising from the brakes. The heavy braking on landing had caused the brake pads to glow a deep orange color.

Ground crew from the Presidential Airlift Group had flown into the airport in advance of the President's arrival and were attending to the plane.

Miller waved over a sergeant from the group. "Get fans and position them at each landing gear to cool off the brakes." The crewman ran off in search of large portable fans.

As the fuel truck approached the aircraft, Miller waved it away from the landing gear and hot brakes. Once the truck was in position under the leading edge of the right wing, he went over to direct the refueling.

Agent Zimmerman approached Miller with a briefcase. "Sir, I'm assigned to guard the fuel truck. Here's the fuel testing kit." He opened the case for Miller to examine.

Miller grabbed a beaker and a ladle with a long handle from the case. He climbed up the stairs mounted on the rear of the fuel truck and walked across the catwalk to the round hatch in the center.

The jet fuel had spent the day heating up and expanding inside the stainless-steel tank. When the hatch was opened, the hissing sound of pressurized fuel vapor escaping could be heard and smelled.

Agent Zimmerman ordered the driver to begin preparations for refueling. "Move it, buddy. Get the grounding wire attached to the plane. I want the hose attached to the refueling panel and ready to deliver fuel as soon as the test is complete."

The fuel truck driver had refueled hundreds of planes

in his career and didn't need some snot-nosed rookie
telling him how it was done. Under his breath, he muttered, "Asshole."

Agent Miller returned with a beaker full of fuel. He
handed it to Zimmerman. "Run the tests."

The new agent dipped seven different test strips into
the fuel then waited for a color change indicating a specific chemical reaction. He held up each strip next to a
laminated chart to compare its color to the options on
the chart. Each strip matched its corresponding test sample on the chart exactly. "The fuel hasn't been tampered
with," he declared proudly. No longer needed, Zimmerman resumed his place in the right seat of the truck cab
and unwrapped another stick of gum.

Minutes later, Air Force One had been refueled, its
wings now sagging down under the weight of forty
thousand gallons. Miller ordered the driver to go directly
to the F-22 and refuel it first before any other aircraft.
He raised his left wrist up to his mouth and announced,
"Boy Scout is cleared to exit the aircraft." He hurried
over to the bottom of the mobile stairs.

The president and first lady descended the stairs to the
sound of "Hail to the Chief" played by the Center High
School marching band. The perspiring band members,
outfitted in their traditional heavy wool band uniforms,
did their best to stay in formation and on tempo.

Miller escorted President Kincaid the fifty yards across
the tarmac and up to the side of the stage. The president's armored limousine sat idling nearby, unnecessary
for such a short jaunt.

Politicians had lined the roped-off pathway to the stage.
They reached out in hopes of being the person identified
glad-handing the president in pictures on the front pages
the next day.

An army major trailed closely behind the commander
in chief. He had a metal Zero Halliburton briefcase,

nicknamed "The Football," handcuffed to his left wrist.

Sarah Whitcomb-Kincaid hooked her arm around her husband's and joined him as he strutted up the stage stairs. They took seats next to the podium. His megadonors had places of honor, seated in chairs along the back of the stage.

Secret Service agents were spaced six feet apart in front of the stage. They scanned the crowd with the chilling eyes of a predator, ready to pounce. Their dark sunglasses not only prevented tipping off potential suspects they were looking their way; they also offered protection from any caustic liquids or projectiles thrown at the agents. Undercover law enforcement personnel circulated among the restless crowd.

Once the obligatory introductions were completed by the mayor and governor, Kincaid strode confidently up to the bulletproof podium to give his speech. Gripping the raised sides of the podium, he smiled the movie star smile that had helped get him elected. "It feels wonderful to be back home in Kansas City. But next time I'm in town, I promise to order cooler weather from the National Weather Service for my loyal supporters."

The crowd cheered wildly at the president for showing such concern for their well-being.

Hoping to give the appearance that the wealthy politician was one of them, Kincaid removed his suit jacket and tossed it onto his chair. He rolled up his sleeves and continued speaking.

Agent Miller's earpiece crackled to life. Fellow agents frantically transmitted their concerns about the president removing his jacket.

The nano tracking device embedded inside the American flag pin on the lapel of Kincaid's jacket, used to track the president in case he was separated from his security detail, was now useless. So was the bullet-resistant fabric the president's wardrobe was made of.

Miller started up the stairs. He had to find a discrete way to get the leader of the free world to put his jacket back on while giving a speech on a scorching summer afternoon. One look at the adoring crowd cheering on their favorite son told Miller that wasn't going to happen.

Suddenly, a deep noise like a clap of thunder came from the north end of the field. Black, oily smoke boiled up into the sky from the direction of the F-22 fighter.

Agent Miller snatched his left wrist up to his mouth. "Agent Zimmerman, report. What the hell happened over there?" He waited a few seconds before screaming again into his wrist mic. "Zimmerman, report in immediately!"

Panicked by the blast, law enforcement officers at the airport drew their weapons on the helpless crowd.

In the blink of an eye, Secret Service agents in front of the stage pulled out FN 90 compact submachine guns from under their jackets. The odd-looking weapons looked like they had been designed by a sci-fi comic book artist.

Miller drew his Glock 19 pistol and sprinted toward the president.

A blinding flash, followed a millisecond later by an earth-shaking BOOM, came from fifty yards behind the stage.

Air Force One had just exploded.

CHAPTER 50

BOILING BLACK SMOKE AND A raging inferno of
fire mushroomed into the sky. A river of flaming jet
fuel rushed across the tarmac toward the stage. The president's limo, nicknamed The Beast, was overturned and
engulfed in flames.

A level of pandemonium broke out among the panicked crowd that no amount of preplanning could have
ever anticipated.

Months of careful preparation for every possible con-
tingency now became worthless. The frightened mob
scattered in every direction. Steel barricades were flat-
tened by the rush of bodies. The weak and young became
steppingstones, heartlessly trampled in the melee.

Mothers screamed their children's names while frantically searching for them. The searing heat from the
conflagration on the ramp blistered the skin of people
who didn't shield their faces.

Policeman were knocked to the ground. Unsure how
to react, panicked law enforcement officers raised their
weapons and began firing into the air, thinking this
would help control the crowd. That only terrified the
spectators even more. Radios in the command center
conference room blared out transmissions from cops
screaming, "Shots fired! Shots fired!"

The entrance to the tarmac, which had been carefully
designed to funnel the crowd through security screening,
now became a narrow chokepoint useless for exit.

The nightmare scenario had happened.

The president of the United States was in unimaginable danger, and the Secret Service was powerless to stop it.

CHAPTER 51

THE CONCUSSION FROM THE BLAST caused the portable stage to pancake down onto the ground. Dignitaries and donors were knocked off their feet when it collapsed, suffering serious injuries.

Agent Miller slowly regained his footing. He opened his mouth wide and shook his head, trying to restore some hearing. Miller searched for the president through the thick oily smoke blanketing the stage. Spotting him sprawled out on the stage, he rushed over and threw himself on top of Kincaid.

Some of the panicked crowd had jumped on the stage, looking for a pathway for escape. A large man wearing a faded windbreaker ran across the stage, directly toward the president. Agent Miller raised his Glock, fired off two rounds into the air, and screamed, "Stop, or I'll shoot!"

Too panicked to grasp the seriousness of the warning, the man continued toward Kincaid. Miller lowered his gun and dropped the advancing man with one shot to the heart.

He rolled off the president and asked, "Sir, are you injured?"

Kincaid had gone into shock. He mumbled incoherently about the heat and his hometown. Miller rolled his protectee onto his back and patted Kincaid's body, doing a quick search for any wounds. Finding none, Miller hauled the president to his feet. The agent screamed commands into the mic attached to his left wrist. The airways were so congested with radio traffic that none of his transmissions reached his team. He ripped the earpiece out of his left ear and threw it down in frustration.

The river of flaming jet fuel had advanced across the tarmac and was within feet of the back of the stage. The intense heat warped the metal stage backdrop into a twisted heap.

Miller wrapped the president's arm across his shoulder and helped him stagger across the stage and down the side stairs. He spotted an ambulance parked nearby. A medical team was mandatory at every presidential appearance.

Miller hustled Kincaid over to the ambulance. He flung open the passenger door and screamed, "Everyone out! Secret Service! Everyone out! Now!"

The frightened EMTs jumped out of their commandeered vehicle. Miller stuffed Kincaid in, then ran around to the driver's seat.

President Kincaid grabbed Miller's arm as he started the engine. "Where's Sarah? I'm not leaving without Sarah."

"Mr. President, we're leaving, now!"

"Not without my wife, we're not." He turned and searched the stage. Kincaid spotted Sarah lying on her side, grasping her right ankle. Flames had engulfed the rear of the stage and were advancing toward her. He pointed. "There! She's on the stage."

Miller jumped out and sprinted over to the stage. He lifted the left side of his suit jacket up to protect his face from the scorching heat as he rushed to retrieve the first lady. Miller sat her up and yelled, "Come with me!"

"I can't walk," she answered in a panic. "I think my ankle is broken."

With his muscular arms, Miller hoisted Sarah Whitcomb-Kincaid up off the stage and flung her over his shoulder in a fireman's carry. He dashed across the burning stage and over to the ambulance. In one motion, he opened the back door and deposited the frightened woman onto the floor. After slamming the door shut, Miller jumped into the driver's seat. He searched frantically for an escape route.

Everywhere around the ambulance, chaos reigned. Exits from the field had been purposely locked down before the rally began. Across the runway, Miller spied Mark's Gulfstream sitting alone on the ramp. Without giving any thought to the severely injured bystanders left behind, he slammed the ambulance into gear and sped across the airport toward the jet.

CHAPTER 52

SPEAKER CLAYTON HAD COME OUT of the bathroom and was napping comfortably in a seat in the cool cabin. Everyone else on board had their noses pressed up against the windows, watching in horror at the firestorm across the field.

Agent Miller screeched to a stop at the base of the aircraft stairs. He jumped out with his gun drawn, slowly spinning around in circles searching for any threats. Seeing none, he opened the passenger door and pointed at the aircraft stairs. "Go! Go!"

Kincaid raced up the stairs and into the jet. Miller helped the first lady out of the ambulance and supported her as she limped up the stairs.

Once inside, Miller waved his gun around and yelled, "Secret Service! If you're not a crew member, get off the plane!"

Clayton and his aide jumped to their feet and rushed up the aisle.

Once the two men were on the ramp, Miller ordered Noelle to close the door.

She pressed the switch on the bulkhead inside the entrance. The stairs tucked back into a stowed position, and the door locked closed.

Noelle and Charlotte hustled their ultra-important passengers to seats in the cabin and helped them strap in.

"Get us airborne, now!" Miller shouted at Mark.

He and Andy jumped into their seats in the cockpit

and buckled in. Dispensing with the checklist, they fired up the engines, released the brakes, and taxied toward the runway.

Mark reached out to key the mic switch on his control yoke to request takeoff clearance. Agent Miller stopped him. "No radio transmissions. Until I figure out what the hell is going on, no one can know that the president is on board."

"Understood," Mark responded. He pulled the jet onto the runway.

The controller in the tower saw what was happening and screamed into his microphone. "Gulfstream Three-Two-Two-Lima-Juliet, get off the runway. You do not have clearance to take off. There are people on the runway."

Mark leaned forward and squinted, peering through the black haze caused by the fire. People from the rally had scattered in every direction. Some were burned. Some were injured after being trampled by the mob. Stunned and dazed, a few had wandered onto the runway.

Mark knew he had to escape the catastrophe while he still could. He turned on the landing lights and pushed the throttles up to maximum power while standing on the brakes. He prayed the roar of the engines would scare people off the concrete pathway to safety.

Luckily, they heard the sound of the engines and scattered onto the grass alongside the runway.

Mark released the brakes. The jet leaped forward and rocketed into the sky. After the flaps and landing gear were retracted, Mark switched on the autopilot.

"Take us to Offutt Air Force Base in Omaha," Agent Miller ordered.

The storied base in Nebraska, made famous by numerous movies, was the home of the 55th Wing of the Air Combat Command and what is now called the US Strategic Command.

Mark programmed the flight-management computer for a direct flight to the base. A red warning message flashed on the screen—Insufficient Fuel. Without refueling before taking off, Offutt AFB was out of reach.

"We can't make it to Offutt," Mark informed Miller. "We need to land somewhere else."

"No civilian airports. What is the nearest Air Force base?"

Drawing from his decades of flying experience, Mark had an immediate answer. "Whiteman Air Force Base. But we can't land there."

The bustling base, located near tiny Knob Noster, Missouri, was a short flight from Kansas City. It hosted the 509th Bomb Wing, part of Air Force Global Strike Command. Stationed at the field was a fleet of the most expensive aircraft ever built, a jaw-dropping one and a half billion dollars apiece. Because of their critical mission, the bizarre looking, bat-shaped flying wing airplanes were guarded by the deadliest rapid-response force in the Air Force. Whiteman Air Force Base was the home of the nuclear weapon delivery platform called the B-2 Spirit.

———◆———

Vice President Rodriguez paced nervously in the living room of the Queen Anne-style mansion located on the grounds of the Naval Observatory. He checked his wristwatch for the third time.

Rodriguez walked over to a window and pulled back the lace curtain. He looked out over the manicured grounds of the official residence of the vice president. Despite being the second most powerful person on the planet, the VP felt impotent.

An unmarked black van raced up the circular drive and screeched to a stop at the front steps. The back door flung open. Heavily armed men poured out. Dressed in all black and lugging heavy duffel bags, they fanned out across the grounds.

Rodriguez raced to the front door and stepped out onto the porch. A hulking man in full combat gear and a black ski mask wrapped the vice president in a bear hug, lifted him off his feet. He carried the VP back into the house and slammed the door.

"What the hell is going on!" Rodriguez screamed, still suspended in the man's grasp.

"I'm with the Secret Service Counter Assault Team, sir. I need you to stay inside the house and away from the windows." He put Rodriguez back down on his feet and pushed him toward the middle of the house.

The VP swatted his hands away and yelled, "Agent, I demand to know what is going on!"

The Secret Service agent pulled off his ski mask. "Sir, there has been an assassination attempt on President Kincaid. He is missing and presumed dead. As of right now, you are the president of the United States."

CHAPTER 53

MAJOR ALFRED NEUMEIER CLIMBED OUT of the motor pool vehicle. Four separate radio antennas sprouted up from the roof of the dark blue Air Force sedan. The thin, pasty-looking officer was often asked if he was a relative of the late actor Don Knotts. The comparison wasn't meant to be a compliment.

Neumeier unclipped his Whiteman AFB ID badge from his shirt and tucked into his pocket. He approached the guard at the base of the control tower and gave a friendly wave.

"Happy Fourth of July, Airman. Looks like you drew the short straw, pulling guard duty on a holiday."

The enlisted man saluted. "Yes, sir, Major Neumeier. Looks like you did, as well."

"Rank has its privileges," he scoffed. "The damned general and colonels are all out partying at the Lake of the Ozarks. I'm stuck babysitting their base. I'm going up in the tower to see how things are going. Let me by." He reached for the door.

The airman moved over to block his hand. "Um... sir...I need to see your ID before I can let you pass."

Neumeier's pasty face went red. "Dammit, Airman, I'm in no mood for games. You know who I am. Get out of my way."

The quivering teenager reached for his holstered pistol. "I'm sorry, sir. Protocol requires that everyone entering a secure facility on this base present a valid ID."

"This is your last warning, Airman. If you don't move aside right now, I'll have you shipped off to Thule Air Base in Greenland for the rest of your tour. Do I make myself clear?"

The guard's hand tremored as he gripped his pistol. His voice cracked. "Major Neumeier, I can't let you pass without seeing your ID. That's the rule."

A huge grin formed on Neumeier's face. He slapped the trembling airman on the back. "Well done, Sonny. You passed."

The guard shook his head in disbelief. "What?"

"We have the most powerful weapons ever built on my base, ready to be used at a moment's notice. Following security regulations to the letter every single time is our most important job. As the temporary acting commander, it's my solemn duty to keep those weapons safe. Congratulations, you did your job and passed my test." He reached out for the door again.

The guard cleared his throat. "ID, sir."

"Damn. I can't get anything past you, Son. Well done." Neumeier fished his ID badge out of his pocket and presented it for inspection. After the guard examined it, the major was allowed entry to the control tower.

After the door closed, the guard grumbled under his breath, "Prick."

———◆———

"This isn't a debate!" agent Miller barked. "Take the plane to Whiteman!" He unholstered his Glock pistol for extra emphasis. "And no radio transmissions."

"Agent…?" Mark looked back over his shoulder.

"Miller," he responded. "Agent Dirk Miller. I am the personal bodyguard of the president of the United States, and you are going to follow my orders, or so help me God you are not going to survive the day." His hand shook as he tightly gripped the Glock 19.

After the horrific incident at the rally, the last thing Mark wanted to do was challenge the agitated and armed Secret Service agent. In a calm voice, he said, "Andy, program the autopilot to fly to Whiteman Air Force Base."

Andy tapped the keyboard on the FMS. The plane began a turn to the east.

Mark pointed at the gun. "Would you mind putting that thing away? We're on the same team, Agent Miller. I don't want an accidental discharge."

Miller took a deep breath, attempting to slow down his racing heartbeat. He holstered his gun.

Drawing from his experience ambushing the enemy during his tour with Delta Force, Miller formulated plans to avoid detection as they approached the base. "Descend to treetop level to avoid radar detection. Maintain radio silence." He pointed at the center console. "Which switch controls the transponder?"

Andy pointed at the switch.

Miller turned off the piece of equipment that broadcast the plane's position to air traffic control. Just like the terrorists had done on the airliners they commandeered on 9/11.

——◆——

Vice President Sergio Rodriguez wasted no time. He had the chief justice of the Supreme Court on the phone within minutes. "Justice Holbrook, it is with a heavy heart that I am calling you. The president is missing and presumed dead. Reluctantly, I am hereby invoking Section Three of the Twenty-Fifth Amendment to the Constitution and assuming the Office of the President. A car is on the way to pick you up and drive you to my residence. After arriving, you will administer the oath of office." He listened for a moment, then said, "Thank you, sir, and may God bless America."

CHAPTER 54

IN THE TOWER AT WHITEMAN, the direct line from the Kansas City Air Traffic Control Center rang. One of the controllers on duty picked up the handset. His eyes opened wide as he listened.

Slamming the phone down, he shouted, "Major Neumeier, center is tracking an unidentified aircraft flying directly toward the base at high speed. The controller hasn't been able to raise the plane on the radio, and it just disappeared from his radar. He estimates the plane will arrive at Whiteman in nine minutes if it doesn't change course. What are your orders, sir?"

Major Neumeier's throat seized up. His mind went into a fog.

"I need your orders, sir!"

Neumeier muttered, "The base...we're under attack. Terrorists are...I think terrorist are attacking the base."

"Sir?"

"Battle stations!" He rushed over to the console and slammed his fist down on a large red button. Speakers around the base came to life. A shrill tone pierced the air. The few airmen remaining on base for the holiday looked at each other in disbelief.

"Launch the alert bird!" Neumeier screamed.

———◆———

The klaxon inside the alert shack at the north end of

the field went off. The two pilots on duty jumped up from their game of cards, grabbed their flight bags, and sprinted out to the car waiting outside. Tires squealed as the car sped off for the B-2 bomber waiting on the alert pad. It skidded to a stop under the right wingtip. The pilots climbed the stairs dangling down under the belly of the plane, immediately retracting them once inside. Twenty-three seconds later, the engines came to life.

Two minutes and nineteen seconds after the klaxon sounded, the most lethal bomber ever built lifted off the runway and flew west. Inside its bomb bay were sixteen B83 nuclear bombs, each with a yield of 1.2 megatons.

The aircraft commander and copilot each entered their unique combination codes into the two separate padlocks attached to a red box. The combinations were correct, and the box was opened. The commander pulled out a plastic holder and cracked it open. Inside were the coordinates of their top-secret target. He programmed their destination into the flight computer.

The plane turned slightly and headed directly for Beijing, China.

CHAPTER 55

SEEING THE B-2 STREAK AWAY, the airmen on the base sprang into action. Each person sprinted to the duty positions assigned to them in case of an attack on the base.

Fire trucks and snowplows sped out to the runway and parked at preplanned intervals, blocking it for landing by an aircraft.

Security police fanned out across the base, their semiautomatic M4 carbines at the ready. Up-armored Humvees with M2 heavy machine guns mounted in turrets on their roofs blocked the entrance to the base as well as critical intersections.

Controllers in the tower scanned the horizon with large binoculars for any sign of the approaching plane.

A glint of sunlight reflected off the windshield of the approaching Gulfstream, giving away its location.

One of the controllers grabbed the hand microphone. "Aircraft approaching Whiteman Air Force Base from the west, identify yourself. You are about to enter restricted airspace. Turn away immediately or you will be reported to the FAA."

After all that had happened back in Kansas City, Mark had to chuckle at the prospect of getting a harshly worded letter from the FAA when the president, and commander in chief, was his passenger.

Mark lined up with runway one nine. As he configured the jet for landing the trucks blocking the runway came into sight. With no other viable option, Mark veered to the right and headed for the massive apron next to the runway. He touched down and came to a stop with plenty of concrete remaining. Andy started the APU then shut down the engines.

Security police swarmed out onto the apron and surrounded the plane. Armed Humvees backed up the men. Major Neumeier drove up to the ring of security forces in his car and skidded to a stop.

He jumped out of the car and grabbed a bullhorn from the officer in charge. Facing the cockpit, Neumeier yelled, "This is the commander of Whiteman Air Force Base! I order everyone on the plane to come out with your hands up!"

Agent Miller was in the cockpit and heard the command. He rushed back to the cabin. "Everyone stay on the plane and away from the door. It's too dangerous for you to show your face yet, Mr. President. I'm going to go out and defuse the situation. Once I get things under control, I'll return and get you. If I don't say your code name, Boy Scout, when I return, *do not* get off the plane. Understood?"

President Kincaid had recovered his senses from the assassination attempt at the rally. He gladly let his bodyguard take control until the chaotic and dangerous situation on the ramp was brought down a few million notches.

"Understood," he replied, nodding his head.

Miller pushed the switch to open the door. The stairs unfurled until coming to rest on the ramp.

Major Neumeier repeated his warning over the bullhorn.

Miller stood to the side of the open door, out of the direct line of fire. He shouted, "Secret Service! The president of the United States is on board! I order you to stand down! Lower your weapons! Now!"

Laughter could be heard coming from the ranks of heavily armed airmen.

Miller stepped out into the doorway, raising his arms. He repeated his statement announcing who he was and walked slowly down the stairs.

Agent Miller reached inside his suit jacket.

An eighteen-year-old security policeman, with adrenaline coursing through his veins, yelled "Gun!" Before his sergeant could stop him, the frightened kid raised up his M4 carbine and fired a three-round burst into Agent Miller's skull.

Lead agent for the President's Protective Detail, Dirk Miller, tumbled down the stairs. He landed face down on the concrete, dead.

Inside his jacket, his hand gripped the leather wallet containing his Secret Service shield. Inscribed on the cover of the wallet, in bold letters, were the words: Duty and Honor. Three inches away, his Glock 19 handgun remained safely tucked away in its holster.

CHAPTER 56

NOELLE DARTED FOR A WINDOW in the cabin. She shrieked in horror at the gruesome sight of Agent Miller lying in a pool of blood with the back of his skull blown off.

President Kincaid was enraged. He bolted out of his seat and sprinted up the aisle.

The first lady reached out to stop him. "Jack, no. Don't go out there."

He slapped away her hand. Before Mark could get out of his seat in the cockpit and block him, Kincaid had started down the stairs.

He looked disheveled, with a large rip in the left knee of his pants and his shirt drenched in sweat after his narrow escape from the tragedy in Kansas City. The Commander in Chief looked wildly around the ramp. "Who's in charge here? I demand to speak to the officer in charge!"

The security forces kept their guns trained on the man and didn't respond.

Kincaid screamed hysterically at the armed men surrounding him. "Don't you know who I am? I'm the president of the United States!"

Not surprisingly, his peculiar appearance and histrionics did little to convince the airmen to lower their weapons and provide the man claiming to be their commander in chief a hearty Whiteman welcome.

Three men rushed the president and tackled him to the

ground, breaking his nose in the process. To add insult to injury, Major Neumeier knelt over the president and planted his knee in the small of Kincaid's back, pinning him to the ground until he was handcuffed.

Spittle flew from the president's mouth as he cursed at the men who lifted him up off the concrete. "I'll have every last one of you court-martialed!"

Neumeier got right in Kincaid's face. "You and your filthy band of terrorists are going away for a long time for attacking my base, pal."

Blood gushed from Kincaid's broken and swollen nose, making recognition even more difficult. "You are relieved of command immediately, Major!" Kincaid bellowed.

Neumeier laughed in his face. "Relieved of command? I just prevented a terrorist attack on my base. The B-2 sitting on alert launched successfully and is on its way to its target. Hell, I'll probably get promoted to colonel for this."

Kincaid's face went pale. "Oh God, no. You have to contact the plane. Tell it to turn around."

"You tell it to turn around," Neumeier said mockingly. "You're the president, aren't you? Prove it. Have your military aide carrying the football send out the top-secret abort code."

In the pandemonium escaping the dangerous situation at the airport, no one had thought to bring along the army major carrying the nuclear codes. He'd been crushed by the stampede of panicked spectators after Air Force One exploded. The metal case lay next to his dead body, still firmly handcuffed to his left wrist.

Kincaid's head sank. "I can't. He's not on my plane."

"Toss this lunatic into the back seat of my car," Neumeier ordered.

They dragged him off to the car.

Sarah rushed up to the cockpit and looked out the left-side window. "Agent Miller! Jack! Oh my God, someone do something." She slapped Mark across the side of his head. "I order you to get out there and stop this."

Noelle had followed the first lady into the cockpit. She grabbed the woman's wrists and yanked them back, twisting both her arms behind her back.

Earlier, when she had warned the obnoxious passenger back at Teterboro that she knew close-quarters self-defense tactics, Noelle wasn't bluffing.

"Stop resisting, or I'll break your arms," Noelle ordered the agitated woman.

As payback for slapping her ex-husband, Noelle applied extra pressure upward on Sarah's arms until she cried out in pain. She backed the first lady out of the cockpit and pushed her down into a passenger seat. "Don't you dare get out of this seat again!" Noelle yelled.

The ring of security police closed in on the jet.

Charlotte looked out at the advancing forces. "The hell with this."

She pressed the door switch.

The stairs retracted, and the door locked shut.

Everyone on the ramp looked at each other, unsure what their next move should be now that the entrance to the plane was closed tight.

Mark grabbed his hand mic. He dialed frequency 121.5 into the VHF radio. Pushing the transmit button, he said, "MAYDAY, MAYDAY, this is Captain Mark Smith. I just evacuated the president of the United States from Kansas City after an assassination attempt, and I'm now on the ground at Whiteman Air Force Base. The president has mistakenly been arrested by the commander of the base. I need any aircraft hearing this distress call to contact the Pentagon and get them to stop what is happening before it's too late."

Every aircraft within one hundred miles of the base heard the panicked call.

A Delta captain flying a B-777 overhead jumped on

the radio. "Get off this frequency, you idiot. It's for use in case of real emergencies, not practical jokes. If you continue making crank radio calls on the universal distress frequency, I will report you to the authorities."

Other pilots nearby echoed the sentiments of the Delta pilot and warned Mark to knock off the crank radio calls.

Major Neumeier picked up the bullhorn and announced, "Everyone on board come out with your hands up, or you will be fired upon. Open the door and exit the plane now!"

The gunners manning the roof mounted .50-caliber M2 machine guns racked and released the charging handles on their weapons. They rotated their turrets, aiming their guns directly at the cockpit windows.

Frantic, Noelle yelled up to the cockpit. "Try calling for help on the radio again!"

Mark threw his hands up. "I'll try. But don't hold your breath. No one will believe me."

Noelle raced up to the cockpit. "Tell the planes out there to relay your message to the Pentagon."

"I already did that."

"This time, tell them to relay the president's code name. Boy Scout."

CHAPTER 57

B Y SUNRISE ON SUNDAY MORNING, west central Missouri had become the center of the universe. The FBI and ATF had descended on the Kansas City airport. The entire field was roped off with yellow crime-scene tape.

ATF agents went to work examining the fuel truck that had exploded near the F-22 and the charred mound of smoking metal that had once been Air Force One.

Thirteen spectators and two local cops had been trampled to death during the melee. The FBI took control of that part of the investigation.

The backup Air Force One was sent to Whiteman and had whisked the president and first lady back to the safety of the White House.

Vice President Rodriguez canceled the press conference he'd called to notify the country that he was now in charge. He was persona non grata in the Kincaid administration from that day forward.

The secretary of defense, all members of the Joint Chiefs of Staff, and the secretary of the Air Force were on the base, demanding answers about the debacle.

The B-2 bomber had been successfully stopped from launching World War III.

Every single service member present on the tarmac during the standoff was locked behind bars in the brig.

The director of the Secret Service and his top deputies were at the base directing the collection of evidence.

Mark, Noelle, Charlotte, and Andy had spent the night being interrogated in separate rooms by agents.

Anthony Lombardo, the number-two agent in the PPD, conducted Mark's interrogation. Lombardo was short with an olive complexion and was built like a tank. He'd gone over every minute of Mark's day and every line from the cockpit voice recorder transcript trying to understand what had happened.

Lombardo closed the folder laying on the metal table. "Mark, you've been more than cooperative. I appreciate you helping me get a clear picture of what happened. Hang tight for a few more minutes. I'll be right back." He got up and took the folder with him as he left the room.

Lombardo entered the small dark room on the opposite side of the one-way mirrored window that looked into the interrogation room.

The Director of the Secret Service, Miles Sanders, was waiting. "Well, what's your assessment?"

"I was able to gain his trust early on during the interrogation. Turns out Smith and my old man were in the same squadron in the Air Force. I used that common bond to my advantage, asking every question I could think of. I didn't get a single suspicious answer from Smith. He's telling the truth, sir. He and his crew had nothing to do with this. Hell, he's a hero in my book. Smith deserves a medal for saving the president if you ask me."

"A medal?" Director Sanders angrily snapped his fingers at the technician seated at the control panel and gave him the cut sign by waving his hand in front of his throat.

The technician understood and paused the recording.

Sanders glared at Lombardo. "Saving the president's ass was our job, not his. After Congress gets done ripping me a new one and slashing the Secret Service budget because of this fiasco, I'll be lucky if I could afford to give him an agency pen for his help. Set up wiretaps on all their phones by the end of business today. I don't care what it takes, but I want the last six months of phone records, text messages, and emails for every crewmember. That's an order. Do I make myself clear, Agent?"

"I don't imagine you're planning on putting your order in writing or getting signoff from a judge first, are you, sir?"

The searing look from his boss could have drilled through granite.

Lombardo clenched his jaw. "I didn't think so."

Director Sanders held his withering glare for a few more seconds then turned and nodded at the technician.

The technician turned the camera back on.

In a clear loud voice, the director said, "Unfortunately, their plane needs to stay here until the forensics team is finished tearing it apart. The crew has been very cooperative. I want to get them back to their families as soon as possible. Requisition a plane from the 89th to take them back to New York City."

Lombardo left in a huff and reentered the interrogation room. He pulled out his business card. "If you think of anything else, anything at all, this is my cell phone number. Call me day or night. You and your crew are free to go."

Mark looked over at the one-way mirror then back at Lombardo. "That's it? I'm free to go?"

Agent Lombardo walked over to Mark's side of the table. "The Secret Service is in debt to you for saving the president, Captain Smith. Of course, you are to speak to no one about what happened. Understood?"

"Sure. No problem," Mark responded.

"Your plane needs to stay here until forensics is done with it. A government plane will take you and your crew back home." Lombardo positioned himself between the camera behind the glass and Mark. He shook Mark's hand, gave him his business card, and silently mouthed, "Thank you."

CHAPTER 58

EXHAUSTED, MARK AND NOELLE TRUDGED into their apartment late Sunday night and plopped their bags down on the floor. Mary came flying out of her bedroom and hugged them both. Tears streamed down her face.

"Thank goodness your alive," she cried. "What a horrible thing to have to see, an assassination attempt on the president. My phone has been going crazy. The media has been calling nonstop for details on what happened." She pulled back to look over her parents. "Are you guys okay?"

"Been better," Mark deadpanned.

"We're fine, sweetie. Just a little shaken up," Noelle said. "I hope your Fourth of July went better than ours."

She wiped her eyes and sighed. "It was a total bust. All the guys wanted to talk about was April's money. Then the jerks took her Maserati out for a joyride and wrecked it. They wouldn't even pay for an Uber so we could get back home." Mary rolled her eyes. "Losers."

Mary's phone rang for the hundredth time. She answered, listened for a few seconds, then shouted, "I don't know anything! Stop calling me!"

She was about to hang up when she asked, "Who?" Mary pressed her fist against her mouth to force back a laugh. She held out the phone in the direction of her father. "It's ABC News. They want to speak to Captain Courageous."

Mark's radio call on the universal emergency frequency had been recorded and posted to every social media site on the internet. He was being hailed as a hero for saving the president, where the Secret Service had failed. His new made-for-the-headlines nickname had gone viral.

———◆———

The situation in Washington, DC, was decidedly less amusing. Not since 9/11 had the government been thrown into such chaos. Despite billions of dollars wasted, and years spent mapping out how to deal with another traumatic national event, the overly bureaucratic plan failed miserably during the time President Kincaid was missing.

The Federal Reserve froze the banking system for six hours, paralyzing financial systems around the entire world. The military grossly overreacted and had gone to DEFCON 1, the highest state of alert. The State Department diplomatic corps directed wild, groundless accusations of blame at allies and enemies alike. Oil-rich countries temporarily stopped all exports to the US in retaliation, sending the price into the stratosphere.

One by one, as stock markets around the world opened for business Monday morning, they immediately crashed. Circuit breakers, put in place after previous meltdowns of the New York Stock Exchange and the NASDAQ, tripped within five seconds of the opening bell, halting trading.

Inexplicably, panicked citizens raided grocery stores, snapping up months' worth of toilet paper, peanut butter, and bottled water.

President Kincaid decided an address from the Oval Office that evening was needed to calm a jittery nation. Sitting behind the famed Resolute Desk with his hands calmly folded in front of him, Kincaid waited for the signal from the cameraman. He reached up and gingerly touched his broken nose, hoping the makeup had done its job camouflaging the bruising.

When the red light came on, the cameraman pointed at Jack.

"My fellow Americans, the last thirty-six hours have been a scary and uncertain time for all of us. Regardless of your party, none of those political labels matter today. Today we are all Americans. Know that the full resources and might of the United States will be brought to bear in finding and holding accountable those responsible for this heinous act. The first lady and I are safely back in the White House and ask that everyone stay calm as we go about returning your government to business as usual. I ask that you join me in praying for the families of the victims of this senseless tragedy. Good evening and may God bless America."

The red light on the camera went out. The crew disassembled the video equipment and packed it away.

Sarah Kincaid hobbled over on her crutches to the side of the desk. Addressing the crowded room, she said, "The president has a monumental task in front of him, and he appreciates everyone's support as his administration begins the investigation into this evil act. I'm sure you won't mind if I spend a few minutes alone with my husband before he devotes his full attention to catching the perpetrators and bringing them to justice."

Aides in the room quickly herded everyone out of the Oval Office, leaving Sarah and Jack the rare opportunity to be alone.

Husband and wife sat on opposite couches in the middle of the room, separated by an antique oval coffee table. The furniture in the historic room had a heavy, sturdy character from a bygone era.

Sarah laid her crutches on the floor and leaned forward. "I've got good news and bad news."

"More bad news?"

"Campaign funds are getting disturbingly low. And now the spigot has completely dried up from your biggest donors. The cowards are claiming that having their name associated with the assassination attempt in any way would be bad for business. Their PR agencies are telling them to lie low until the election is over."

Rage flashed in Jack's eyes. "You tell those weaklings they can kiss any chance of an ambassadorship goodbye if they abandon me."

"It won't help. Most of them said they already own the politicians in the countries that their plants are in anyway, so why take the risk."

He let out a frustrated sigh. "So much for loyalty. What's the good news?"

"The latest poll numbers came in this morning. You are in a statistical tie with your opponent after what happened. RPs across the country are mad as hell that someone would try to assassinate their president and have rallied around you in a big way. The good news is those *real people* will hopefully get off their fat asses and vote in November." She leaned forward and lowered her voice. "If you can stretch out this investigation for three months, you could announce the names of the criminals that did this just before Election Day. You'd win in a landslide."

Jack got up and went to her side. He clasped her hands. "You've always been my number one supporter. Without you, I wouldn't be sitting here. I trust your advice completely. But it can't look to the public like I'm concerned with getting reelected right now. It's bad optics. Finding out who did this has to take precedence."

She patted his hand. "You're right. I was just looking out for your future, as always. The investigation must come first. You need to show the voters you have the balls to clean house if that's what it takes to restore confidence in your leadership."

"I knew you'd understand." He looked down at her leg. "How's the ankle?"

She tapped the plaster cast encasing her right ankle. "It hurts like hell. That quack of a doctor prescribed fentanyl pills to help take the edge off, but they're barely working. I wouldn't mind a stiff drink right about now." Sarah reached for a crystal decanter on the table.

Jack quickly pushed it away. "Absolutely no alcohol until you are off those opioids. Doctor's orders."

Sarah crossed her arms and plopped back against the couch. "I feel so useless."

The President stood and paced the floor. "The investigation needs to begin right away. I need someone I can trust to lead it. Someone who had nothing to gain from me being killed." He turned excitedly to his wife. "I want you to do it."

She recoiled back. "Why me?"

"You know the behind-the-scenes maneuvering that goes on in this town better than anyone. Every day, I deal with members of the other party who'd make Brutus and his pals in the Roman Senate look trustworthy. I'm constantly getting self-serving advice from prostitutes masquerading as politicians and their pimps masquerading as lobbyists. Even my own staff isn't above suspicion."

"Are you worried someone in the administration was behind this?"

"That's exactly what I'm worried about. That's why it makes perfect sense for you to run the investigation."

The first lady's eyes narrowed. In her mind she calculated the potential advantages running the investigation would give her when making the move to realize her own political ambitions. Although certain she was entitled to carry on the family dynasty, a little insurance never hurt.

With the backing of the president, she could weaponize the formidable resources of the federal government and no one could stop her.

Potential future rivals could be easily eliminated if they were named as suspects. Smearing their names—even without any actual evidence of wrongdoing—would ruin their chances of winning any election in the future. In the toxic waters of the DC swamp no tactic to harm your political opponents was beyond consideration.

Sarah Whitcomb-Kincaid leaned over and gave her husband a peck on the cheek. "If that's what you want, dear, I accept. It's my duty as a patriotic American to help bring the people who did this to justice." A disturbing smirk formed on her face. "I know just where to start."

CHAPTER 59

Two weeks later

JACK KINCAID WASHED DOWN THE last of his spinach, feta, and egg white omelet with coffee made from a special blend of arabica beans, a gift from the Ethiopian ambassador. He was so fixated on the two CNN anchors discussing the recent shakeups in his administration that he didn't notice the White House butler take his breakfast tray away.

Sarah walked into the sitting room located off to the side of their master suite and turned her back to the president. "Jack, we're late. Would you zip me up?" She lifted the back of her hair and waited.

He didn't even realize she was in the room. "Sarah!" he yelled over his shoulder.

"Jack, I'm right here."

He turned to see his wife glaring at him with both hands planted on her hips.

"Oh, there you are." He pointed at the TV. "Those bastards in the media are at it again. It's no wonder my poll numbers have been dropping."

On the set, a distinguished-looking silver-haired man in his late fifties sat opposite a former beauty pageant contestant half his age. Between the two anchors, the procedures peddled by the plastic surgery industry were well represented.

The man cradled a stack of papers as he read the teleprompter. "The Washington political establishment has been paralyzed by the ongoing purge of the struggling Kincaid administration. Vice President Rodriguez resigned yesterday, claiming a desire to spend more time with his family as the reason for his unprecedented decision. The president appointed Thomas Jackson, HUD secretary, to serve out the remainder of his term—making him the first African American vice president in American history.

"Chief of Staff Harry Wilcox was given his walking papers the day after the incident in Kansas City. Rumors are circulating inside the beltway that Speaker of the House Wilber Clayton is also under investigation by the commission headed up by the first lady. His perplexing absence from the rally—because of a claimed upset stomach—has investigators focusing on the person second in the line of succession. Speaker Clayton's office had no comment on the rumors."

The bubbly anchor assumed a serious expression when the camera switched to her. "Today, President Kincaid will be making his first foray outside the White House since the assassination attempt. He will be attending the funeral for Secret Service agent Dirk Miller. The actions of the president's personal bodyguard on the day of the incident are being scrutinized by the commission as well. Let's go to our DC correspondent, Isabella Fuentes, for the latest."

The screen switched to a live shot with the White House in the background. The spunky, raven-haired reporter breathlessly brought the television audience up to date. "I am standing outside the fence surrounding the White House, rather than on the grounds as I have in the past. New security measures put in place have barred all nonessential personnel from the grounds, even journalists." She pointed over her shoulder at a gleaming Sikorsky VH-92A helicopter. "Marine One sits on the helipad ready to take the president and first lady to Joint

Base Andrews, where the remaining Air Force One will fly them to New York City for the funeral. It has been confirmed that the brave pilot who saved the president, Mark Smith, will be attending as well."

The bottle blonde anchor flashed back up on the screen. "Isabella, is the new presidential protection detail, put in place just this week, concerned about President Kincaid leaving the safety of the White House so soon after the embarrassing debacle in Missouri?"

Fuentes responded just as she'd practiced for the planted question. "My sources inside the White House tell me they feel confident that if there was another attempt on the President's life, the pilot, who some have dubbed Captain Courageous, would be there to save the day again. Back to you in the studio."

The coffee cup Kincaid hurled at the TV shattered the screen.

———————

Jack and Sarah Kincaid walked across the South Lawn up to Marine One. An impeccably dressed Marine snapped to attention, holding his salute as the couple boarded.

As soon as the door was closed, the rotors began to spin up to speed. The skilled pilot lifted the large heli-copter straight up into a hover, twenty feet above the pad. He smoothly pressed his left foot forward on the anti-torque pedal. The craft spun counterclockwise 180 degrees without deviating from the center of the helipad.

An ambulance crew and fire truck stood at the ready off to the side in case of emergency. The pilot looked south toward the Potomac River. All streets under the intended flight path had been blocked off by DC police. With the path to the river clear, the pilot simultaneously eased the collective up and the cyclic stick forward. Marine One began its short flight to Joint Base Andrews.

Thirteen minutes later, Air Force One lifted off and turned north.

———————

It didn't take long for Noelle to pick out a suit for Mark to wear to the funeral. He only owned one. And it was twenty years old. She was the fashion aficionado in the family, not Mark. One benefit of being an airline pilot had been no need to buy an extensive wardrobe for work. The uniform never changed. With only one tie on the rack, picking it out was just as quick.

Mark walked into the bedroom to get dressed.

"I need to take you shopping now that you're a celebrity," Noelle teased. "I can't be seen standing next to Captain Courageous wearing the same suit for every network TV interview. It would ruin my reputation."

"That settles it then," Mark replied. "As much as I love talking to those jackasses in the press, no interviews. Your status as a fashionista is safe."

Noelle went over and wrapped her arms around Mark's neck. Turning on the charm, she manufactured a seductive smile, accompanied by a loving gaze from her alluring crystal blue eyes. "Speaking of my status. Before things got so crazy, we talked about getting remarried."

"We did?" Mark said in mock surprise.

Noelle pinched him. "Yes, we did. When do you plan on making good on your promise, flyboy? I'm not getting any younger."

Never accused of being a hopeless romantic, Mark off-handedly answered, "You busy Thursday?"

"Mark!" Noelle pushed him away. "You can't just ask a girl if she wants to get married in a few days. It takes months to plan a wedding. There's the flowers, finding the perfect reception hall, catering, my dress…"

Noelle was so occupied rattling off the tasks needed to pull off a proper wedding that she didn't notice Mark get down on one knee in front of her. He reached out and took her hands.

Noelle stopped in mid-sentence when she realized what was about to happen. Her eyes teared up.

Mark looked up at his ex-wife. "I've been such an idiot. You didn't deserve the terrible way I behaved when we were married. Noelle, you are the best thing that ever happened in my life. Without you in it, what's the point? These past few months have shown me that you are my true soul mate. You said it yourself; we make a great team. If you'll have me—"

"I do."

Mark rolled his eyes. "*Wait*, I haven't popped the question yet."

Noelle grimaced. "Sorry." Her hands were shaking. "Hurry up already."

"Noelle will you—"

Mary and April burst into the bedroom.

"Mom! Dad! You're not going to believe what happened!" Mary blurted out.

"Ever heard of knocking?" Mark said as he got back up on his feet.

"You know those two brothers who wrecked my Maserati on the Fourth of July?" April asked rhetorically. "I just received a summons from their dad's law office. They're suing me. He claims his sons suffered emotional distress from the accident and that I should have known not to let them drive my car. Can you believe that crap?"

"It turns out their dad is that lowlife ambulance chaser who put up those sleazy billboards all over the city," Mary informed her parents.

Mark shook his head. "Sorry, kid, I warned you about this type of thing. Unfortunately, you have a big target on your back now that you're rich."

"I was just trying to be nice and let them take my Maserati for a spin, and this is how they thank me," April grumbled. "They wreck my new car, then they sue me."

"Sorry, Sis. You don't deserve this." Mary put her arm around April. "I'm here for you."

April's glum mood brightened up some. "Thanks. I can always count on my little sister to cheer me up."

"Tell them about the mayor."

April pulled an embossed invitation out of her back pocket. "The mayor invited me to his gala at the Met next week. I don't even know the guy." She ripped it in half. "He probably only invited me so I would donate money to his campaign."

"Speaking of money. Have you heard back from the Treasury Department yet?" Mark asked.

"Special Agent Reed called me yesterday," April answered. "He found even more criminal activity in my father's past, so the Treasury Department has extended the investigation."

"For how long?"

"He laughed when I asked that. He said government red tape can be a real pain in the you-know-what and that he couldn't give me a time frame." A look of desperation blanketed her face. "And the investment company keeps calling me asking when I plan on repaying the one hundred million-dollar loan." April let out a heavy sigh. "I wish I'd never inherited the money. It's become nothing but a curse. Life was so much simpler before I got it."

Noelle embraced her dispirited daughter. "No matter how crazy the rest of the world acts, your family is always here for you. Don't forget that."

April nodded. "Thanks, Mom."

Noelle pulled back from April with an excited look on her face. "Mark and I have some exciting news to tell you guys. We're getting married."

CHAPTER 60

THE THREE WOMEN BOUNCED UP and down, squealing loud enough to cause hearing damage to anyone nearby. They gleefully hugged each other at the announcement of the upcoming nuptials.

"What colors have you picked out for your wedding?" Mary asked.

"Have you booked the church yet?" April inquired. Her eyes lit up. "I know, you guys should have it at Saint Patrick's Cathedral in Manhattan. It's the perfect venue for a wedding."

"We really haven't had a chance to plan any of the details yet," Noelle said.

"We?" Mark put up his hands. "You girls leave me out of this. Just tell me where and when to show up. That's as involved as I want to be."

The three women went right back to discussing wedding plans, ignoring Mark. He shooed them out of his bedroom and got dressed.

———

Mark presented their driver's licenses to the NYPD SWAT officer stationed outside the entrance to Woodlawn Cemetery in the Bronx. The entire four hundred-acre property had been shut down and sealed off for the funeral because the president was attending. Only people on the official list were allowed in.

A repeat of the fiasco in Missouri was not going to happen.

Noelle looked out the windshield of their minivan. A large contingent of military equipment sat on high alert. Two AH-64 Apache attack helicopters circled slowly overhead, like birds of prey hunting for their next meal. If World War III happened to kick off during the funeral, the Bronx would be well protected.

After getting the licenses back, they were waved through the checkpoint. Mark drove twenty feet before being stopped again. Mark and Noelle were ordered out of the van. Metal-detecting wands were waved over every inch of their bodies. EOD technicians slid mirrors on rollers under the car, checking for bombs. A cream-colored Labrador retriever, specially trained in explosives detection, jumped into the minivan and sniffed around. A camera hidden behind the glass in the door of an unmarked van nearby recorded their images and checked them against government databases.

The officer in charge received an all-clear transmission in his headset and gave his team a thumbs-up. Mark slowly pulled away and entered the cemetery.

The bucolic resting place of both the famous and the ordinary stood out as a rural oasis in one of the most densely packed urban areas in America. Massive marble mausoleums dotted the grounds, each more ornate and statelier than the last.

Mark weaved the minivan along the tree-lined road leading to the gravesite, passing armored vehicles and snipers. The president's helicopter came into view as they crested a small hill. It was parked on the lawn, nearby the open grave.

Jack Kincaid and his entourage were seated in a roped-off area separate from the other mourners. There was nothing between the president and his helicopter that could prevent a quick exit.

Newly widowed mother of two, Tiffani Miller, sat in the front row with her twelve-year-old daughter and ten-year-old son. She tried to put on a brave front for her kids, but the look on her face gave a more accurate reading of how heartbroken she was. Behind her, an overflow crowd filled every fold-up metal chair set out in rows on the lawn. Fellow agents, military buddies in their crisp dress uniforms, and grieving family members had all come out to pay their respects and honor the popular man.

Mark and Noelle stood to the side of the large crowd. Dirk Miller's parents sat next to Tiffani. His father looked over at Mark then whispered something in his daughter-in-law's ear. She nodded her head.

He walked over to Mark. "You're the pilot who flew the president and my son out of harm's way in Kansas City, correct?"

"Yes, sir, I am."

"Tiffani would like to thank you personally for what you did." He pointed back at the widow. "Would you mind coming with me?"

"Of course." Mark followed Dirk's father over to the gravesite. He walked up to the widow and cleared his throat. "Mrs. Miller, I'm Mark Smith, the pilot of the plane your husband was on when he was…"

The overwhelming look of sadness and grief on her face caused Mark to pause. A knot formed in his throat. The last thing he wanted to do was say something that would worsen the pain she was feeling. He opted for the standard platitudes.

"I'm so sorry for your loss. Your husband was a brave man. I'm sure he was a good father and husband."

Tiffani Miller looked up at Mark. The sad expression on her face was suddenly replaced with one reflecting a different kind of pain. One that Mark had seen before but couldn't quite place at this awkward moment. Her eyes narrowed as she glared at him with contempt.

Mark looked around, confused by her behavior. "I'm sorry. Did I say something…"

Dirk's father shooed Mark away from his daughter-in-law. "Please. You've said enough."

Mark excused himself and quickly returned to Noelle's side.

With full military honors, the funeral of Dirk Miller began. A solo drummer began a slow-cadence drum roll on his snare drum as he led the procession up the center aisle. Six members of the United States Army Honor Guard served as pallbearers for the flag-draped coffin. An army chaplain outfitted in a white smock trailed behind.

Clouds drifted over the cemetery, blocking the sun. The scene took on an unnerving, ominous mood.

As he'd done too many times before, the chaplain performed the funeral rites using the standardized text authorized by the Department of Defense.

President Kincaid got up and offered a few remarks. He talked about how grateful he was that brave men and women like Dirk Miller were willing to pay the ultimate sacrifice to protect our American way of life. Anthony Lombardo, new lead agent on the PPD, was positioned on the left side of the podium as the president spoke. Kincaid finished his brief eulogy and went back to his seat.

The honor guard lifted the American flag off the casket and meticulously folded it thirteen times. The triangular package was handed off to the army chief of staff. The four-star general knelt on one knee in front of Mrs. Miller and recited the heart wrenching words no one ever wants to hear: "On behalf of the president of the United States, the United States Army, the Secret Service, and a grateful nation, please accept this flag as a symbol of our appreciation for your loved one's honorable and faithful service."

A lone bugler played "Taps" while the coffin was lowered into the ground. There wasn't a dry eye in the crowd.

Conspicuously absent from the ceremony was the traditional twenty-one-volley rifle salute, at the request of the Secret Service. Even ceremonial rifles loaded with blanks was more than it could allow so soon.

At the end of the service, Jack and Sarah Kincaid left the roped-off area and walked up to Tiffani Miller. Jack knelt and clasped her hands. Speaking softly, he again expressed his condolences for the death of her husband. He stood and moved aside. Sarah Kincaid leaned on her crutches and reached out for the widow's hand.

Tiffani Miller looked up at the first lady. Tears streamed down her cheeks. She cried out, "To hell with all of you!" Tiffani grabbed a child in each hand and stormed off to the black stretch limousine provided to her by the funeral home.

CHAPTER 61

SARAH KINCAID HAD SUMMONED EVERY member of the commission investigating the assassination attempt to the White House at 8 a.m. sharp the following Monday.

The meeting took place in the basement under the West Wing. The ultra-secure Situation Room was the logical place to hold a meeting of such importance.

Everyone attending had been through the security protocols before. They knew not to wear a watch, a wedding ring, a necklace, or any other type of jewelry. One by one, the most recognizable people in the country placed their right hands on the glass panel of the biometric scanner to prove who they were. Only after they were positively identified could they enter the reception area outside the Situation Room.

Cell phones and other electronic devices were locked away in a lead-lined cabinet. Anyone foolish enough to smuggle a device into the Situation Room would be ratted out by the sensors hidden in the ceiling that detected cellular signals.

A narrow mahogany table ran the length of the room. High-backed leather chairs ringed the table. Attendees jockeyed for seats near the president.

Once the door was closed and the SECURE sign illuminated, Jack Kincaid took command of the meeting. "Thank you for coming this morning. The people in this room represent every facet of the government. Focusing on your specific areas of expertise, you've all had time to investigate what happened. I have entrusted the chairmanship of this commission to the capable hands of the first lady. I expect every one of you to show her the same loyalty and dedication to finding the truth as you would me." He nodded at his wife.

Sarah Kincaid stood up and crossed her arms. She slowly walked around the perimeter of the room looking each person in the eye. Despite being some of the most powerful people in the world, attendees squirmed in their seats. They knew their reign could end in an instant with one wrong comment. The primary goal of each leader was to shift blame to any agency other than their own for failing to identify the culprits.

"It's been three weeks since that fiasco in Kansas City," she growled. "And all I'm hearing from you people are excuses as to why you haven't found out who the sons of bitches are who did this. The American public has temporarily rallied around your president. That won't last forever. They are demanding that their government find the perpetrators and find them soon. If we let this moment of unity in the country slip away, it could cost us the election."

"Me. Not *us*."

All heads turned toward the president.

"It could cost *me* the election."

The scowl on Sarah Kincaid's face quickly reversed to a smile. "Of course, darling. Cost *you* the election. That's what I meant." The scowl returned as she faced the participants. "In case there is any doubt in your minds, let me be clear about one thing: If Jack doesn't get a second term, neither will any of you." She returned to her seat. "Someone is going to prison in handcuffs soon, or your heads will be mounted on spikes on the South Lawn. No more excuses. I want answers. Secret Service, you're first."

Miles Sanders nervously cleared his throat after that

gruesome warning. "Madam First Lady, my agency has done a complete review of the procedures used to protect the president. Big changes have already been implemented. First, we will deploy more decoy motorcades every time the president leaves the White House. Second, a new agent has been assigned—"

The head of the CIA interrupted. "I must reiterate my objections to the Secret Service being put in charge of this investigation. If the agency had done its job correctly, we wouldn't be here today."

The battle to sway the president and first lady had begun. All the big guns in the bureaucratic arsenal were there, shoulder to shoulder, battling for the spotlight. The normally spacious room strained to hold all the participants. An aircraft hangar wouldn't have been large enough to contain all the inflated egos. It was a turf war on steroids.

Sarah Kincaid leaned forward in her chair and repeatedly stabbed at the table with her index finger. "The Secret Service is the lead agency during this investigation. There won't be any more discussion about my decision." She regained her composure and sat back with her arms tightly crossed. "NSA, what do you have?"

The NSA director wisely changed his plans and avoided recommending his agency take over the investigation. "The NSA has gone back and pulled all the intercepted phone calls from the last six months from our database and had them reanalyzed. We are using different search terms this time that we feel would be more germane to the incident. So far, none of the calls have set off any red flags."

"CIA?"

"Nothing definitive yet, ma'am," Director Mary Powell said meekly as she stood. "No terrorist groups have stepped forward and claimed responsibility for the attack. Of course, Russia was first on our list of state actors possibly involved in this. To try to convince us that it wasn't them, Russia has been using diplomatic back channels to volunteer to help with the investigation in any way it can."

The first lady didn't suffer fools gladly. "Please tell me you declined their offer," Sarah said, sarcasm dripping from her words.

Others around the table cast their eyes downward, suddenly feeling compelled to scribble on notepads in front of themselves.

The confident facade Powell wore on her face melted away. "Yes, ma'am, I did."

"Sit down."

Mary Powell spent the rest of the meeting thinking about what her next job might be after she was fired.

"SEC, you're next."

A thin, tall man seated near the end of the table stood up. He pushed his glasses back up the bridge of his nose. "The Securities and Exchange Commission has been coming at this investigation from a different angle than my esteemed colleagues. We have a team of forensic investigators searching for unusual trading activity. We're looking at anyone who shorted the stock market recently. As you know, markets around the world crashed after learning about the assassination attempt. We think anyone brazen enough to try to kill the president would also be greedy enough to try to profit from it. If the person or persons responsible for this placed an order to short certain stocks in high volumes right before they crashed, they could make millions, possibly even billions of dollars."

Sarah nodded approvingly. "Nice work. Keep searching for any signs of someone manipulating the markets. Let me know if you need any additional money to fund your search."

"Yes, ma'am." The SEC commissioner sat down with

a self-satisfied look on his face, having one-upped the heads of the more glamourous agencies in the room.

Sarah's complimentary demeanor vanished as she called upon the next department head. "Secretary of Defense, do you have anything, anything at all, positive to report?"

Of all the branches of the government, the military had come out of the incident looking the worst.

Every member of the military took an oath when they enlisted. Part of that oath included a statement pledging to obey the orders of the president of the United States. The troops at Whiteman Air Force Base hadn't even recognized their commander in chief when he had stood right in front of them. Needless to say, they failed to obey his orders, as pledged.

Everyone else seated at the table was thankful the glare of the spotlight wasn't focused on them at that moment.

The DOD secretary rose hesitantly from his seat. "Madam First Lady, I assure you everyone involved in that unfortunate incident at the base has been dealt with appropriately. Again, I want to express my deepest regrets about what happened. There was no excuse—"

"FBI, you're up."

After being so rudely interrupted, the secretary of defense sat down and began his own follow-on career planning.

The meeting dragged on as the heads of the FBI, DIA, DHS, ATF, PID, DOJ, FAA, and other agencies gave their reports until all the letters of the alphabet had been exhausted.

CHAPTER 62

MARY SAT ON THE COUCH, her computer balanced on her lap, watching the twentieth adorable cat video in a row on YouTube. Mark and Noelle were at the kitchen table poring over a mounting stack of overdue bills.

Mark's cell phone skittered across the table as it vibrated. He picked it up and tapped the speakerphone icon on the screen. "Hello."

"Is this Mark Smith?"

"Yes."

"This is Linda Peterson, calling from the White House."

He rolled his eyes and reached out for his phone. "Very funny. I wasn't born yesterday. Goodbye."

"Wait. I assure you this isn't a prank. I work in the office of Public Liaison—"

Mark tapped the screen and disconnected the call. "Damned prank phone calls. That's the tenth one this week."

"Have you heard anything from Marty about charter flights we can work? We need the money," Noelle said.

Mark plopped the stack of bills down on the table. "No, nothing yet."

"Dad, it wasn't a prank call." Mary held up her laptop. "She was telling the truth. I just Googled her name. Linda Peterson works in the office that coordinates visits to the White House for invited guests."

Mark cocked his head. "What?"

"Congratulations. You just hung up on the White House."

With a confused look, he turned to Noelle for help. She poked him. "Well, call her back. Call her back!"

Mark tapped the redial icon on his phone. The call was answered in one ring.

"White House office of Public Liaison, Linda Peterson speaking. I'm going to take a wild guess and say this is Mark Smith calling."

"Um, yes," Mark said sheepishly.

"Forty-two seconds. Not bad, Mr. Smith."

"Come again?"

"Normally, people I contact take over five minutes before they convince themselves my call was legitimate and call me back. You beat that by a wide margin. Congratulations."

"Thanks," Mark said, unsure if her comment was meant as a compliment or if she was being sarcastic.

"Now, like I was saying, I'm calling from the White House to invite you, your crew, and immediate family members to the White House. President Kincaid has decided to award you the Presidential Citizens Medal, Mr. Smith, for your brave actions on the Fourth of July."

He was speechless.

A rare occurrence for Mark.

"Hello?" Peterson could be heard talking to a coworker in the background. "I think he hung up on me again."

"I'm here," Mark said quickly, before being disconnected. "I'm just a little...I'm a little surprised...that's all. Sorry."

"That's okay, it happens to most of the people I call. I'm used to it. It might be best if you grab a pen and paper before I go ahead with the details of your visit. That way, you won't miss anything."

Mark jumped up from the table and pulled open a cabinet drawer, returning with a pen and paper.

"Okay, go ahead. I'm ready." Before she could proceed, he asked, "By the way, how did you get my cell phone number?"

Peterson chuckled. "I do believe I mentioned this is the White House calling. We have a few resources at our disposal to help find information we want."

Mark didn't find her explanation very comforting.

"Each crew member on your plane and their immediate family members are invited to the White House for the award ceremony at 10 a.m. on August 7. I will email you all the details and a form for each person to fill out and return. The Secret Service will need to do a full background check on everyone attending. Return the forms to me as soon as possible. And yes, before you ask, I already have your email address. Any questions I can answer at this time?"

Mark raised his index finger. "I have a question. Money is a little tight for us right now. I assume the White House will be paying for the airfare and hotel rooms. Correct?"

"No, sir, we can't pay your expenses."

"You can't?"

"It's against the law. Don't worry, though. We have private donors who help in situations like this. They cover costs the White House is not allowed to pay. Everything will be taken care of. The travel office will contact you to make all the arrangements. And please, don't hang up on them when they call. Good day, Mr. Smith."

Mark disconnected the call. The apartment went silent as each person digested what had just happened.

Mary tossed her laptop aside and jumped up. "We're going to the White House!" She dashed over to the kitchen table. "The president of the United States is giving you a medal, Dad. How cool is that?"

Mark was at a loss for words again.

Noelle wasn't. "I can't be seen at the White House wearing any of my old rags. I need a new dress. Mary, you and I are going shopping."

Mark stood up and wandered around the kitchen in a daze. "Wow. This is nuts. The White House. A medal." He turned to his family. "I don't think I really *deserve* a medal for what I did. I was just in the wrong place at the right time."

Noelle went to his side. "Flyboy, in this life, somebody is always ready to criticize. Since you asked for my opinion," Noelle gave him a playful wink, "I think you should proudly accept the award for what you did. You deserve that medal." She gave him a soft peck on the cheek.

CHAPTER 63

WITH GIDDY ENTHUSIASM, NOELLE, CHAR-LOTTE, Mary, and April pulled their new dresses out of the store bags and held them up against themselves. They marveled at each dress as if they hadn't just spent the entire day shopping for them.

Mark had passed on the offer to join the women on their shopping spree due to an important errand he suddenly remembered he had to run.

Noelle decided Mark's old suit would never do for such an important occasion. She bought him a stylish charcoal-gray, double-breasted Armani. It was easier than trying to find a tactful way to tell him his old suit didn't quite fit as well as it used to after he'd put on a few pounds.

"Can y'all believe we're actually going to the *White House?*" Charlotte said with awe. "My mamma, God rest her soul, would never have believed her baby girl would be invited to meet the president of these United States."

"Is Bubba excited to go to Washington?" Noelle asked.

"He ain't going. The stubborn old mule said he didn't vote for the president and he'd be damned if he'd go all that way just to shake the rascal's hand."

Noelle shook her head. "That's Bubba for you."

"Thanks for including me on this trip," April said to Noelle.

"Of course, sweetie. Immediate family was included in

the invitation. You're my daughter. There was never any question you'd be going."

"I've never been to Washington, DC," April said excitedly. "What should we see when we're there?"

"I'm sure Dad will insist on going to the Smithsonian Air and Space Museum *again*," Mary said.

"Count me out," Noelle whined.

"He's already taken me to it three times," Mary groaned. "Says it's nirvana for pilots." She mimicked gagging herself with her index finger.

"I want to pay a visit to the Vietnam Veterans Memorial," Charlotte said. "My Uncle Dewey's name is on it."

"I've never been to the top of the Washington Monument. I hear the view is amazing. April, what do you want to see?" Noelle asked.

She rubbed her chin. "I did a paper on Abe Lincoln in high school. It would be cool to see the Lincoln Memorial."

April's phone buzzed in her back pocket. She pulled it out and answered. "Hello. Yes, this is April Parker." She listened for a moment. "But…there's nothing I can do about it. The Treasury Department still hasn't released my money." April gestured in frustration with her free hand as she talked. "Have Lowell Huntington call his buddy. Get him to finish the review." Her face grew redder by the second. "That's not fair. I don't have—" She dropped the phone to her side after the caller hung up on her.

"What in the world is going on?" Noelle asked.

"That was my lawyer from my family office. He said he has no choice but to resign. It would be a conflict of interest if he represented me while working for his firm."

"Why?"

"JP Goldman is demanding the money back they loaned me. He said their patience has run out. The firm is suing me for one hundred million dollars, plus inter est." April's eyes teared up. A terrified expression washed across her face. She wasn't used to playing hardball in the big leagues. "He said I would go to jail if I don't repay it."

CHAPTER 64

M ARY SCANNED THE SCREEN ON her laptop as it balanced on the tray table.

She narrated the information she'd found to her seatmates, Mark and Noelle. "The Wikipedia article about President Kincaid says his grandfather, Joseph 'Tuffy' Kincaid, cut his teeth under the tutelage of Tom Pendergast, the corrupt political boss in Kansas City. He even took the rap for him and went to prison for two years rather than testify against Pendergast. After he got out, the Pendergast machine rewarded Kincaid by securing votes for him as he shot up through the political ranks. Anyone foolish enough to run against him in an election usually decided to bow out before Election Day or they conveniently committed 'suicide' the night before. Joe Kincaid eventually became governor of Missouri. His father was a little shrewder. He became a US Senator by blackmailing others into doing his dirty work for him rather than having them killed. That way, he stayed above suspicion while other people took the fall. Impressive family tree," Mary said sarcastically.

"There's DC," Mark said, pointing out the window of the Boeing 737.

Mary leaned across her father to take in the view.

The plane jerked back and forth above the Potomac River on the approach to Reagan National Airport like it was running an airborne obstacle course. At the last second, its right wing dipped, and the plane planted itself onto the short runway. Passengers were pushed forward in their seats as the pilot brought the plane to an abrupt stop. After a short taxi, the plane pulled up to the jetway and shut down its engines.

Well-dressed passengers rushed off the plane to conduct business in the nation's capital before the opposing viewpoint could get an audience with the same politicians.

After the stampede of lobbyists was over, everyone grabbed their luggage from the overhead bins and marched up the narrow aisle. Andy Wilson helped Mary with her bag. The six special guests of the president of the United States made their way out to the curb and waited. Thirty minutes later, the Drury Inn van arrived and whisked them off to downtown Washington.

———◆———

The next morning, everyone met in the lobby, dressed in their finest. Everyone except Mary and April. Since his days in the Air Force, Mark had been a stickler for being on time. His family, not so much. As Mark picked up the house phone to call their room, the women came around the corner. They were still applying the last touches of makeup.

"You're late," Mark growled, tapping his watch.

"You want us to look our best when we meet the president, don't you?" Mary quipped.

"The President? Or is it the handsome young men on his staff you're more concerned about?" Mark asked.

The two twentysomethings giggled and linked arms as they walked away, effectively answering his question.

The group walked outside and piled into the hotel van for the short trip.

"Where to, folks?" the driver asked.

"The northwest gate at the White House," Mark said. "We have a meeting with the president."

The driver rolled his eyes. "Real original, pal. Never heard that one before." He looked back over his left shoulder then pulled out into traffic. "Seriously. Where to?"

"Show him the invitation," Noelle said from the middle bench seat.

Mark pulled out it out. The invitation was printed on official White House card stock. He waved it in front of the driver's face.

His eyes widened. "Holy Toledo. You weren't kidding. You folks *are* meeting the president. Who are you people?"

Noelle leaned forward until she was next to the driver. In a low, cautious voice she said, "Can you keep a secret"—she looked at his name tag—"Terrance?"

"Absolutely, ma'am." He crossed his heart.

"You strike me as a man who can keep top-secret battle plans against the Russians to himself, no matter how long they torture you."

His head snapped to the right. "Say what?"

"You look pretty tough. I'm sure you can handle it. Don't worry. After thirty-six hours straight without any information from you, they usually stop the torture and...well...you know." Noelle simulated putting a gun to her temple with her hand and pulling the trigger.

Mark turned his head to the side and chuckled.

The driver cleared his throat. "You know what? I think I'd better stop being so nosey, drop you nice folks off, then be on my way." He pulled the van over to the curb a block away from the White House and kicked everyone out. Before the side door on the van was even closed, he peeled out, made a U-turn on Pennsylvania Avenue, and sped back to the hotel.

The group walked the remaining block to the White House. All along the fence on Pennsylvania Avenue, tourists gaped in awe at the historic house. Cell phones snapped family photos and selfies with the building in the background.

Vying for the attention of tourists were small bands of political activists standing across the street in Lafayette Square Park. They held homemade signs with messages either praising the president as a saint who could do no wrong or demonized him as the devil incarnate.

Two-man teams of Secret Service agents stood evenly spaced along the street, keeping a close watch on the daily circus. Other agents, in plain clothes, circulated among the tourist.

The van driver's peculiar exit from the scene had attracted plenty of attention from the security detachment patrolling the White House roof. Several pairs of cartoonishly large Steiner binoculars were trained on Mark and the others.

As they approached the fortified fence, Mark looked up. A small army of Secret Service snipers, clad in black BDUs, stared back down at him from the roof.

Mark had heard rumors during his career as an airline pilot that the White House was defended by antiaircraft guns mounted on the roof. The airspace around it was labeled Prohibited on aviation charts. No planes were allowed to fly in the vicinity of the White House for any reason. If one did, it would be the pilot's last flight.

An armed Secret Service Uniformed Division officer, dressed in a starched white shirt over black uniform pants, stepped out of the guard shack and eyed the group as they approached the closed gate. He held out his hand. "You folks will need to turn around. This gate is reserved for people on the pre-cleared visitors list only."

When Mark reached inside his suit jacket the guard tensed up. Upon seeing the invitation Mark pulled out, he relaxed slightly.

Mark held out the invitation through the bars. "We are here to see the president. I'm getting an award today."

The guard didn't take the invitation. He scanned his clipboard. A big grin flashed across his face. "Well, I'll be damned. You're the pilot who saved the president's ass. Welcome to the White House." He went back to the shack and pressed a big red button. The heavily fortified fence creaked and groaned as it inched back across the metal tracks embedded in the pavement. The guard waved everyone through then immediately closed the gate.

They were suddenly surrounded by heavily armed security personnel in black BDUs who appeared out of nowhere. Each visitor was ushered through an airport-style metal detector. Their hands were swabbed with a small damp cloth. Then the cloth was analyzed for any traces of explosives. Next, a German shepherd meandered through the group, sniffing for who-knew-what.

Once through the checkpoint, Mark and his group were escorted down a long sidewalk between the White House grounds and the Eisenhower Executive Office Building. They reached the entrance to the West Wing and were subjected to a secondary screening process more invasive than the first.

The guards turned the group over to Secret Service agents dressed in dark business suits after they finished the screening.

Lead presidential protection agent Anthony Lombardo entered the security screening room. "Mark, great to see you again." He reached out in a gesture of friendship. "Congratulations on receiving the award from the president today. It's well deserved."

Mark left his hands at his side and muttered, "Agent Lombardo, we meet again." He looked suspiciously around the room then pointed at the one-way mirror on the wall. "When does the interrogation start?"

"I was just doing my job, Mark. Had to do it. You guys were caught up in a bad situation beyond your control.

That's all." Lombardo forced a grin. "No hard feelings?"

Mark inhaled deeply.

He let the breath out slowly.

"No hard feelings." A smile formed on Mark's face. He gripped Lombardo's hand and said, "Tell your dad hi for me."

"I'll do that. Let's get your special day started."

He handed out visitor badges on lanyards to each member of the group. The badges were color coded and had a large letter F in the center. Wafer-thin RFID chips were embedded in each badge, allowing the precise location of each guest to be tracked by the Secret Service.

Lombardo pointed to the entrance to the famed West Wing. "Follow me."

The group formed into a single-file line and followed Agent Lombardo down the narrow corridors. Lining the walls were some of the most significant pieces of American art and sculpture.

Lombardo stopped at the desk of the president's executive secretary. "Ms. Wilkins, these people are guests of the president. They're here for the awards ceremony."

She stood and gave a warm smile. "Welcome to the White House."

Ms. Wilkins was dressed in a prim and proper gray pantsuit. Upon closer examination, the woman was obviously more than just an executive secretary. She was the same height as Mark and was remarkably fit. Her muscular build was evident through her jacket. If she was just a "secretary," then a well-known bridge in New York City would be coming on the market soon.

Wilkins gestured toward the door to the Oval Office. "Please go in. The president will be joining you shortly."

Mark grabbed the knob and pushed the door open.

Something felt odd about the door. Not because of the slightly curved shape, or that it led to the office of the most powerful man on earth. The weight of the door didn't match its size. He shrugged and continued into the Oval Office.

Unknown to Mark was that all doors and walls of the Oval Office had Kevlar panels embedded in them.

"Wow," April said as she rotated in circles, the significance of where she was standing overwhelming her.

Mary had her phone out and was capturing the moment on video for all her followers on Instagram to see.

Andy was more interested in checking out Mary than the historic surroundings.

Charlotte sniffed around. "Smells like my Granny Myrtle's house in here; old and musty. The only thing missing is the clear plastic slip covers."

"It's bigger than it looks on TV," Mark observed.

He took in the grandeur of the room, amazed that a poor kid from Long Island would ever end up in such a historic and significant spot, let alone be there as the guest of the leader of the free world.

Frederic Remington's bronze sculpture *The Bronco Buster* sat on a cabinet, its cowboy struggling mightily to tame the wild horse he rode. The sculpture was an apt allegory for the challenges of leading modern-day America. A bust of Honest Abe Lincoln cast a wary eye on the room from the opposite side of the Oval Office.

Mark went behind the desk and walked up to the full-height bulletproof windows. He looked out over the Rose Garden. Not a single petal or leaf dared to deposit itself on the immaculately maintained grounds.

A small stage had been set up with rows of chairs in front of it. White House aides were ushering people to their seats as the last of the preparations were made before the ceremony started.

Mark turned around and ran his hand across the intricate carvings on the nineteenth-century Resolute Desk.

"Impressive, isn't it?"

Everyone wheeled around. Jack Kincaid stood in the

doorway to the Oval Office, flashing a big politician's smile.

CHAPTER 65

PRESIDENT KINCAID STRODE CONFIDENTLY INTO his office, followed closely by the first lady, his newly appointed chief of staff, and an assortment of minions toting clipboards.

Mark quickly moved out from behind the desk. "Sorry sir, I was just admiring the view." He reached out his hand. "Hello, Mr. President, I'm Mark Smith."

The president let out a laugh. "I know who you are. You don't think they let just anyone wander into my office, do you?"

"Uh…no…of course not," Mark replied timidly, embarrassed to be the butt of the joke.

Kincaid took Mark's hand and gave a weak handshake. "Captain Smith, good to see you again. Unquestionably, it's under much more pleasant circumstances this time."

Mark regained his composure. "It's a great honor to be here, Mr. President. I can't tell you how humbled I am to be chosen to receive the award today."

"I'm grateful that you and your crew were able to get me out of that terrible situation in Kansas City. It's about time I publicly thanked you." With a pained expression, he reluctantly added, "Congratulations on all the favorable press you've been getting from the incident."

"Look this way, please." The White House photographer had requested the two men turn to face him. He snapped a few pictures of Kincaid glad-handing Mark, then said, "Thank you, Mr. President."

Kincaid dropped his grip with Mark, then turned to the others. "I'm so glad everyone could come today to celebrate this special occasion." He reached out for Noelle's hand. "Ms. Parker, I'm told you were the person responsible for getting the Pentagon to take Mark's distress call seriously."

Noelle blushed at the praise as she returned the handshake. "Yes, sir."

Kincaid's grasp on her hand lingered for an uncomfortably long interval. He winked and patted Noelle's hand. "Let's keep my Secret Service code name just between us, if you don't mind."

Since puberty, Noelle had attracted a lot of attention from the opposite sex because of her looks. She'd seen every disingenuous smile and heard every lame pickup line from men with more than platonic intentions. Noelle could easily spot a wolf in sheep's clothing.

Noelle yanked her hand away from his grasp. Miffed at the president for teasing Mark on his special day, she loudly said, "I won't tell a soul. Boy Scout's honor."

There was a collective gasp from the staff members in the room.

From brutal dictators to battle-hardened generals, visitors to the Oval Office were expected to bow and scrape in the presence of the president. Apparently, Noelle never got that memo.

A nervous silence enveloped the room as everyone waited for Jack Kincaid's famous temper to erupt.

Instead, his phony smile widened even more. "I see that the personality profile I had my security staff produce on you was spot-on."

He held her gaze and let the ominous implications of his comment hang in the air long enough to leave no doubt in her mind who Noelle was messing with.

Kincaid gestured toward the door leading to the Rose Garden. "Why don't we go outside and get started."

CHAPTER 66

SUMMER ANNUALS PLANTED IN THE Rose Garden were in full bloom, providing a kaleidoscope of vibrant colors and sweet fragrances.

Bright sunlight had already heated up the air. Another sticky, humid August day—the type that DC was infamous for—was underway.

President Kincaid led the way to the stage. Mark and his group lined up along the back edge. The first lady hobbled over to the front row on her crutches and sat in a seat labeled FLOTUS.

While the customary introductions were being made, Mark looked out at the small crowd. Oddly, the leaders of practically every law enforcement and intelligence agency in DC made up much of the gathering. And they were all staring at him.

When he focused on the front row, Mark recoiled back. The secretary of the Treasury sat on Sarah Kincaid's left. On her right was Lowell Huntington, the CEO of JP Goldman.

His attention was drawn back to the ceremony when Mark heard his name mentioned by the president.

"Captain Mark Smith and his crew are true heroes for what they did on that dark day in our nation's history." Kincaid was in full campaign-speech mode. "I was fortunate that they were able to get me to safety, and I consider myself privileged to call each of them my friends." He opened a decorative wooden case and picked up the medal. Kincaid dangled the gold disk adorned with an eagle surrounded by a wreath of leaves by its dark blue ribbon. "The Presidential Citizens Medal is the second-highest honor that a president can award to a civilian. It recognizes an individual who has performed an exemplary deed for his country. I can't think of a more deserving recipient than Mark Smith."

Kincaid swept his hand back and said, "Please join me in welcoming Mark to the podium."

The crowd gave a polite round of applause as Mark came forward. Kincaid unclasped the ribbon and encircled Mark's neck with it. He fumbled for a few seconds trying to get the clasp to reclose. Once it was secured, Kincaid grabbed Mark's hand and made a big production of posing for the press.

Cameras whirred and clicked. Mark tried to hide his discomfort with being in the spotlight. The last thing he wanted to do was give a speech in front of the national press corps. He forced a smile. "Thank you very much for this award, Mr. President." He turned to return to his spot at the back of the stage.

Kincaid put his hand on Mark's shoulder, preventing him from walking away. "Not so fast, Mark."

Mark turned back and swallowed hard.

"I realize we haven't discussed this in advance, but there is one other thing I want to announce while you are up here."

Mark looked back at Noelle, uncertainty apparent on his face. She shrugged, unsure what was coming. A trickle of sweat rolled down his forehead.

Kincaid continued. "If there is one thing I've learned since coming to Washington, it is to surround yourself with the best people and then let them do their jobs. If I am fortunate to be entrusted with a second term by the citizens of this great country, I'd like you to be my next FAA administrator, Mark."

Mark's mouth fell open.

"An experienced pilot like yourself at the helm is just what the FAA needs." Kincaid slapped him on the back. "What do you say, Mark? Will you do me the honor of joining my administration?"

CHAPTER 67

THE WALK BACK TO THE Oval Office was a blur for Mark. Being asked in such a public way to lead a massive, powerful government agency had caused his head to spin. Embarrassing video clips on the news later that night would show him unable to put together an intelligible response to the surprise request by the president.

Copilot Andy Wilson opened the door for Mark. "Can you believe it? My former roommate, the next FAA Administrator. Way to go, man. If you need a sharp young pilot to serve as your right-hand man, I know just the guy for the job."

"What's his name?" Mark joked.

President Kincaid walked up to Mark. "Sorry to spring the announcement on you like that. My wife suggested you for the job just before you arrived. We both think it would be the perfect way to reward you for what you did." He slapped Mark on the back. "The Kincaids take care of their friends."

Mark cleared his throat, stalling for a suitable answer to come to mind.

"In politics, people are either your friend or your foe. There's no gray area. I do hope I can think of you as a friend, Mark."

"I'm flattered you would consider me for such an important position, Mr. President. To be honest with you, I'm a bit in shock right now."

"I completely understand. I'm a good judge of people, Mark. You impress me as a straight shooter. I can tell you are just the kind of man I want on my team."

Mark looked down at his shoes and didn't respond.

"You *are* planning on accepting my appointment to the FAA, aren't you?" Kincaid asked in a less friendly tone.

Mark continued to study the tops of his shoes in silence.

"It's a *very* generous offer. You'd have a cushy, high-paying job as FAA Administrator for a few years. After that, a run for Congress would be a natural next step. With my backing, you couldn't lose. If a career in politics doesn't interest you, you're sure to be recruited by any number of aerospace companies after you leave the FAA, each willing to pay you ten times your government salary. No more hoping for an occasional charter flight so you can pay the rent and keep the lights on."

Mark grimaced. "You know about that, huh?"

"Of course I know. I'm the president."

Noelle walked up to Mark and hooked her arm through his. "Can he have a few days to think about it?"

The politician's insincere smile returned. "Certainly. I imagine today has been quite overwhelming for you, Mark. You don't have to give me an answer right now. Talk it over with your family. When you're ready, let me know."

The president's executive secretary knocked, then opened the door. "Mr. President, the tour guide is here."

Kincaid nodded. "Thank you, Ms. Wilkins." He pointed at the door. "I've arranged for a private tour of the White House for you fine folks. After that you'll have lunch. Please follow my secretary. She'll show you the way." Kincaid went behind his desk and sat in his chair, not bothering to shake everyone's hand as they left his office. The group shuffled toward the door.

"Mark, would you mind sticking around for a minute?" Sarah Kincaid called out. "I never got a chance to personally thank you."

Mark turned to see the first lady lumbering toward him on her crutches. "Of course." He looked back at Noelle. "I'll catch up to you in a minute."

The secretary closed the door to the Oval Office, leaving only Mark, the first lady, and the president in the ornate room.

Sarah Kincaid sat on one of the couches in the middle of the room. She gestured for Mark to do the same. He took a seat on the opposite couch.

"I am forever in your debt because of what you did for my husband and me," she said. "I don't think Jack would be here today if it wasn't for you."

Jack Kincaid sat down next to his wife. "I do hope you seriously consider my offer. An outsider like you would be a breath of fresh air in this town. As I've come to find out, Washington can be a frustrating and bureaucratic nightmare. The red tape in this town can be a real bitch."

Sensing an opportunity, Mark smiled and nodded. "I hear you there, Mr. President. I've seen glaciers move faster than most government agencies. My niece, April Parker, has been battling the Treasury Department for weeks to get money released that she inherited. There's no legitimate reason for them to have delayed their decision for as long as they have." He leaned forward with a hopeful look. "Mr. President, by any chance would you be willing to put in a good word for April?"

"I'd be happy to. It's my job to represent the fine citizens of this country. Making sure hard-working people like your niece get treated fairly by their government is a duty I take very seriously." He stood up and walked briskly toward his desk. "I'll have my chief of staff draft an executive order right away. April will have her six hundred million dollars released within the hour."

Mark sat up straight. "Thank you, Mr. President. That's very kind of you. April will be so—" He stopped in mid-sentence. Mark cocked his head. Deep furrows formed on his forehead. "How did you know how much money April inherited?"

CHAPTER 68

JACK KINCAID WALKED UP BEHIND Mark. "That's not important." He clamped his hands down on Mark's shoulders, pinning him to the couch. "Let's not get off on the wrong foot today. What's important is knowing I can count on you to be a team player in my administration. I'm just the coach. I need people I can count on to do whatever it takes to win at this game."

Kincaid released his grip on Mark and took a seat next to his wife. He leaned back with a smug look, arms crossed. "I hate that politics has come to this, but it can be a vicious and merciless game."

"And expensive," Sarah Kincaid added. "The cost of running for president is ludicrous. Contributions from our major donors has dried up, and there are only a few months left before the election. We could really use your help."

Mark cocked his head to the side. "I can barely afford to pay my rent. How could I possibly help you?"

Sarah moved to the front of the cushion. "After her inheritance is released, we'd like you to convince your niece to contribute to Jack's reelection campaign."

Mark looked down at the medal dangling from his neck. He recalled the intimidating makeup of the crowd at the ceremony. The surprise he felt seeing Lowell Huntington and the treasury secretary sitting together. As Mark began to connect the dots, he felt the spacious room closing in on him.

He struggled to respond. "How much money are you talking about?"

"Three hundred million dollars," Sarah Kincaid answered, as if it were pocket change.

"You can't be serious?" Mark replied, outraged at the audacity of her asking for such an enormous amount of money.

"Your niece would still have three hundred *million* dollars left. Think about that. That's more money than most people could imagine having in their wildest dreams."

Mark felt like he'd been punched in the gut by Mike Tyson. He shook his head. "I don't have any say on how April spends her money." He glared at President Kincaid. "If you want her to contribute to your campaign, you'll need to ask her yourself."

Kincaid bolted up off the couch. "The one thing I demand above all else from people on my team is honesty, Mark. I thought we were friends. Friend's don't lie to each other. We both know you can authorize any expenditures you want from April's estate. You have power of attorney."

CHAPTER 69

MARK FELT LIKE THROWING UP. He didn't even bother asking how the president knew Mark could authorize the extortive demand for half of April's money. The real reason he was sitting in the Oval Office crystalized in his mind.

An unnerving grin formed on Jack Kincaid's face. "It's a win-win situation. I get reelected. You are the next FAA Administrator. April gets her money and becomes filthy rich." He held up his index finger to emphasize his next point. "And she avoids going to prison for not paying back the bridge loan to Lowell's firm."

"You conniving son of a ..." Mark started toward Kincaid but quickly realized what a monumental mistake it would be to lay a hand on him. He pulled back and shook his head in disgust. "You orchestrated all of this. Locking up April's money. The loan from JP Goldman. Dangling the FAA job in front of me." He looked down at his chest. "And this." Mark yanked the medal off his neck and threw it across the room. It bounced off the wall with a loud clang.

Within seconds, Agent Lombardo burst through the doorway, his hand hovering near his pistol. "Is everything okay, Mr. President?"

Kincaid angrily waved him away. "Everything's fine. Leave us alone."

Lombardo slowly backed out of the room, eyeing Mark with every step.

After the door closed, Kincaid continued. "My administration would be remiss if it didn't do a thorough background check before submitting your name to Congress for approval as the new FAA Administrator. You have a very checkered past, Mark. The booze, the women, the gambling. I'd hate to see all that ugliness dredged up. That's just the kind of thing the cutthroat journalists in this town live for. God forbid it was somehow leaked to them. It would devastate your reputation."

Mark stood to leave. "What makes you think I'm not going to tell the press everything you've done the minute I leave?"

Kincaid sniffed. "Who do you think they'd believe, the *Boy Scout* or someone with your dubious past?" He went over and sat behind his imposing desk. "You have until noon tomorrow to give me your answer."

Sarah Kincaid used her crutches to lift herself to her feet. She smiled at Mark. "Given the incredible amount of money April would still have, I think our request is very reasonable. I do hope you give it serious consideration. I certainly wouldn't want you, or your family, to be the personal enemies of the president of the United States." She turned toward the door and yelled, "Agent Lombardo!"

Lombardo burst into the room in two seconds. He'd been hovering outside the door to the Oval Office.

The first lady glared at Mark. "Mr. Smith is leaving now."

CHAPTER 70

AGENT LOMBARDO GRABBED MARK'S ARM and forcefully led him out of the Oval Office. Once they were down the corridor and out of earshot of the president's secretary, he lightened his grip. "What the hell is going on?"

Mark yanked his arm away from Lombardo. "None of your damned business."

"If it involves the president, it *is* my business." Lombardo put some space between them to appear less threatening. "Look, I don't know what happened in there, but…" He lowered his voice, "hear me when I say this. Whatever the problem is between you and Kincaid, be smart. You aren't going to beat him. Give him what he wants and walk away."

Mark's head drooped. "I can't. I made a promise to my niece."

"Dammit, Smith, this isn't some old black-and-white movie. And you aren't Jimmy Stewart."

Mark didn't respond.

Lombardo gave up trying to reason with Mark. "Fine. It's your funeral. Let's find your family and get you on the tour." He started down the hallway.

"No. I don't want to spend another minute in this snake pit."

Lombardo shook his head in resignation. "Follow me." He led Mark back to the entrance to the West Wing, stripped him of his visitors' badge, and handed him off to the uniformed officer. "Escort Mr. Smith to the gate."

The burly officer pointed at the door. "This way, sir." He stayed within two feet of Mark during the long walk back out to the fortified gate.

The guard who'd let Mark and his family in when they arrived had a sympathetic look on his face as he opened the gate. Word had gotten out about the dustup in the Oval Office. "Have a nice day, sir" was the best he could come up with as Mark passed by.

The security team on the roof of the White House kept a close eye on Mark until he was out of sight.

Mark wandered aimlessly around the nation's capital for an hour. He couldn't stop thinking about how devastated April would be if he betrayed the trust she'd put in him. He'd been through that before with Noelle. His life had lurched into a downward spiral for years after that.

The threatening words of the president and first lady echoed relentlessly in Mark's head as he walked. He stopped on a street corner and looked up. A flashing neon sign beckoned him. The sign read: Murphy's Bar.

CHAPTER 71

SOUNDS OF CAREFREE LAUGHTER FILTERED through the door to Murphy's Bar. The walls pulsated to the beat of the lively music from the jukebox.

Swarms of busy people rushed by on the sidewalk as Mark stood at the corner. They were too preoccupied with their own agenda to notice Mark. He felt anonymous. Just a few feet away lay an escape from all the turmoil in his life.

The door to the bar swung open. An inebriated couple and loud music poured out of the establishment.

Painful memories of rehab, relapse, and then finally defeating his addiction to alcohol came flooding back.

Occasionally, the skeletons in his closet couldn't resist opening the door and peeking out to see if there was some fun to be had.

To distract his cravings for a drink, Mark pulled out his phone and brought up an old family photo of him, Noelle, and Mary. He smiled at the thought of having April Photoshopped into the picture.

Mark nearly dropped the phone when it suddenly rang. He put it up to his ear. "Hello?"

"Hey, flyboy, where are you?"

"Um...I'm..."

An impeccably groomed middle-aged man stumbled out of Murphy's, sufficiently recharged by his liquid lunch to endure the rest of his day as a lobbyist. Music blared out into the neighborhood as he held the door open, shielding his eyes from the bright sunlight.

"Is that music I hear? Where are you? Is everything okay?"

Mark took another look at the picture. He smiled and nodded. "Everything's okay. I'll be back at the hotel in a few minutes." He walked away from the bar.

———————

As soon as Mark entered their hotel room, Noelle wrapped her arms around him. "I've been worried about you. What happened after we left the Oval Office?"

He debated whether to tell Noelle about the extortion plot. Just as he was about to tell her, Mary and April burst in.

"Look what we got after the tour." They held up small gift bags.

Mark let out a frustrated breath. "Didn't I talk to you guys about knocking?"

The excited women ignored Mark and dumped the contents of their bags onto the bed.

Mary held up each prized possession as she rattled off the contents. "We got a deck of playing cards, a calendar, bookmarks with the Pledge of Allegiance. And they all have the official seal of the president on them. Wait until I post pictures on Instagram. My friends will be so jealous."

Mark chuckled at the Millennial generations' obsession with bragging about their lives. Somehow, if you believed social media, every Millennial lived a never-ending highlight reel of a life.

"The best part was lunch," Mary continued. "We ate in the White House mess in the basement. The room looks like an old-time Navy ship. The tables were covered with fine linens and we ate lunch on the official White House china."

Mark nodded absently. "That's nice."

"We're going to go sightseeing," April said excitedly. "What do you want to see first, Uncle Mark?"

He was lost in his thoughts and didn't answer.

"Earth to Mark." Noelle snapped her fingers, trying to get his attention.

He looked up. "What? Did you say something?"

"Where do you want to go first, Uncle Mark? Washington is such a fascinating place."

The naïve and trusting look on April's face made Mark feel even worse about the tight spot he was in. "You guys go without me. It's been a long day. I'm going to hang out here at the hotel."

Noelle gave him a suspicious look. "We could spend a few hours at the Air and Space Museum if you want."

"I'll pass. Maybe some other time."

Noelle knew something was wrong. Mark would never pass up an opportunity to see his favorite museum. She steered her daughters toward the door. "Why don't you grab Andy and Charlotte and take them with you? I'm sure they'd like to see the city. I'll stay here and keep Mark company."

Both girls shrugged and walked away, planning out their itinerary.

Noelle closed the door and walked up to Mark. "You want to tell me what's really going on? You left the White House without us. I get back to the hotel, and you're not here. When I called, it sounded like you were at a bar. And then you say you don't want to go to the Air and Space Museum." She looked at his chest and cocked her head. "Where's your medal?"

Mark looked away. "I lost it."

She planted her hands on her hips. "You *lost* the medal the president of the United States gave you?"

"Yes, I lost it," Mark replied angrily. "Get off my back." He opened his suitcase. "I need some air. I'm going for a run." Mark changed into his T-shirt and running shorts.

Before Noelle could pry any further, Mark dashed out of the room.

———————◆———————

Mark stepped outside the hotel and drew in a deep breath. The hot, humid air burned his throat as it made its way to his lungs. Or it could have been the bitter pill President Kincaid had asked him to swallow instead.

He started down the sidewalk at a brisk walk to warm up his stiff muscles. After only a few blocks, Mark heard an odd buzzing noise. It sounded like a swarm of angry bees. He pulled back the bushes along the street looking for any sign of the annoying insects. No hive was hidden among the bushes. When he looked up, Mark saw a small, black drone hovering overhead, its six electric rotors buzzing away.

Mark shook his head. *I wonder if the kid flying that thing realizes his toy is in prohibited airspace? The feds don't have a sense of humor when it comes to pilots violating the No Drone Zone.*

He sped up to a jog and turned the corner. A few blocks later, he heard the buzzing sound again. The same aerial prowler lurked overhead. Its camera lens stared right at him, as if daring Mark to challenge it.

He took off in a full run, dashing across the next intersection. Each block, Mark randomly changed direction.

The drone changed direction as well, remaining overhead.

Mark stopped and pulled out his phone. With his heart racing, he fumbled with the device, trying to pull up its camera. If this electronic vulture was going to stalk him in prohibited airspace, he was going to get proof and turn it into the FAA for prosecution.

Mark looked skyward to aim his phone.

The drone had disappeared.

Mark backtracked a few blocks looking for it. The

high-tech surveillance platform was gone.

The ominous warning from the first lady echoed in his head as Mark returned to his run. The oppressive heat made his anger at the president burn even greater.

Mark kept up a torrid pace as he ran the full two-mile length of the National Mall. He flew past the Capitol Building, the Washington Monument, and the Reflecting Pool. Exhausted, Mark stopped to catch his breath. He bent over and put his hands on his knees, gulping in oxygen. Other joggers altered their course to get around him. After a few minutes of rest, Mark stood up straight and looked around. He was standing at the base of the stairs leading up to the Lincoln Memorial.

The Parthenon-inspired monument, built as a tribute to the sixteenth president, loomed large. Honest Abe seemed to be glaring right at him from his lofty perch, disappointed with Mark for what he was considering.

He held up both hands and implored, "He's the friggin' president. What do you what me to do, go to war with him?"

People nearby heard Mark rambling to himself and promptly moved away from him.

———◆———

Mark returned to his hotel room and jumped in the shower before Noelle could interrogate him. At dinner, he kept to himself and pushed the food on his plate around with his fork, barely eating.

When they returned to their room, Noelle locked the door and cornered Mark. "Enough with the drama, flyboy. You're not leaving this room again until you tell me what happened in the Oval Office."

CHAPTER 72

"THAT BASTARD." NOELLE GRABBED A pillow from the bed and hurled it against the wall. "We can't let him get away with this. We'll go to the press."

"And tell them what? The President of the United States is a manipulative politician? That a mysterious black drone followed me? I'll be a laughingstock. They'll say I'm naïve, paranoid, or delusional." He plopped down on the bed. "And that would be nothing compared with what Kincaid could do to me. To us. I won't let that happen. Guys like him get off on using their limitless power to annihilate their enemies. It's like an aphrodisiac."

Noelle sat down next to Mark. "You're not seriously considering doing what he wants, are you? April trusted you. It would devastate her if you betrayed that trust."

Mark threw up his hands. "This isn't like taking on City Hall. You're asking me to go up against the president of the United States. Can you even fathom the damage he could do to our lives?"

She gently clasped his hands. The disappointment on Noelle's face wounded Mark down to his soul. "The Mark Smith I know today would never consider what Kincaid is demanding." Tears formed in her eyes. "When we were at Benoit's estate in France and his bodyguard was going to kill me, you offered your life in exchange for mine. That's when I knew you weren't the same man you were back when we divorced. You're better than that now. That's the Mark Smith I want to remarry and spend the rest of my life with."

Mark looked away and didn't answer.

She let go and dabbed at her tears.

A mixture of anger and sadness emerged on her face. "Nothing can erase the past. I can't completely forget how you betrayed the trust I had in you when you cheated on me. How terrible that made me feel. Women aren't wired that way. But our future…"

Mark studied his ex-wife's face intently as she recounted those painful memories from the past.

"Why are you looking at me like that?"

His face went ghost white. "Oh my God." Mark jumped up from the bed. "I have to go see the president." Mark opened the door and looked back.

"I'm sorry, Noelle."

CHAPTER 73

THE SUN DIPPED BELOW THE horizon as the hot August day turned into a pleasant evening. Lovers strolled hand in hand on the sidewalk. Mark didn't notice anyone around him as he contemplated what he was about to do. He jogged the mile to the northwest entrance to the White House grounds. As he approached, Mark noticed the new, taller fence for the first time. Anti-climb features and intrusion-detection sensors were installed on it to prevent anyone from making it over. From either side.

The guard who'd greeted Mark and his family earlier in the day walked warily up to the closed gate. The safety strap over the top of his pistol was unsnapped.

"Hey, Captain Smith. What are you doing here?"

Breathless, Mark implored, "I need to talk to the president."

The guard took a step back and eyed Mark suspiciously. "I'm afraid that's not possible." He looked down. As if his clipboard was the final authority on these types of situations, he said, "You're not on the guest list for tonight."

"I realize that, but he'll know why I'm here. Kincaid will see me."

The guard moved closer to the fence and sniffed twice. "You been drinking, sir?"

"No, I haven't had a drink in a long time."

Mark winced inside remembering how many times in the past he'd told that lie before he successfully completed rehab.

"Please, call the president. It's extremely important."

The guard shrugged as he shook his head. "I'm sorry, you're not on the list. I can't let you in. Why don't you go back to your hotel and enjoy this wonderful evening with your family? And please, stay off the sauce."

Dejected, Mark turned to leave. He took a few steps then turned back. "Could you at least call Agent Lombardo and let him know I'm here? He can give me authorization to see the president."

The guard exhaled in frustration. Glad to be able to dump this problem in someone else's lap, he replied, "Wait here." He went back to his shack and picked up the phone. The guard talked in a low voice with his hand shielding the handset. When he returned to the gate, he said, "You better not be yanking my chain, Smith. I'm sticking my neck out for you."

Mark gave a weak smile and paced outside the gate.

Two minutes later, Agent Lombardo stormed up to the gate. "Mark, what are you doing here at this time of the night demanding to see the president?"

He pressed himself up against the gate. "You have to let me in."

"Like hell I do," Lombardo shot back.

Mark grabbed the bars on the gate. "I know who tried to assassinate the president."

CHAPTER 74

"YOU KNOW?" LOMBARDO LOOKED AROUND suspiciously. "Keep your voice down." He pressed up against the fence in front of Mark. In a low voice, he said, "The entire government has been investigating the assassination attempt and hasn't come up with any names yet. Why should I believe that you know who did it?"

"Because I was there. At first, I didn't see all the pieces of the puzzle. But now I do. You've got to let me in. I have to tell the president."

Lombardo looked around a second time to see if anyone was nearby. Convinced they were alone, he walked over to the guard, put his arm around the man's shoulder, and led him away from the gate. He whispered instructions to the guard that Mark was unable to hear. When he finished, Lombardo marched back over to the gate.

"Smith, I could lose my job over this. I'm going to let you in—on one condition. You follow my orders without question. If you even *think* about pulling some sort of stunt or endanger the president, I'll make sure you do hard time in a federal prison. That is, if you're still alive." He reached out between the bars. "Deal?"

Mark vigorously shook the agent's hand. "Deal."

Lombardo signaled the guard. The heavy gate unlocked and slid across the track until there was a gap wide enough for Mark to slip through.

As soon as he was on the White House grounds, the

gate locked securely closed with a resounding jolt.

"Follow me." Agent Lombardo started up the sidewalk. He paused to speak to the guard. "There's no need to enter this in the visitors log. I'll take responsibility for Captain Smith while he's on the grounds."

The guard rubbed the back of his neck, aware he'd already broken too many rules to back out now. He avoided looking at Mark. "Who?"

"Smart decision." Lombardo turned and waved Mark forward. "Let's go."

The two made their way down the well-lit sidewalk leading to the West Wing entrance. Halfway there, Lombardo reached out to stop Mark.

"We can't go through the security checkpoint. You're not on the visitors list."

"Tell the president I need to talk to him. He'll clear me."

"I'll call him. But first I need to get you out of sight and into the White House." Lombardo scanned the grounds then pointed. "The basement service entrance. The kitchen staff will have left by now. No one will see us enter there."

They disappeared into the shadows. He guided Mark along the exterior wall of the majestic building until reaching the stairs leading down into the basement. Lombardo waved his ID badge past the scanner to unlock the door.

Once inside, the lead Secret Service agent responsible for safeguarding the president's life led Mark down a confusing maze of dark hallways. When they came to the base of the stairs leading up to the first floor, Lombardo turned to Mark and said, "Kincaid is in the Oval Office. Before I take you to see him, you need to tell me everything you know. Who do you think was behind the assassination attempt?"

CHAPTER 75

LOMBARDO'S EYES NARROWED AS MARK told him everything he knew. He stroked his chin. "Do you have any proof?"

"No. But I know someone who does."

"Who?"

"You." Mark put his hand into his pant pocket.

Lombardo reached inside the left breast area of his suit jacket.

His hand came to rest on the Glock 19 tucked into its holster.

Mark pulled out the business card agent Lombardo had given him after the interrogation at Whiteman Air Force Base. "I need a pen."

He moved the gun aside and pulled out a pen.

Mark grabbed it and scribbled on the back of the card. He handed it to Lombardo. "Get me this document."

Agent Lombardo cocked his head as he read the card. "Why this?"

"The proof I need is buried in plain sight. I just didn't realize it until tonight." Mark handed the pen back and started up the stairs. "Let's go see the president."

Lombardo tucked the pen away and followed Mark. The stairway door creaked as it opened into a narrow corridor on the main floor.

The usual hustle and bustle of people was gone. They navigated the labyrinth of hallways in the West Wing without passing another soul. Minutes later, Mark and

Lombardo arrived at Ms. Wilkins's desk outside the Oval Office. She was packing up to leave for the night.

Wilkins eyed them suspiciously as they approached. "Agent Lombardo, why is Captain Smith back? The president isn't expecting any guests."

"I couldn't wait until tomorrow," Mark said, trying to appear excited but not nervous. "The president wanted my answer about joining his administration by noon tomorrow, but I knew I'd never sleep unless I talked to him tonight. If you'd let him know I'm here, I'm sure he'd be pleased to spare a few minutes of his time." Mark jammed his hands into his pockets, hoping Ms. Wilkins hadn't noticed how badly they were shaking.

She picked up her phone, never taking her eyes off Mark. "Mr. President, I'm so sorry to bother you. Captain Smith is here. He insists on speaking with you." She listened for a moment. "Yes, sir." Wilkins hung up and pointed at a chair. "Have a seat."

Mark went over to it and sat down. His hands were sandwiched between the cushion and his legs.

"I'll be right back, Ms. Wilkins," Lombardo said. He disappeared down the hallway.

Wilkins retook her chair. Her right hand rested lightly on the armrest, inches from the panic button installed on the underside of the desk. She and Mark held each other's stare.

Five minutes later, Jack Kincaid opened the door to the Oval Office. As if he were greeting a long-lost relative, Kincaid gushed, "Mark, it's so great to see you. To what do I owe this unexpected visit?"

Mark stood. "I have something very important to tell you, sir."

"I see you've come to your senses," Kincaid said with a smirk. "Please, come in."

Mark followed Kincaid into the Oval Office. Ms. Wilkins closed the door behind him.

"Hello, Mark."
Mark turned toward the female voice.
A look of astonishment flashed across his face.

CHAPTER 76

MARK STOOD FROZEN IN PLACE. "Mrs. Kincaid, I didn't see you enter the office."

Sarah Whitcomb-Kincaid didn't get up from the chair in the corner. She nodded toward the opposite side of the room. "There's more than one door to the Oval Office, Smith."

He had failed to notice the four separate doors in the room during his first visit due to his excitement.

"Jack called and told me you insisted on seeing him. I came down right away to see what this was all about."

Stalling for time until Agent Lombardo returned with the incriminating document, Mark pointed and asked, "What room does that door lead to?"

The president glared at Mark. "Forget the damned doors. I don't appreciate visitors showing up after hours like this. You had better be here to deliver good news."

"Believe me, Mr. President, you will be very interested in what I have to say." He glanced down at his wristwatch and nervously rotated it back and forth on his wrist.

After one knock at the door, Agent Lombardo let himself into the Oval Office. He held a manila folder in his hand.

Before Lombardo could speak, President Kincaid barked, "Wait outside, Agent."

Lombardo held his ground. "I think it would be best if I were present in the room, sir. Given the unusual circumstances of Mr. Smith showing up uninvited like this,

I believe it would be prudent. For your own safety, of course."

Kincaid thought about the agent's recommendation. Having forced Mark into a trap, it would probably be wise to have a trained killer on his side in case Mark lost his temper. "Fine. You may stay. I don't have to remind you, Agent Lombardo, you swore an oath to keep secret anything you hear or see while you are my bodyguard. Under penalty of jail time."

Lombardo held his temper in check. "You are correct, Mr. President, you don't have to remind me of the oath I took."

Kincaid turned back to Mark. "My patience is wearing thin, Smith. Give me your answer. Now."

"Not until you give me something I want." Mark buried his trembling hands deep into his pockets.

Jack Kincaid let out a snide laugh. "You're a quick learner. Nobody in this town gives anything without getting something in return. What is it you want?"

"An executive order releasing April's money."

The president gave a dismissive wave. "Done. I'll have the order typed up first thing tomorrow morning." He grinned like the Cheshire Cat. "You have my word on it."

"Not tomorrow. I want you to give the order verbally. Now. No order, no deal."

Sarah Kincaid jumped up out of her chair. "Watch yourself, Smith. You're talking to the president of the United States."

The president waved at his wife. "Sit down."

"Like you, the one thing I demand above all else from my friends is honesty, Jack." Mark glared at Kincaid. "You and I are not friends." He looked skeptically around the room. "Seeing as how I can't rely on anyone to be my witness, I'm going to video you issuing the executive order."

"Are you going to put up with this, Jack?" Sarah snarled. "I said sit down!"

The first lady grudgingly planted herself back in the chair.

Mark pulled out his phone and pointed it at Kincaid. He tapped the screen, looking confused. "Hold on," Mark said sheepishly, "I need to figure out how to get this thing working."

Kincaid rolled his eyes and shook his head.

"Okay, I got it." Mark pointed at him. "Go ahead, Mr. President."

The scowl on Kincaid's face instantly evaporated, replaced with a forced smile. "I'm in the Oval Office with a good friend and true American hero, Mark Smith. As a servant of the people, it is my duty to stand up for the great citizens of this country when I feel they have been wronged by our government. I am pleased to announce that by executive order I am releasing all funds of Mark's niece, April Parker, held by the Treasury Department. This order is effective immediately. Thank you, and may God bless America."

"Cut." Mark fumbled with the phone for a few moments, tapping at the screen repeatedly. "Okay, I think I did everything right on my end." Mark put the phone in his pocket.

Kincaid leaned back, sat on the edge of his desk, and crossed his arms. "You've gotten what you wanted. Now it's your turn. And remember, I don't need a video as proof. I can rely completely on the other people in this room to be impartial and faithful witnesses to what you are about to say."

Mark grimaced. "Yah, about that. You might have misunderstood why I'm here. I'm not taking the job at the FAA. And I'm sure as hell not letting you extort April out of half her money so you can get reelected."

Kincaid shot to his feet. "You son of a bitch. You lied

to me."

Mark shrugged. "I told you, Jack, you and I are not friends."

The anger erupting inside Kincaid caused his entire body to tremble. He screamed, "No one gets away with double-crossing me! You have no idea how badly you are going to regret this, Smith!" He turned to his bodyguard. "Agent, confiscate his phone!"

Lombardo recoiled. "Sir?"

"I said take his phone!"

Mark instinctively covered his pocket with his hand to protect his valuable evidence.

Lombardo was torn between his sense of right and wrong and his duty to obey the president. He shifted back and forth. "Everyone calm down. I'm sure there is a reasonable—"

"I ordered you to confiscate his phone!" Kincaid bellowed.

Lombardo pinched the bridge of his nose. "I heard you, sir." He shook his head in resignation. "I'm sorry, Mark." He held out his left hand. "Please give me your phone."

"Like hell I will."

"If I have to use force to get it, I will. All bets are off if that happens. Use your head, Mark. You are standing in the middle of the most heavily secured building in the country. You only walk out of here a free man if you do the smart thing and give me your phone."

Mark's head sank. He thought about how far he'd come since the dark days of his past. How eager Noelle was to start a new chapter in their lives. How devastated April was going to be.

He reached in his pocket and pulled out his phone. Mark stared at the floor as he reluctantly handed it to Lombardo.

The agent took it and held it out in front of himself. President Kincaid snatched it out of Lombardo's hand.

He threw the phone down and ground it into the floor with his heel.

With an arrogant expression, he crowed, "Go and say goodbye to your niece, Smith. She's going to prison for a long time. Her money is going to be tied up in red tape for years now."

Mark cocked his head. "But Mr. President, you just promised to release April's money."

Kincaid gave a sarcastic laugh and looked directly at Mark. "Apparently, you haven't learned how things really work in Washington. I don't *recall* saying any such thing." He looked at his wife. "Sarah, did I say I'd release April's money?"

She shook her head. "I don't *recall* you saying that either, dear."

"You see, Mark, unless you have proof, it's your word against the president and first lady. And I think you know who will win that battle."

Mark let out a deep sigh. "You're right about that, Jack. In this room it's two against one. But here's the problem. You also told the whole world you'd release the money. So technically, you and your lovely wife are outnumbered."

"What the hell are you talking about?" Kincaid barked.

Mark chuckled. "You got to hand it to Millennials. Occasionally, they have a good idea. My daughter installed an app on my phone called *Instant Gram*. The video I took wasn't just stored on my phone. It was broadcast live to the whole social media–obsessed world. By now, it has probably gone viral."

CHAPTER 77

PRESIDENT JACK KINCAID DREW IN a sharp breath. He tapped his index finger against his lips as he paced back and forth in front of the Resolute Desk. The political wheels were spinning in his head. He stopped and turned. "I underestimated you, Mark. You *do* understand how this town works. I could use a man like you on my team. I want you to reconsider. Come work for me."

Mark rolled his eyes. "I think you have this Democracy thing backward. You work for me, Mr. President."

Kincaid marched up to Mark and got right in his face. "Look who's the Boy Scout now. You're willing to throw away the opportunity of a lifetime because of some misguided notion of how life works. It isn't that simple. The world is gray, Mark. The problem with idealists like you is that you don't look at the big picture. You see everything in black and white."

Mark stood toe-to-toe with the most powerful man on earth. "Not black and white. I see right and wrong."

Kincaid flinched. He retreated a few steps back. "Agent Lombardo, Mr. Smith is leaving now. Escort him out of my office."

Lombardo tossed the manila folder onto the coffee table, crossed his arms, and glared back at the president.

Kincaid looked perplexed. "I said escort Mr. Smith out of my office. Now, Agent Lombardo."

Lombardo stood tall. "Sir, Mark has something important to tell you. I took an oath to never reveal anything I hear or see while on duty. I believe it would be in the best interests of both of us if I wasn't present in the room at this time. You'll excuse me, sir." He left the room before Kincaid could respond.

"Are you going to let that insubordinate little mall cop get away with that?" Sarah Kincaid yelled at her husband.

Kincaid held up his hand to silence his wife. "Trust me, he will never work in a government job again. Apparently, there is something so important Mark needs to tell me that Agent Lombardo is willing to lose his job over it." He turned toward Mark. "Let's hear it."

Mark picked up the manila folder.

President Kincaid glance nervously at it.

"I've made a lot of mistakes in my life, as you've so bluntly reminded me, Mr. President. I've tried to learn from them and become a better man. One of the things I've learned is that once you've lost the trust of a spouse, it is exceedingly difficult to regain. I'll never forget the look on Noelle's face when she found out I was cheating on her. I saw a glimpse of it again when we were talking in our hotel room earlier."

"Is there a point to this melodramatic rehashing of your sordid past?" Sarah Kincaid asked impatiently.

"There is, Madam First Lady. I will never profess to understand women, but I know from experience what it looks like when they've been deeply hurt. I didn't recognize it at the time, but when I spoke to Tiffani Miller at the funeral what I saw wasn't the look of sadness and grief. It was the look of a spouse betrayed. Her face said it all. Dirk Miller was having an affair, and she knew it."

The president circled his desk and sat down. "Go on. Who was Agent Miller having an affair with?"

"He was having an affair with your wife."

CHAPTER 78

DESPITE HER INJURY, SARAH KINCAID shot out of her chair. "How dare you accuse me of such a thing? In a hallowed place like the Oval Office, no less. Jack, I demand that you have this charlatan arrested immediately."

Jack Kincaid remained seated behind his desk, surprisingly calm after such an explosive revelation. "That's a very serious accusation you're leveling against my wife, Smith. You damn well better have proof."

"I have proof. As you may recall, Agent Miller left the plane first at Whiteman Air Force Base. Unfortunately, we all know what happened next. After you went down to the tarmac, you were violently tackled to the ground by the soldiers. When your wife looked out the window, I remember that she screamed out Miller's name first, and then yours, Mr. President." He looked at Sarah. "Your heart was quicker than your brain, Madam First Lady. In your panic, you shouted the name of the man that mattered most to you first. And it wasn't your husband."

"You *remember*? You call that proof?" Sarah sniffed. "I distinctly remember saying Jack's name first. He's my husband. Miller was just another overpaid mall cop. Obviously, your memory is as deplorable as your past, Smith."

Mark went up to the desk and tossed the folder on it. "Here's my proof."

The president reached across the desk and opened

the folder. He pulled the document out and studied it. Kincaid's face reddened "What the hell are you trying to pull, Smith? This is the transcript from the cockpit voice recorder the day you flew me out of Kansas City. It doesn't prove a thing."

"Oh, I believe it does, sir. After we landed, I shut down the engines. But the cockpit voice recorder continued to run as long as the APU was powering the electrical system. Everything that was said in the cockpit was recorded. Your wife was in the cockpit when she said it."

"Jack, are you going to allow this delusional fool to fabricate this outlandish nonsense?" Sarah pleaded.

Kincaid didn't respond.

Mark pointed at the transcript. "It's there in black and white if you don't believe me."

Jack Kincaid tossed the transcript onto his desk. His shoulders drooped. The color drained from his face. Kincaid looked at his wife and shook his head. "Is it true, Sarah?"

"I was hysterical. I couldn't be expected to be clearheaded in such a traumatic situation. So I said Miller's name first. So what? That doesn't prove a thing." She went to his side and reached out. "Jack, I love you. You can't possibly believe I'd cheat on you, can you?"

He looked at her outstretched hand. Kincaid reached out and took it. "I believe you." The president stood and faced Mark. "She's right. A slip of the tongue in a stressful situation doesn't prove a thing. If that's all you are basing your outrageous accusation on, then I'm afraid you've just sealed your fate."

"Enjoy spending the rest of your miserable life in prison with your own kind, Smith." Sarah Kincaid yelled out, "Agent Lombardo, get in here!"

Tense silence filled the room as they waited for the agent to come busting through the door.

No one came.

She yelled even louder.

"Agent Lombardo won't be coming," Mark announced. "He's busy making a copy of some very important data from the White House server." Mark had a victorious smirk on his face. "The whereabouts of every person in this building is tracked continuously and stored on the server. We stopped in his office before coming to the Oval Office. I asked Lombardo if he could filter past tracking data to only include times when Agent Miller and your wife were together. Turns out you can. The results were very surprising. They spent an unusual amount of time alone together. In your bedroom, Mr. President."

CHAPTER 79

JACK KINCAID DROPPED HIS HAND from Sarah's and backed away. She moved toward him, but he put up his hand to stop her. "Stay away from me." He paced the room, contemplating his next move. Kincaid steepled his fingers and brought them to his lips. After a long, awkward silence, he said, "This is very embarrassing. A president's *wife* cheating on *him*. Maybe I can still spin this in a way that won't hurt me too bad politically. The public has gotten so numb to news of philandering politicians that the fallout from this should only last until the next celebrity train wreck grabs the headlines."

"I'm afraid it might go deeper than just adultery," Mark said. "I can't prove it, but I think Miller and your wife are the ones behind the assassination attempt."

Kincaid looked stunned. "That's impossible."

"Think about it, sir. It was a classic love triangle, and you were the odd man out. They wanted to get rid of you. Who better to make that happen than the people who had the greatest access to you? People who'd be completely above suspicion."

Kincaid's head sank. "I don't believe you."

Despite what he had said to Mark, he actually felt sorry for Kincaid. "You wouldn't be the first guy to suffer that fate at the hands of illicit lovers. It's an all-too-common scenario as old as humanity itself, sir." Mark looked him in the eye. "Like I said, I can't prove they were behind the assassination attempt, but I'm sure once the investigators target the right people, a little digging will uncover the necessary evidence to identify the real culprits." He turned to Sarah. "Once that happens, you're the one going to prison."

Kincaid sat on the edge of his desk. He glared at Mark and crossed his arms. "You mean *if* they target the right people. There is no guarantee that will happen. It is a government committee, after all. Controlled by Sarah. One never knows what might happen. When the investigation ends without finding out who did it, there will be an uproar. The citizens will lose all faith in their government." Kincaid stood up. "Nobody wants that. It would be in the best interest of the country if this whole sordid mess just went away, don't you think, Mark?"

"Hardly," Mark replied.

"You seem like a shrewd guy. Tuck away this valuable chip you just found and use it in the future when you might need it. I'd be happy to cash it in for you when that time comes."

Mark pondered the benefits of having the most powerful man in the world indebted to him. The temptation of being in such a strong position battled with his common sense. Fortunately, he recalled the past when he was foolhardy enough to believe he could make a deal with the devil and not lose his soul in the process. That past choice hadn't turned out very well for him.

Mark shook his head. "Keep it. I've learned the hard way that gamblers always lose." He started toward the one door in the Oval Office he was certain would lead him back to safety. "And in case you two do try to cover this up, don't forget about the press. As you said, Jack, a scandal like this is just the kind of thing the cutthroat journalists in this town live for. God forbid it was somehow leaked to them."

He pulled open the door and looked back at the historic room. The chamber where so many honorable men—and a few less so—had guided the country through challenging times. With a clear voice, Mark said, "There's one more thing, Mr. President. I'm not voting for you in November."

CHAPTER 80

MARK ENTERED THE RECEPTION AREA. Ms. Wilkins wasn't at her desk. He looked to his left. She stood at the opening to the hallway leading away from the Oval Office, blocking Mark's path.

He approached the imposing woman. "Thanks for helping me get in to see the president. I'll be going now."

"No, you won't."

Mark swallowed hard at her menacing response, anticipating a physical confrontation.

Wilkins spread her feet shoulder width apart. Her eyes narrowed. "I was suspicious after you showed up unannounced, so I called the front gate. The guard said he had no record of you entering the White House grounds."

A bead of sweat formed on Mark's forehead. "There must be some mistake. I clearly remember entering. Is Agent Lombardo around? He can vouch for me."

"He's in his office." She stepped aggressively toward Mark. Suddenly, her expression changed. What could almost be described as a smile formed on the face of the intensely serious woman. "Anthony told me why you're here. He said you were willing to risk your freedom to expose what Agent Miller and the first lady did. Before I let you pass, I want to tell you how much I respect that." She gave Mark a congratulatory punch on the arm. "Oorah, sir."

Mark winced in pain from the blow. But as a former Air Force pilot, he was too proud to reach up and rub the bruise on his arm. "Semper Fi, Marine," he replied through gritted teeth.

Wilkins stepped aside and let Mark leave.

———————◆———————

Lombardo was in his office packing the contents of his desk in a cardboard box when Mark walked in. "There you are. I was getting worried about you. I'll take you back the way we came in and get you out to the gate."

"The sooner I get out of here, the better," Mark responded. "I'll never understand how the people in this town think. The way power and money change them." He paused. "So, what's next for you? Obviously, you won't be working here anymore."

A dejected look washed over Lombardo's face. "I'm not sure. This is all I know how to do. I've had enough of risking my life protecting slimy politicians, though. Maybe I'll start my own security consulting business and protect slimy rich people instead. Might as well get paid well if I'm going to put my butt on the line." He nodded toward Mark. "How about you?"

"You were right earlier. I'm not Jimmy Stewart. And this"—he waved his index finger in a circle— "is not some black-and-white movie. This Mr. Smith is *leaving* Washington."

That brought a smile to Lombardo's face.

The two surreptitiously made their way back out to the northwest gate.

Before Mark slipped through the narrow opening, he reached out is hand. "Say hi to your dad for me."

Agent Lombardo responded with a firm handshake. "Will do, sir."

———————◆———————

Jack Kincaid sank into a couch in the center of the Oval Office. He pulled the stopper from a crystal decanter on the table and poured himself three fingers of Jameson Irish Whiskey.

Using her crutches to assist her, Sarah Kincaid hobbled over to the opposite couch and sat down. "My ankle is killing me." She pulled a pill bottle out of her purse and downed a fentanyl tablet with water from the other decanter on the table.

Husband and wife sat silently, avoiding eye contact.

Ten minutes and two drinks later, Jack let out a deep sigh. "Why?"

Sarah Kincaid stared at the floor. "I know you are going to find this hard to believe, but we did it for you. Dirk and I were so dedicated to seeing you get reelected that we were naturally drawn to each other. Things just spiraled out of control after that. We never meant for anyone to get hurt."

President Kincaid slammed his glass down on the table, shattering it. "Bullshit!"

Sarah recoiled back on the couch.

"With me out of the way, you could finally achieve your political ambitions. That's why you did it!"

"Okay! Yes, that's why I did it!" Her face reddened. "It's time for *my* turn in the spotlight! Do you have a clue about all the sacrifices I've made for you over the years? How many times I've had to swallow my dignity and pretend to be the doting, supportive wife while you spouted off one bad policy idea after another? When I came up with better ideas, all I got from you were patronizing comments and dismissive criticisms. I felt like a little girl being patted on the head and told to go out and play while the adults talked."

"So, you blow up Air Force One to get revenge?"

"That was Dirk's idea, not mine. He said you deserved to die for how you treated me."

"Well, I'm still here. Looks like your boyfriend failed."

"That's what I get for relying on a gung-ho Snake

Eater. If he'd just reined in his damned aggression and not tried to take on an entire security force, Dirk would be alive today and hailed as a hero for saving you."

"Hero? Twenty-three people in and around Air Force One died when it exploded."

"Collateral damage," Sarah said without any hint of remorse. "Couldn't be helped."

"How the hell could he blow up my plane, anyway? He was ten yards away from me when it happened."

"His Delta Force training. He drew out the fuel sample from the truck first so it wouldn't be contaminated, then poured in some exotic chemical compound the Special Forces Command developed. They've been blowing up enemy fuel trucks and storage tanks for years and making it look like an accident. The tainted fuel was pumped into Air Force One, and thirty minutes later…boom."

Kincaid looked ill. "I trusted that man with my life. How could he do such a despicable thing?"

"Grow up, Jack. Why does anyone in this town do anything? Power. He was no saint. Once I promised Dirk that I'd recommend him for Secretary of Defense after you were gone, he gladly planned everything."

Jack hauled himself up off the couch and headed for his desk. "I need to tell the investigation committee who was behind all this."

"Wait." Sarah reached out for her husband. "We can still make this work to our advantage. You tell the committee you were the one who figured out your bodyguard had turned against you. I'll admit to having an affair but swear that I knew nothing about what Miller was planning. He was going to get caught anyway. This way, you get the credit."

"What makes you so sure he would get caught?"

"That was the easy part. I told him he'd get rich if he shorted the stock market before the attack. I knew the SEC would investigate large trades betting against the market. I let greed do the rest." Sarah was obviously pleased with herself. "It's genius. We pin everything on him. Your poll numbers shoot through the roof. You win in a landslide."

Kincaid shook his head. "Jesus. You two were a match made in hell."

"Like I said, I'll do whatever it takes to get you reelected."

He sat down across from his wife. "It's not that simple. You betrayed me and you betrayed our country. No one is above the law. Someone must go to prison for what happened. We both know the country won't be satisfied until that happens. Miller is dead. That leaves you."

For one of the few times in her life, Sarah Whit-comb-Kincaid was speechless. She struggled to breath as her mind digested the stunning words her husband had just uttered.

She shook her head. "Absolutely not. I refuse to go to prison. A Whitcomb has never served jail time regardless of what they've done. I'm an alumna of Brown University, for God's sake. I can't be seen with *those kinds of people.*"

Jack thought about her response then let out a heavy sigh. "You're probably right. You'd never survive prison. And think of the disgrace you'd bring on your family name. They'd never forgive you."

Sarah broke down crying. She buried her face in her hands.

Jack checked that the doors to the Oval Office were closed then went to her side. "Everything will be okay."

"How! How will everything be okay?"

"There's a much more honorable option than spending the rest of your life locked up with those dreadful people."

Sarah lifted her head. "There is?"

"You trust me, don't you?" he asked.

Sarah nodded her head.

He found the pill bottle in her purse.

Kincaid laid six fentanyl tablets on the table.

"What are you doing?"

Next, he filled a tumbler with whiskey.

He put his arm around Sarah's shoulder. "You're distraught. Have a drink. You'll feel better."

She looked at the lethal combination on the table. The color drained from her face.

"This whole episode has been more than anyone could be expected to handle. Even someone as strong as you," Jack said sympathetically. "Being used and misled by a cunning, traitorous Secret Service agent. It's positively awful. Given the circumstances, no one could blame you for forgetting exactly how many pills you've taken today."

Sarah looked over at her husband of thirty years. In his eyes she saw the real man she'd married. Her face lacked any trace of astonishment or shock at what Jack's eyes revealed. Hell, with her shrewd political skills, she'd done more to mold him into the monster he'd become than anyone.

This rat wasn't about to be caught on a sinking ship.

Sarah Whitcomb-Kincaid sat up straight with perfect posture. She smoothed out the wrinkles in her dress and picked up one of the powerful opioids. Her hand trembled as she picked up the tumbler. Expensive whiskey splashed onto the table.

She placed the pill on her tongue then washed it down.

One by one, she downed the remaining pills. Tears streaming down her cheeks mixed with the Jameson. A minute later, the tumbler was empty.

President Kincaid wiped his fingerprints off the pill bottle then placed it back in his wife's purse. "Go upstairs and get ready for bed. I'll be up in"—he looked at his watch—"two hours should be enough. By morning, everything will be fine."

She stood and wiped away the last of her tears. "I did this for you, Jack."

"I believe you." Jack Kincaid embraced his wife and softly kissed her on the forehead. "Goodbye."

Sarah Whitcomb-Kincaid, first lady of the United States, walked out of the Oval Office, closing the door behind her for the final time.

CHAPTER 81

Two weeks later

M ARK AND NOELLE WERE SNUGGLED together on the couch watching *Forrest Gump* on their sixty-five-inch TV. The new leather furniture in the spacious condo gave off a pleasant, earthy smell.

Noelle held up her left hand and admired the simple, one-third carat wedding ring like it was one of the Crown Jewels. "No changing your mind now, flyboy. We're officially married. I've got a new ring to prove it."

"What are you going to do with your old wedding ring?" he asked.

"What I should have done years ago." Noelle hopped up off the couch, pulled open the top drawer in a rolltop desk, and fished out her twenty-five-year-old ring. She opened the sliding glass door and went out on their balcony, ten stories above the bustling street. Noelle went to the railing and admired the beautiful view of Manhattan Island across the East river.

Mark sidled up alongside her.

She reared back and threw the ring as far as she could.

Noelle turned to Mark. "To new beginnings." She took his face in her hands and gave Mark a passionate kiss.

As the lingering kiss became more sensual, his hands roamed freely over her toned body.

Mary and Andy Wilson burst through the front door, hand in hand.

Mark threw back his head. "What is it with our kids? Don't they ever knock?"

"Hi, Mom and Dad," Mary said cheerfully. "I brought Andy over to show him your new place."

Mark looked over and zeroed in on their clasped hands.

Andy noticed and let go. "Nice place. Sure beats that smelly old commuter pad you used to hang out in with us lowly copilots."

Mark winked at Noelle. "Better roommate, too."

Noelle pointed around the room. "I hope you don't mind. We gave away the furniture you got for our old place to Goodwill. It conjured up too many painful memories from the past."

"No problem, Mrs. S," Andy replied. "I wasn't that attached to it. Garage sale leftovers were all I could afford. I'm not a captain. Yet."

Mary grabbed Andy's hand. "We gotta go. Andy is taking me out for one last night on the town before I go back to medical school."

"Is that right?" Mark said protectively. He walked over to Andy and wrapped his arm around the copilot's shoulder. "What time do you plan on having my daughter back tonight?"

Andy swallowed hard. "Midnight?"

Mark's eyes narrowed.

"Eleven?"

He smiled. "You kids have a good time."

Mary pulled Andy away from Mark's grip and rolled her eyes. "Dads." She opened the door to leave.

April stood in the hallway, just about to knock. "Oh. Hi, Sis. Hi, Andy."

The lovebirds rushed past April without responding, before Mark could delay them any longer.

Noelle hugged her daughter. "Hi, sweetie. What brings you by?"

April produced a box from behind her back. "I've got

something for Mark."

"What more could you possibly give me?" Mark asked as he accepted the box. "You paid for this condo. Furnished it. And bought us a new minivan. You've been more than generous."

"It was the least I could do after all you went through with the president. Besides, I wanted my family out of that dangerous neighborhood. Astoria is a much nicer area."

Noelle reached out for April's hand. "Do you miss your fancy apartment overlooking Central Park?"

"Nah. I was never cut out to rub elbows with the Rockefeller crowd. I'm more of a Queens girl." April clapped her hands excitedly. "Now, my whole family lives in the same building. Tommy and Stephanie are across the hall, and I'm one floor up. Isn't that great?"

Noelle forced a smile. "Wonderful. It was very thoughtful of you to buy your folks a condo right across from ours."

"I feel bad about canceling the order for your new Gulfstream, Uncle Mark."

"That's okay, it was the smart thing to do," he said half-heartedly. "Besides, when you own a plane there's a lot of recordkeeping and paperwork you have to do. And then there's cleaning it after every flight. Who needs their own private jet? Too much work."

His rationales for not wanting the jet weren't the least bit convincing.

April pointed at the box. "I got you this instead. Open it."

Mark pulled back the flaps on the box and lifted out a gleaming model of a Gulfstream 700. The tail number on the model was N711MS.

Mark nodded approvingly. "I love it, kid. Thanks." He carefully placed the model in the center of the kitchen table.

Noelle wagged her finger. "That's not where it goes, flyboy."

With a mischievous grin, Mark responded, "We'll see about that." He looked at April. "Well, what's next for you? Are you going back to work at the VA?"

"Nope. I've decided I don't want to be a nurse assistant anymore."

Mark and Noelle gave each other a concerned look.

"I'm going to medical school. I'm going to be a doctor for the VA!"

Noelle smiled proudly and embraced her. "You're going to make a great doctor."

They led her over to the couch and sat down.

"What about your inheritance? Have you given any thought to what you're going to do with all that money?" Mark asked.

April's buoyant expression disappeared. She shook her head. "I thought inheriting all that money was the most amazing stroke of luck imaginable. Boy, was I wrong. It almost ruined my life and my family's life." She looked around at the lavish new condo. "Now that everyone is taken care of and the loan is paid back, I think I'll donate the rest of it to a charity that helps veterans."

Mark nodded slowly. "That's a lot of money. Any idea who you'll give it to?"

April looked at the TV as she pondered the all-important question. Lieutenant Dan was yelling at his men in a scene in the movie.

April perked up and smiled.

————◆————

The next day

A pleasant-looking woman was opening a stack of mail at her desk. The phone rang. Bringing the handset to her ear, she said, "Gary Sinise Foundation, can I help you?"

The woman listened for a moment. "Yes, I'd be happy to accept a donation over the phone. How much would you like to give?"

She dropped the phone and fainted.

CHAPTER 82

JACK KINCAID TRUDGED INTO THE Oval Office with a melancholy look on his face. He tossed his suit jacket at the back of the couch in the center of the room. He missed, sending the bullet-resistant jacket tumbling to the floor. Kincaid cursed under his breath and poured himself a hefty portion of Jameson.

He strolled over to the large windows and looked out on the normally pristine gardens. The wilting flowers combined with the gloomy, overcast skies to create a depressing landscape.

The American flag flew at half-staff.

After a moment of reflection, Kincaid sat behind his desk.

Jack pushed the intercom button on his desk phone. "Ms. Lopez?"

"Yes, Mr. President."

"Hold all my calls."

"Yes, sir. You can count on me, sir. I appreciate the opportunity to serve you during this—" He released the intercom button, tossed back a swig of his drink, and clicked on the TV.

An attractive news anchor was sending the feed to a remote shot. "We go live now to our White House correspondent, Isabella Fuentes."

"Candace, I'm standing outside the fence surrounding the White House. President Kincaid's motorcade entered the grounds a few minutes ago. He just returned from the funeral of his beloved wife, Sarah Whitcomb-Kincaid. The private ceremony was held in her small hometown in eastern Connecticut at the request of her family. White House sources tell me the president is devastated about her death from an accidental overdose and that his administration will do everything possible to find solutions to the opioid crisis in his next term. Back to you in the studio."

Without missing a beat, the anchor in the studio read the next story from the teleprompter. "With President Kincaid's poll numbers skyrocketing since he discovered that his own bodyguard was responsible for the attempt on his life, Vegas oddsmakers are predicting he will win reelection in a landslide."

Kincaid smirked and clicked off the TV. He picked up a framed photo on his desk and studied it. It was an old picture of Jack as a toddler sitting on the knee of his grandfather, Joe "Tuffy" Kincaid. He nodded appreciatively.

The president picked up the receiver on his desk phone. Just as he was about to dial, he stopped and replaced the handset. Kincaid pulled a cell phone out of his pocket and placed a call.

A female voice answered. "Hello."

"It has been a rough couple of months for me. I've missed you."

"Can we talk freely?"

"Yes, I'm not using my office phone."

"I've missed you too, sweetheart. I haven't seen you since Dirk's funeral."

"I know. It couldn't be helped. Nice performance at the funeral, by the way. Even I thought you were sincere. The best actress award goes to Tiffani Miller."

"Those two years with the local community theater came in handy. But I can't keep acting forever. When can I see you?"

"Be patient. Our plan worked better than either of us could have ever imagined. We can't risk blowing it now that I'm so close. I'll play the grieving husband until the election is over. After that, we can rendezvous. In secret, of course."

With a pouty whine in her voice, she said, "But I can't wait that long. I want you in my bed tonight."

Jack Kincaid leaned back in his chair and picked up his glass. "We'll be together soon enough, darling. Don't worry, I have everything figured out." He downed the last of the whiskey. "You trust me, don't you?"

AUTHOR'S NOTES

Honoring our veterans, first responders, and their families by providing help for those in need is something the Gary Sinise Foundation does exceptionally well. Please consider supporting their efforts.

www.garysinisefoundation.org/donate

——◆——

WANT MORE?

Be the first to know about upcoming book releases, events Dan will be at, and more. Sign up for his email list at: https://danstratmanauthor.com/

Follow the Dan Stratman Facebook page: facebook.com/DanStratmanAuthor

——◆——

Please consider leaving a review. Honest reviews are immensely helpful for self-published authors.

OTHER NOVELS IN THE CAPT. MARK SMITH SERIES

MAYDAY (#1 Best Seller)

HURRICANE (4.7 Stars on Amazon)

ACKNOWLEDGMENTS

Thank you first and foremost to my beautiful wife, Cyndi. Thanks for being my sounding board, first round editor, and constantly challenging me to be the best writer I am capable of being. I love you more than you will ever know.

Several talented people helped me get my manuscript from a rough first draft to a finished novel. Without their help and suggestions *BETRAYAL* wouldn't be nearly the book it is.

Thank you to Phil Heffley for all the time you took reviewing and editing. Your advice and input were invaluable. Thanks to Rob Perschau, a veteran newspaper man, for the in-depth review and insightful suggestions. Thanks to my brother, Paul Stratman. Who knew you had such a keen eye for editing?

Experts in the fields of DNA and adoption provided helpful advice and information to me during my research. Even though you asked not to be credited, I thank you.

Words can't describe how indebted I am to my editor, Jason Whited. Your advice and guidance are irreplaceable in helping my writing shine. I consider you a good friend.

And last but certainly not least, I want to thank my readers. I'm eternally grateful for not only buying my books but also for telling so many people how much you enjoy them. Good word of mouth is the best form of praise there is for an author and is greatly appreciated.

Sincerely,

Dan Stratman

ABOUT THE AUTHOR

Dan Stratman is a # 1 bestselling author and retired major airline Captain with over 39 years of experience in the aviation industry. Before flying for the airlines, he was a decorated Air Force pilot. In addition, Captain Stratman is a highly sought-after aviation consultant and media aviation spokesperson. He is a World traveler, having been to 43 countries so far.

Dan has an entrepreneurial side that stretches back many years. He developed the popular air travel app, Airport Life. The app did something that was sorely needed, it made flying easier and less stressful for passengers. In addition, he created a specialty photo printing eCommerce website, ran a multi-expert aviation consulting company he founded, and has filed numerous patents for consumer products.

Dan is a volunteer pilot with the Civil Air Patrol performing search and rescue missions and disaster response flights when called on. In his spare time he enjoys mentoring budding entrepreneurs and volunteering weekly with Habitat for Humanity.

The two things he is most proud of are his long marriage to his lovely wife and his three wonderful kids.